A New and Different Life

Alison Morant

An Original Publication from Alison Morant

A NEW AND Different LIFE

Written and published by Alison Morant

Cover by VilaDesign
Formatting by Frostbite Publishing
Copyright © 2018 by Alison Morant

www.alisonmorant.com

*For my female friends who are always there providing friendship,
fun times and support ... just like the women in this story*

CHAPTER ONE

'Hey ... what do think about you, me, Gabi and Belle sharing a house together?'

'What ... all of us share a *house* together?' Evie grinned; eyebrows lifting as she looked across at me. 'Are you serious?'

I'd just picked up my long-time friend from Avalon Airport, and we were now heading for Geelong on the Princes Highway.

'Yeah, I'm totally serious,' I smiled. 'Don't you think it's a fab idea?'

'Um ... well ... no ... I'm not sure that it *is* a fab idea. I mean, I haven't shared a house with friends since my *twenties*, and as fun as that was, it's certainly not something I've ever thought about doing since.'

'Well I've been thinking about it for a while now, and I

believe it could be great. I nearly phoned last week to run it by you, but then with Jim dying I knew you'd be here for the funeral so I decided to wait … and that wasn't easy … as you know, patience has never been my strong suite.'

'Ha … *that's* true.'

Noticing a frown on my friend's face I couldn't help but laugh. 'Hey … don't look so serious. I think it's a *wonderful* idea, *and* I think I've found the perfect house. I'm sure once you hear all the details you'll love it too. Now … take a deep breath and just chill for a minute. You don't have to decide right now, although you *do* have to say yes,' I grinned.

Evie turned and looked at my beaming face and couldn't help but smile, saying, 'Okay … I *will* think about it … *later*. But I have to say it's not something that grabs me. I think I like my own space too much, so you might have to count me out.' Suddenly yawning she added, 'Hmm … I'm definitely feeling tired now … I was up at 4am. I tried to have a snooze on the plane but couldn't as I kept wondering how Anna's coping. Have you seen her recently?'

'Yeah I saw her yesterday. We've been dropping in to keep her company ever since we heard about Jim.'

'Oh that's good. What about Sam and Claire? Have they arrived yet?'

'Well apparently Sam was flying in last night … he'd been sick with the flu so couldn't get here any sooner. I haven't spoken to Anna today but I'm assuming he's arrived.'

'And Claire?'

'Yeah, Claire got here yesterday.'

'Hmm … I imagine she'll be feeling devastated. She's always idolised Jim.'

'Yeah, you're not wrong there,' I nodded. 'I have to say she *has* done well - becoming a pilot like her dad - it's just a shame she's never had the same connection with her mum. Poor Anna. All *she's* ever wanted was a close family and grandkids one day. I can't see that happening now though.'

'No, same here. Anna mentioned ages ago that Claire felt no urge to procreate. Can you believe Claire actually said *procreate?*'

'Yeah I *can* believe it actually,' I grinned, thinking it sounded just like the serious, studious Claire. 'And Anna told me a while ago that Sam wasn't interested in having kids either. She was pretty upset about it, but, what can you do?'

Evie shook her head and sighed. 'Hmm … I don't suppose it'd be easy for him to have a long-term relationship though, with all the traveling he does.'

'No it wouldn't be easy. But I bet he's the type to have a girlfriend in every city,' I grinned. 'I met him at Anna's a few years ago and thought he looked gorgeous with his curly black hair. She was sure she'd have grandchildren one day because all the girls loved him.'

'Yes, well, we both know things don't always go to plan.' Evie stared out the window for a moment then added, 'It's hard to believe though isn't it? First Hugh dies and now Jim. Looks like we're *all* single again.' Glancing over at me, Evie went on, 'Sorry Liz … that was probably a bit tactless of me.'

'No, it's okay. It's been eight months already since Hugh

died … part of me still can't believe it … but recently part of me has started to adapt and make plans for the future. You know … the human spirit moving on and all that.'

I had a wry smile on my face as I flicked on the indicator before accelerating past a truck which had 'Geelong Fresh Foods' emblazoned along its side … then smoothly merged back into the centre lane of traffic.

'Which brings me back to my question,' I looked over at Evie and gave her a big smile. 'Now the initial surprise has worn off … what *do* you think about us sharing a house together? I know you're tired but just think about it for a minute. I haven't mentioned it to Gabi and Belle yet, but I'm sure they'll both be interested, and I actually think Anna might consider it now as well.'

'Hmm … well, yes … I suppose it *could* work. It would probably depend on the house though, and how much room everyone had. Like I said before, I really need my own space sometimes, *and* a quiet place when I'm writing. That's why I'm thinking it wouldn't work for me. But I can see Gabi being interested … and maybe Anna … not sure about Belle though.'

'Yeah, well the house in question is huge so we'd *all* have plenty of our own space. After all, I'd need room to make my jewellery, Gabi would need room for all her clothes,' I grinned before going on, 'Belle would need a fair bit of room to do her painting …'

'So how is Belle anyway?' Evie interrupted. 'I didn't get to see her last time I was here. She was visiting Tatiana in Alice Springs I think.'

'Yeah, she's okay. I think she's accepted she's also not going to have grandchildren, now she knows Tatiana's gay. It *was* bit of a shock to her at the time, not that she's worried about *that*. It was realising she wouldn't be a grandmother that got her down.'

'Yes, she *was* pretty upset about it.'

'Yeah. Anyway she seems reconciled to the fact now and is getting on with her life. At least she was able to be with them when they got married. Actually I think that's why she was in Alice Springs the last time you were here.'

'Oh yes that's right; Belle emailed me the photos. Didn't Tatiana and Naomi look *gorgeous*? I wish we could have all gone, but … it was their day and they just wanted a small ceremony. Bloody shame it's not a *legal* marriage though.'

'Yeah, it's ridiculous. Apparently they're going to invite *everyone* when they can do it again, legally.'

'Yes, that'll be fantastic. Hopefully we won't have to wait *too* long.'

We drove in silence for a few minutes, before Evie said, 'So … tell me about this house … where is it anyway?

I tried to keep my excitement at bay as I replied, 'Anglesea.'

'Oh … Anglesea … I *love* Anglesea.'

'Yeah well who doesn't love Anglesea? It's got so much going for it. The beach for a start, and the river, and the markets, and there's a great arty community, and …'

'Yes okay, okay, I get the picture. I *do* actually know what's there you know.'

'Yeah I know, I just love the place though,' I smiled over at my best friend. Not being able to contain myself I went on, 'It's only about thirty minutes to the Waurn Ponds shopping centre too, which has everything you might want, so there's no need to drive into Geelong very often either. I know how much you hate those parking meters in the city,' I finished with a grin.

'Yes, bloody parking meters,' Evie frowned. 'They're so *expensive* these days.'

Now on the ring-road which by-passed Geelong, Evie noticed all the houses which had popped up since her last visit.

'Goodness, looks like *all* that farmland will used for housing pretty soon.'

'Yep, suburban sprawl is on its way,' I shook my head. 'Well, we should be at Anna's in about ten minutes ... we won't stay long though. Apparently it's been ages since Sam and Claire have been there at the same time, so no doubt she'll want to spend as much time with them as she can.'

'Yes okay.'

'So, by the time we get to Belle's we should have an hour and a half before the funeral. You'll have plenty of time for a shower *and* a nap if you want one.'

'Okay, sounds good.'

We both sat quietly for a bit then, each with our own

thoughts. Mine were of Evie's second last visit when she'd made the trip to attend Hugh's funeral.

'Okay,' Evie broke into my reminiscing, 'tell me more about the house before we get to Anna's. You said it was big, so *how* big? How many bedrooms and bathrooms?'

'Four big bedrooms, two with ensuites, plus a large bathroom and separate toilet *upstairs* ... and downstairs there's another *huge* room which I thought could be converted into a big bedroom and studio for Belle. There's also another toilet and separate shower room, *and* a lovely sunroom.' Turning to see Evie's reaction, I smiled, happy to see the surprised look on her face.

'Oh ... wow ... that sounds good.'

'Yep. It also has a big kitchen and dining room, and two lounge areas upstairs ... *and* a fantastic balcony which goes right around the house. Oh yeah ... did I mention it has a fabulous view of the ocean?'

'You're kidding? It sounds *awesome*! No wonder you're thinking of buying it.'

'Well ... no. I'm actually *not* thinking of buying it anymore.' I paused and looked at Evie; puzzlement evident on her face. With a big grin I went on. 'I've actually *bought* it ... I put the deposit on it two days ago.'

'Oh my God! You've actually *bought* it already! Liz you are *crazy* ... but that's fantastic ... I think.'

'Yep, and I got it at a really good price as I know the previous owners - George was a work colleague of Hugh's and I often played golf with Iris. I'd already been thinking of moving, and how good it would be for us to share a place, so when I found out they're house was on the market I just *knew* it would be perfect for us. They'd wanted a quick sale as they were ready to relocate overseas, and as I'd been to their place heaps times I knew exactly what I'd be getting.'

I merged into the left-hand lane and then took the exit for Newtown, while Evie sat there, still appearing a little stunned. Slowing down to adjust to the 60 kilometre speed zone, I then continued on.

'They were only selling because their kids have left home and are scattered all over Europe. So they decided to move to the south of France, firstly because they love the area, and also because they'll be closer to their kids.'

'Oh, okay.'

'Yeah. They'd already put a deposit on a place and were keen to move, so when I said I was interested in *their* place they were happy to reduce the price *quite a lot* if I committed to buying it then and there. So, I did, and everybody's ended up happy,' I concluded smiling.

'Wow, I can't believe you bought a *house* just like that … no, hang on … I *can* believe it actually … you are *mad*. But what are you going to do if no one wants to move in with you?'

'I'll cross that bridge if I have too,' I replied. 'One step at a time for now though. But I think when you see it you'll fall in love with it too. And you *did* say you'll be ready to move back to the Geelong area once Blue finishes Uni. You'd go crazy living in that big house by yourself. That's one of the reasons I'm moving from Eastern View.'

'Yes ... I *think* I'm ready to downsize,' Evie nodded as I stopped out the front of a red brick, Federation style house; just visible through the foliage of several large trees.

'Well, we're here,' I said, stretching my neck from side to side. 'I have to say I'll be glad when today's over ... funerals are never good.'

'No, they're not.' Evie's thoughts were elsewhere though; an image of the house taking shape in her mind. 'So what's the address of this wonderful house in Angelsea?'

'Eleven Seaview Avenue.'

'Hmm ... well I still don't think I'm up for *sharing* the house, but I'd love to see it after hearing your description.'

'Okay, well I'll tell the others about it after the funeral, then we can all drive there tomorrow and check it out. But for now ... let's go in and see how Anna's faring ... it's going to be a long day for her.'

CHAPTER TWO

I let my eyes wander over the array of faces I could see from my position in the church; two rows behind Anna and her immediate family.

'Wow,' Evie said quietly to me, 'I thought there'd be quite a few people here, but not *this* many. Jim certainly knew a lot of people.'

'Yeah well, with him travelling all over the world for the last thirty odd years, you'd expect him to know a lot.'

Belle, who was sitting on my other side, turned towards me and spoke in a low voice. 'Liz, see that Asian lady sitting in the front row over there?'

'Yeah.'

'She's very pretty isn't she? And she looks so upset. I wonder who she is.'

'No idea. That young girl next to her is beautiful as well isn't she? Gorgeous dark hair.'

I craned my neck around and scanned the room. 'There're people from heaps of different nationalities here. That woman in the second row over there looks Scandinavian, don't you think?'

'Yeah, and isn't she *attractive*. She *could* be a model,' Belle mused for a moment before continuing *her* scan of the church. 'And look over there … I think that couple are Nigerian … I love her gorgeous clothes. I suppose Anna would be happy to see so many of Jim's friends and colleagues here.'

Nodding in agreement, I then leant forward to get the attention of my friend sitting on the other side of Belle. 'Gabi do you know any of these people?'

'Oh yes, I know quite a few,' she whispered back. 'Remember I went with Anna and Jim to the Airline Christmas party a couple of years ago. I was trying to catch myself a pilot,' she smiled, 'not that I had the luck. The single ones were all the playboys; I think they had the different womens in every country.'

'Hmmm … well at least Anna didn't have to worry about that with Jim,' I stated. 'He *adored* her.'

The soft music that had been playing came to an abrupt end as the celebrant took up her position at the front of the assembled people. She had an extremely worried expression on her face as she glanced left to right at the two front rows, then taking a deep breath she began the service.

'Oh. My. God!' Evie's eyes were round as saucers.

'Oh my God alright.' I was fuming. 'What the *hell* was he thinking? How could he have done that to Anna?'

We were at the cemetery, the four of us standing in a huddle, all completely stunned. The eighty or so other people who'd gone to the cemetery seemed completely stunned as well.

The coffin had been lowered into the ground about ten minutes ago, and it had been then that IT had happened. Anna, Sam and Claire had just sprinkled in some dirt, and then a handful each of yellow rose petals, when the Asian lady had been unable to control her grief any longer. She'd let out an awful moan and began to sob uncontrollably, the young girl beside her having trouble to keep her upright.

Everyone had stared, momentarily shocked into silence, before everyone then shifted their gaze to Anna. The celebrant had then moved to Anna's side and gently moved Anna, Sam and Claire slightly away from the gravesite; speaking quietly to them as she did so.

A minute later Anna looked completely puzzled, then blank, then horrified. She'd stared open-mouthed at the Asian woman for a moment, then with Sam and Claire holding her around her shoulders they'd all turned and walked off in the direction of the limousine in which they'd arrived.

After they'd all hopped into the back of the vehicle, Sam suddenly stepped out and walked back to the Asian woman and young girl; both of whom were obviously distraught. Everyone couldn't help but stare as the sobbing woman talked with Sam for a minute or two before he escorted them towards a waiting taxi. He then walked grim-faced back to the limo and got in beside his mum and sister.

After watching the limousine drive off, most of the mourners wandered over to their own cars, all appearing rather shocked, while a few stood in huddles, still talking quietly amongst themselves.

'Come on then … let us all go to Anna's place and see if there is anything we can do for her,' Gabi said, taking charge as usual. 'Not that I can think of a single thing which could help at this minute.'

We all turned and walked the short distance in silence to where my and Gabi's cars were parked side by side. Before getting into Gabi's car, Belle shook her head in disbelief.

'I can't believe it … I just *can't* believe it. It's so bloody obvious there was something going on between Jim and that woman. Poor Anna. I wonder how long it had been going on for.'

'I don't know and I don't care how long it's been,' Evie said angrily as she opened my car door. 'That *bastard* …

doing that to Anna. She adored him. Always having everything perfect for him … *doting* on him … looking forward to having him all to herself when he retired next year. Ha! What was going to happen *then* I wonder?'

'Yeah,' I nodded. 'Maybe he subconsciously created that heart attack to save himself from the upcoming consequences.'

We were shaking our heads in dismay as we got into the two cars then drove out of the cemetery towards Anna's home.

CHAPTER THREE

The wake was a disastrous affair. Firstly, as soon as Claire had arrived back at her mum's home she'd packed her bag and said she had to go. Sam had tried to stop her but she'd been beyond reasoning with. Her tear streaked face had held a stony expression as she'd said goodbye before walking out.

The majority of mourners had then arrived at Anna's to commiserate and have refreshments, however there was such an atmosphere of unease they hadn't felt inclined to stay very long.

It was only early afternoon but everyone had now gone except for the four of us and Sam. Belle had just made a fresh pot of tea when, to everyone's surprise, Anna asked for a glass of whiskey.

'Are you sure Mum?' Sam looked a little surprised as he knew she didn't drink much alcohol.

'Oh I'm sure. I want a glass of his best whiskey ... the one he always said was *so* special. And one for everybody,' she said, looking at each of us. 'You'll all have one with me won't you?'

'Of course we will Anna,' Evie replied, eyeballing everyone as if daring them to refuse. No one spoke while Sam poured the amber liquid into crystal glasses and then handed them around.

'Thanks Sam.' I took my glass and raised it towards Anna. 'What would you like to drink to Anna?'

'To new beginnings.'

'Okay.'

Everyone raised their glasses and repeated, 'to new beginnings,' then drank some of the strong but smooth whiskey. Anna took a big mouthful, coughed a little, thanked everyone for coming and being such wonderful friends ... then burst into tears. Sam said he thought it best if his mum had a lie down, so after saying we'd be back tomorrow, we left.

'Well I know I've said it a dozen times now ... but I still don't believe it.' Belle was opening the windows and sliding doors to allow the cool breeze entry to her slightly stuffy home.

We all nodded in agreement as we dropped our bags onto the kitchen bench, then slipped our shoes off.

'Come out to the patio, it's lovely and shady out there. Now, who wants what? Coffee, tea, beer, wine ... more whiskey?' she asked, eyebrows raised.

'Ha … no more whiskey for me thanks, although it was rather nice, yes?' Gabi replied as she gracefully lowered herself into a banana lounge.

'Yes, it was rather nice,' both Evie and I agreed as we not so gracefully maneuvered ourselves into our outstretched seats.

'So, I think I am better to stick with the coffee as I have to drive home later,' Gabi smiled.

'Yeah same for me thanks,' I said. 'What about you Evie?'

'I'll have a beer thanks Belle … I don't have to drive anywhere as I have my chauffeur,' she said grinning at me.

'You could all stay here tonight if you like,' Belle suggested. 'There's the spare bed, the couch and that big inflatable bed I bought ages ago.'

We all looked at each other, then smiled, and it was unanimously agreed with nods of our heads.

'Okay, I will have the drink then … a wine please Belle,' Gabi stood up saying, 'and one for you Liz?' Without waiting to see me nod my head, she followed Belle inside to give her a hand.

Half an hour later we were on our second round of drinks; still rehashing the day's events. Several large trees were providing dappled shade, while lavender and rose bushes subtly scented the air with their distinctive fragrances. Stretched out on the four identical sun lounges, drinks in hand, we then sat in silence for a moment.

We'd heard most of the details of Jim's double life from Sam. He'd unfortunately discovered his father's infidelity after he'd made a surprise visit to catch up with him in Singapore, nearly six years ago. Jim had sworn his son to secrecy, but only after Sam had extracted a promise that the affair would end.

'Poor Sam,' Belle then sighed. 'What a crappy thing for Jim to do, asking him to say nothing to his mum.'

'Yes, and poor Claire,' Evie nodded. 'Finding out her hero dad is a liar and a cheat. But I still don't think she should have left like she did. She wasn't thinking of her mum *at all*.'

'What a bastard Jim's turned out to be,' I scowled. 'Just goes to show how little you can really know a person … and he *obviously* didn't keep up his end of the bargain and *end* the affair.'

'No,' Gabi shook her head. 'Bastard.'

'Yeah, absolute bastard,' Belle nodded. 'And I feel sorry for that woman too … *and* her daughter … can you believe Jim actually had a *daughter* with her?'

'No,' Gabi shook her head again. 'Bastard.'

'Yeah, absolute bastard,' Belle agreed again.

Evie and I looked at each other and grinned.

'Okay, I think we've established that Jim was a bastard,' I said, then after pausing a moment I went on, 'but I also feel sorry for that woman. After all, she's been fooled as well.'

'Yes but she *did* know he was married,' Evie responded.

'Yeah, but remember when Sam talked to her after the funeral? She said Jim had convinced her that Anna was being looked after in a nursing home; completely bed-ridden and near death.' I shook my head in disgust and continued on. 'Even though it went on for years, Jim apparently kept telling her it wouldn't be long before Anna died. She certainly hadn't expected to see her at the funeral. It was only when she realised that it was Anna at the cemetery, and not at death's door, that she lost it.'

Evie sighed and shook her head. 'But how did she even know that Jim had died? I mean, it happened on his lay over in Sydney.'

'Oh yeah, Sam asked her that. A colleague of Jim's who was with him at the time, and knew about the affair, phoned her. *Huh* … she probably knew about it before *Anna*.'

'Hmm … that was pretty disrespectful. He could have at least phoned *Sam* first. Poor Sam … I can still see the look on his face when he realised that girl is his *half*-sister.'

Belle nodded. 'Yeah, his dad had evidently failed to fill him in about *that* little detail … bastard.'

'Yes. Bastard,' Gabi echoed.

We all had bit of a laugh about our continual use of the same descriptive word, prompting me to suggest we should eat something, so we de-camped and headed indoors. Belle had prepared a heap of food to have on hand - which was good as we'd eaten very little at the wake - so Evie and I heated up what needed heating, while Belle and Gabi retrieved the other goodies from the fridge.

After deciding to eat indoors to avoid the pesky flies, we sat around the dining table and began our assault on the appetizing array in front of us. All talk was down to a minimum then, and while I savoured a delectable club sandwich I let my eyes wander; contemplating how lucky I was to have these smart, funny women as my friends.

Gabi, the most exuberant of us all, was tall and skinny with short red hair and a flawless pale complexion. She usually wore flamboyant creations of many colours but had toned herself down for the funeral, wearing a simple, russet brown shift dress and a matching short-sleeved jacket. Having never fully grasped the intricacies of the English language, she often had us laughing at her funny mispronunciations.

Belle, in complete contrast, was of average height and a little overweight – or *extra* curvy as she liked to describe herself. Her shoulder length, greyish brown hair, normally pulled up into a topknot or ponytail, was today worn loose. She generally favoured conservative, easy-to-wear casual clothes; today's being grey slacks and a simple black jacket, with a pale pink, silk t-shirt underneath. She'd ditched the jacket straight after the funeral though, saying it had been too warm.

And Evie … well I thought she *always* looked smart no matter *what* she wore. The pinstripe pants she was wearing today had been bought because she thought they might look slimming, and she'd teamed them with an unusual yellow and purple floral top. She often laughingly said that her weight would be perfect if she could just grow from five foot four to five foot eight. I once again admired the silvery white colour of her short shaved hairstyle, wishing I had the nerve to copy it, but knowing I never would. I was born a blonde and always joked that I would *die* a blonde.

I smiled a little then, thinking of how different we all looked from each other, then sighed as I reached forward and placed my empty plate on the coffee table. I don't mind being the shortest of my friends, but I'm not thrilled at being the heaviest. Having initially lost weight after Hugh died, I'd then put it all back on, *plus* some, and knew that comfort eating had led to my preference for 'comfortable' clothing. I'm quite happy though, with my range of stretchy Capri pants, leggings and loose tops, and will only have an outfit made-to-measure if the occasion calls for it. Even though I don't have to worry about money I still *love* getting a bargain, as I had with today's outfit of slim fitting, black pants and a midnight blue, silk tunic top; buying them both for half price! Noticing Gabi smiling as she reached towards the cheese platter, I stopped my musings and asked her what she was thinking about.

'Well, yes ... I *was* just doing the thinking ... about how *happy* I am to have all of you as my friends. We are all very different, but I think this is a very good thing, yes?' She then smiled at each of us in turn.

'Yes, it *is* a very good thing,' I replied, surprised at having just been thinking the same.

The other two nodded in agreement while happily munching on their scrumptious mini quiches.

'Yes,' Gabi went on, 'I love that we are all having our

different interests, even though you three are *so* creative and I am not creative *at all*.'

'Yeah, but you're still quite creative with your mastery of the English language,' Belle grinned. '*And* you're also good at other things … like organizing events. I'm totally useless at that.'

'Yes, same here,' Evie nodded.

'Me too,' I also agreed. 'We couldn't possibly manage without your expert help when we have our openings and exhibitions.'

'Hmm … yes that is true. So, yes, it *is* good we are all different. Imagine if we were all the same … how boring.'

We all agreed to that, then filled each other in about the state of our current projects until we'd finished eating; putting the leftovers in the fridge. Deciding to have one more glass of wine, we took them back out to the patio; stretching out once more onto the thickly padded sun lounges.

'Hey you know how much I love words, and finding just the right one when I'm writing,' Evie then asked.

We all nodded; sipping our drinks and waiting for her to go on.

'Well I was just wondering if any of you have any favourite words. I have a few but one I used recently is 'hence'. You don't hear it much these days, but for some reason I like it … *hence* me bringing it up now,' she grinned.

We all smiled at that, but before I could say anything

Belle said one of her favourite words is 'peccadillo', just because of the way it sounded.

'Ooh yes … *peccadillo* … that does sound good to say doesn't it,' Evie agreed.

Belle then went on, saying 'And another favourite of mine would be 'cumquat'. I bought a cumquat tree a while ago and the word stuck in my head for ages.'

'Cumquat? Hmmm … yes, that too is a good word,' Gabi nodded. 'But I think my favourite is 'zabka'. My papa used to call me that when I was still the child. I loved hearing him say it, but of course I never hear it anymore now.'

'Oh, what does it mean Gabi?' Evie asked, quite interested.

Smiling, Gabi replied, 'well, it does have a few of the meanings, but one is an affectionate term for 'frog'. It always used to make me giggle when he called me that.'

We all smiled, saying it was a lovely memory to have of her father. I then announced that my favourite word was 'shopping', to which they all rolled their eyes, saying, 'that'd be right.'

After a few more hours of chatting and laughing, interspersed with worrying about Anna, the sun began to set and the ensuing mosquitoes forced us indoors. Belle ordered in Thai food and we ate until we were all finally full, then leaned back in our chairs and appraised the assemblage of empty containers on the table. Evie cheerfully offered to do the dishes before collecting all the plasticware and heading outside to deposit them in the bin. After gathering the used cutlery, bowls and now empty glasses, she put them in Belle's dishwasher, filled the kettle, then asked, 'Who's for a cup of tea?'

Everyone was now enjoying their cuppa, settled in Belle's comfy lounge room. Being a little cooler now, Belle had provided cardigans for those of us who'd left their jackets in the car. It was quiet for a moment, and I became aware of the scent of boronia wafting in through the open window, as the curtain gently drifted in and out with the slight breeze.

'You know … funerals make you feel more *alive* somehow … don't you think?' I looked at everybody, as they looked back at me quizzically.

'Hmmm … I know what you mean Liz,' Belle then replied. 'I think the thought of no longer existing makes a person think about exerting their presence somehow … leave a mark for posterity maybe. *Or* … maybe just live for the moment and enjoy every day.'

'Yeah exactly, thank you Belle,' I smiled. Then a funny feeling came over me as I exclaimed, '*Oh* … I forgot to tell you all something. Well actually I already told Evie on the way from the airport … but with everything else that's happened today I forgot all about it.'

'What is it?' Gabi and Belle said in unison; smiling with obvious curiosity on their faces.

'Well … I've bought a house … a huge house … and I

thought we could all live in it together … with Anna too hopefully.'

Smiling at the stunned expressions on their faces, I settled back to once more give a description of the house I'd bought; fingers crossed they'd be open to my idea.

CHAPTER FOUR

It was dark outside now, and Anna was lying on her bed staring at the ceiling. The glow from her bedside lamp illuminated the room sufficiently for her to see several long cracks in the paintwork near the overhead light. She wondered how long they'd been there without her noticing before.

'Humph … I wonder what else I haven't seen that's been right under my nose.'

She still felt numb, and was surprised when she was able to get up and walk to the bathroom, accepting that her body must be operating under some sort of automatic function. That thought made her smile, but when she caught a glimpse of herself in the bathroom mirror she saw that the smile was more of a grimace. Her short brown hair was sticking out at all angles, and her normally plumpish, round face looked haggard and drawn.

'Oh … you ugly old cow. No wonder Jim found himself another woman.'

After using the loo, she stared at her reflection in the mirror for a moment, then watched as fresh tears made their way down the creases in her cheeks. She must have zoned out for a while then, because she suddenly became aware that her skin was now mostly dry. Straightening her posture, it felt like her whole body had seized up and she had to make a concerted effort to turn around and walk back into her bedroom.

She was lying down again, once more staring at the ceiling, but couldn't remember actually getting onto the bed.

'That's right … I'm going crazy now … just what I need.' A strangled sounding laugh came out of her mouth, the sound so odd that she immediately stopped herself. Not wanting to think about anything anymore, she closed her eyes, hoping the sleeping tablet Sam had given her would kick in soon. Sleep … she just wanted to sleep and sleep … and hopefully when she woke up she'd discover that today had just been a bad dream.

But her eyes must have opened of their own accord as she realised they were focused on the ceiling cracks again. An image of Claire storming out of the house then filled her mind, bringing with it a new level of sadness to weigh her down.

'Poor girl … she idolised her father. She may never be

able to acknowledge what he's done. *Huh* … it wouldn't even surprise me if she blames *me* somehow … she always took *his* side in things.'

Her thoughts then went once more to the scene at the cemetery, and to the words the celebrant had spoken to her.

'I'm so, so sorry Anna … but apparently that lady has been living with Jim for some time. I just found out about it before the service. She asked me where she should sit … being his partner.'

'Partner. Wife. Partner. Wife.'

The words rolled through her mind over and over.

'Did I ever mean anything to him I wonder? Or was I just one of many? Maybe this was just a convenient place for him stay and be pampered for a while, on his stop-over to someone else.'

The thought that Sam had known but hadn't told her hurt immensely. She'd understood his reasoning though, when he'd told her that he'd only promised his dad he'd say nothing if he swore to end the affair.

'Bastard,' she said out loud, the word startling her slightly. Then, 'what a bastard … putting that on Sam. What sort of a father expects that from their own son?'

Her thoughts then went to the young girl … Jim's daughter.

'How could he, how could he, how *could* he? He knew how much I'd always wanted more children,' she whispered to herself; tears streaming down her face again. Rolling over onto her stomach, her face now pressed into the pillow, she let the tears flow. Thankfully the sleeping tablet finally took effect and she slipped into a deep, exhausted sleep.

It was getting on for midday when she woke, still feeling tired, and with just one thing on her mind. Contacting Claire. After quickly washing her face, she pulled on her dressing gown and headed to the dining room where she'd left her laptop. Sam had left a note on the table saying he'd gone to get milk and the newspaper, so she made herself a black tea while waiting for the computer to boot up.

It wasn't long before she had a blank email page in front of her and was contemplating what to write. With the time difference between countries, Claire had said a long time ago she'd prefer they emailed each other, rather than phoned. Anna had always thought it was terribly impersonal but went along with what her daughter wanted. Taking a deep breath she put her fingers on the keys.

From *annanowiki@gmail.com*
To *clairebaumann@yahoo.com.au*

Hello Claire,

I'm so sorry you felt you had to leave here so quickly yesterday. I hope you're okay, although I know you must be feeling as devastated as Sam and I are. I don't know what to say about your father, so I won't say anything. I know you loved him very much. Please contact me as soon as you're able, as I can't rest properly until I know you're home safe. Please say hello to Gunther for me.
Take care … I love you.
Mum xx

Closing the lid of her laptop, she took a sip of her now luke-warm tea, grimaced, and tipped it down the sink. Deciding to get dressed before making another, she was heading for her bedroom when she heard the doorbell ring. Not really feeling like seeing anyone she considered ignoring it, but then thought maybe Sam had locked himself out. So, turning around she sighed before slowly making her way down the passageway towards the front door.

Gabi had arrived at Anna's place just on midday. She was hoping to be able to cheer up her friend before leaving for her one o'clock lunch date at Eastern Beach. As soon as Anna opened the front door though, Gabi knew it was going to be a difficult mission.

'Anna …hi …I hope you were not lying down. Did I wake you? Where is Sam? I thought he would be here.'

'Hi Gabi ... come in. No you didn't wake me. Sam just walked to the shop, he won't be long.'

Even though it was pleasantly cool inside with all the curtains and blinds closed, Gabi felt a heavy gloom in the air as well. It was as though Anna's sadness was hovering above, waiting for somewhere to settle.

'It is so cool in here Anna ... outside is so hot now.' Gabi knew she was prattling on but couldn't stop. 'We are having so many hot days lately, yes?'

'Yes ... coffee? Or tea? We've run out of milk so it will have to be black.'

'Yes I drink the black tea, so that would be lovely ... thank you Anna.'

There was a lull in the conversation then as Anna turned the kettle on and scooped tea into a small teapot. Gabi sat at the dining table, placing her bag on a chair beside her, then studied her friend for a moment. Seeing how sad Anna looked - as if all joy had been completely wrung out of her - she spoke.

'How are you Anna? Really.'

'*Really?* I still feel a bit numb actually.' Then, stopping what she was doing with the cups and teapot, she went on. 'But you know what? I'm just now realising how *angry* I am. And I feel betrayed and humiliated and sickened.' Turning round to look at Gabi the words continued to flow. 'I feel stupid too. How stupid of me to have waited on him hand and foot whenever he *deigned* to come home. *Home!* I wonder how many *homes* he actually had.'

'Please do not think of yourself as being stupid Anna. He fooled all of us … none of us can *believe* what he has done!'

Anna surprised herself then with her sudden need to give voice to the many jangling thoughts which had been tormenting her since the funeral. Stepping from behind the kitchen bench she sat down opposite her friend, then, buoyed by Gabi's presence she continued to unburden herself.

'He used to say how we'd live three or four months of the year in that apartment in Singapore when he retired next year … how it would be our base when we travelled through Europe and Asia … how we could have our friends come and stay with us there. Ha! What a liar. He'd been living there with *them* for *years*. God only knows what he did with them the times I went over for a holiday. Bastard.'

'*Anna* … I think that is the first time I have ever heard you swear,' Gabi grinned.

Anna looked at her friend's startled face and couldn't help but smile.

'Yes, well I'm not the same old Anna anymore. I'm not sure who I am yet … but I'm not going to be so … *agreeable* anymore.' She looked at Gabi as if daring her to disagree … but smiled again when she saw the look of admiration on her face.

'But that is fantastic, good on you.'

Sam walked in then with the milk and newspaper but stopped in his tracks as soon as he saw his mum smiling.

'What's going on here then? Hi Gabi … good to see you

again.' He'd left the house fifteen minutes ago, seriously worried about his mum ... and now here she was actually *smiling*!

'Hi Sam, how is everything with you? How long are you staying? Do you have to go back soon? And where are you living these days?'

'I'm good thanks Gabi.' He grinned at the number of questions she'd just asked him. 'I'm actually living in Vancouver now but I'll be back in Australia soon for a twelve month job contract in Alice Springs. I'm really looking forward to it. I hope you'll be able to come for a few visits while I'm there Mum.'

'Of course ... I'd love to come for a visit.'

'And to answer your other question Gabi, I can stay here as long as Mum needs me.'

'Well I think you should go back next week,' Anna said, standing up to attend to the now whistling kettle. 'There's no need to stay till the will's sorted; I can manage all that. And as you said, you'll be back in Australia in no time.'

Sam looked a bit worried at the mention of his dad's will, but Anna didn't notice as she was intent on pouring the boiling water over the aromatic tea leaves. He made himself a coffee as his mum placed the teapot and cups on the table, then excused himself to read the paper outside.

The two women talked for another half hour or so; Gabi saying that Evie, Liz and Belle were dropping round to visit Anna about two o'clock. She even managed to get Anna to smile again before leaving for her date at the Eastern Beach café, by relaying the details of her *last* disastrous date. They were now standing at the open front door, giving each other a hug.

'Thanks for coming Gabi. You've actually cheered me up a bit. I was feeling pretty miserable before.'

'Well that is what friends are for, yes?'

'Yes, I guess so. Well I better have a shower and get dressed before the others get here I suppose.' Smiling she added, 'Let me know how your date goes.'

Driving off, Gabi was pleased that she'd left Anna happier than she was before her visit. She was also excited to be meeting the man she'd been chatting to online for the last week. He'd looked good in his photo, and he seemed to like the same things she did. Of course that was no guarantee the elusive spark would be there though. She'd been on numerous dates; some good, some bad, and some she'd rather not think about *ever* again.

'It is not that I am fussy,' she thought to herself, 'well … yes … I suppose I *am* a *bit* fussy, but there is nothing wrong with that.' Sighing, she then spoke out loud, 'I would just like to find a really nice man … why is that so hard?'

She felt a bit morose then, thinking of her long quest to find a compatible partner, and wondered if she'd caught some of Anna's discarded depression. So, turning up the stereo she began to sing along to *Crazy Little Thing Called*

Love, and it wasn't long before she felt her spirit lift; once more elevated to its usual bubbly state.

Ten minutes later she was lucky to see a car pulling out of a parking space on Eastern Beach Road. Deftly parallel parking in the shade of a large Elm, she sat for a moment and studied the fantastic vista. Her view took in the expanse of Corio Bay, the yacht club, and the huge semi-circular swimming enclosure in front of the café where she was to meet her date. There were heaps of people of all ages out enjoying the summer-like weather, and the sound of children screaming in delight heightened her mood even more. After a quick look at her reflection in the rear view mirror, she took a deep breath, then stepped out of the car.

'Okay,' she breathed out slowly. 'Fingers crossed he at least *looks* like his photo.' She couldn't help but grin a little at the memory of some of the men she'd met in the past, who bore very little similarity to their profile pictures.

Walking down the steep slope towards the agreed rendezvous point, her despondency disappeared completely. She felt that whatever eventuated today she was just happy to be alive. The laughter of the children was contagious and she felt herself smiling as she stood in front of the café looking for 'Trevor'.

CHAPTER FIVE

Belle, Evie and I were nattering away about a variety of subjects as we approached Torquay on our way to Anglesea. I could have taken the other road and bypassed the popular beachside town, but I didn't think of it in time.

'Bugger … we've certainly got a bit of traffic here today,' I muttered as I slowed down to a crawl behind a row of cars.

'Yes, well it's always busy here when we get a bit of hot weather, but don't worry Liz, it's a gorgeous day for a drive and we have plenty of time.' Evie then lowered her window right down and inhaled the ocean air. 'Ahhh … yes … I just love the smell of the beach.'

'Oh me too,' Belle agreed. 'Anna and I often come here in the summer to walk along the beach, especially in the evenings when it's cooler … there aren't the crowds then either. Gabi sometimes comes too. What about you Liz, are you still walking on the beach near you? Or not so much now that Hugh's not with you?'

'I still go sometimes. I have a couple of neighbours that are regular walkers, but I do find it a bit sad without Hugh. You know how much he loved the beach.'

Evie and Belle nodded, and we then drove in silence; all having our own thoughts to dwell on for a while. Ten minutes later we'd left Torquay behind and our conversation returned to the house we were on our way to inspect.

'It's a shame Gabi couldn't come with us to check out your house as well,' Evie said.

'Yeah. I just hope that her date goes well,' I smiled. 'You've really got to give her an A for effort in her pursuit to find a nice man.'

'Yeah definitely an A,' Belle agreed.

'I'd actually hoped that Anna would come for the drive too … you know … not just to see the house, but to take her mind off everything else for a while.' The other two nodded and I sighed and went on. 'But I *do* understand that she's wanting to spend time with Sam while he's here. Never mind though … I'll drop by again to see when she's up for an outing. If she feels like it tomorrow she can come with Gabi as I've promised to show her the house in the afternoon.'

'Well … here it is.' I had a very proud grin on my face as I pulled into the driveway and turned off the car. The others just sat for a moment - eyes focused on the house - before simultaneously opening their doors and stepping out.

'Wow, looks *great*,' was all that Belle could manage. She seemed completely stunned by the size and 'look' of the place.

'Yes … *fantastic*.' Evie too was a bit awed.

I laughed. 'Yeah well I did say it was a fabulous house, did I not? Come on, I'm dying to show you the inside. George and Iris have already removed their furniture, and even though the sale won't be finalised 'til next week they were happy to give me the keys.'

As I stopped to fish around in my bag for the said keys, the other two women took stock of what lay before them. The house was rectangular in shape, with the short end facing the road. The top level had a verandah overhanging the lower area, providing a sheltered walkway right around the house. A combination of three creepers were growing up the supporting posts, entwining with each other to display a delightful mix of yellow, white and orange.

A free standing double garage was to the left, and a large carport, big enough to shelter four cars, abutted the front end of the house. No one spoke as we walked under the carport and to the right, towards the impressive front door which was larger than normal and carved with an intricate sun and waves design.

'Wow,' Belle said again after I inserted the key, opened the door, and we stepped inside.

Even though the spacious entrance was in semi-darkness,

both Evie and Belle commented that it had a very welcoming vibe. The timber flooring exuded a coolness which we all appreciated after the heat outdoors, and as our eyes adjusted to the low light I noticed my friends glancing to the right where a carpeted staircase led their eyes upwards.

I just smiled and immediately set about opening the drapes on the right-hand side wall, revealing petunias of many colours spilling over the edges of hanging baskets which were attached to the underside of the verandah. Then, before the other two had a chance to say anything, I led them through a door on the left into the spacious laundry, then unlocked a security door which opened onto a large outdoor paved area.

An old style, four strand clothes line was strung between two wooden t-shaped posts, behind which a stunning pink bottlebrush stood out amongst a group of other native plants near the fence. A pathway to the right led to a timber seating area, arranged under a couple of tall Eucalypts.

'Oh this is lovely Liz,' Evie exclaimed. 'Anyone would enjoy doing the laundry here.'

'Yeah I know … it's fab isn't it? George and Iris left a couple of outdoor settings here, along with the pot plants. They said it wasn't worth moving them, so that's a bonus,' I grinned. 'Wait 'til you see the rest though. As they say – you aint seen nothin' yet.'

Shooing them back inside to the entrance area, I pointed to a door next to the windows.

'Look through there … it's a gorgeous sunroom. It'd be

sheltered from the hot summer sun, but would be beautifully warm in winter. I *had* thought it could be a spare bedroom if need be, but *now* I'm thinking I'll use it as a workroom to make my jewellery.'

The women stepped into the room as I opened the curtains. A full-width window showcased a large section of the garden, and as it faced northerly, the room was flooded with light.

'Oh this would be an excellent room to work in Liz,' Belle exclaimed. 'A perfect place to make your jewellery, or just sit and enjoy the view.'

The two women then followed me into the entrance area once more before I led them through a doorway on the rear wall. This opened onto a *huge* room which had a wall of curtains to the right, and another smaller room to the left. I pulled a couple of the curtains apart to reveal a sliding door which gave access to outside, and another lovely paved area. Large pots of cyclamen in full bloom stood out against the greenery, but before Evie or Belle could comment on the vivid display, I continued with my commentary.

'They used to have a full size billiard table here, and every type of gym equipment you can imagine. And over there were several couches and a PlayStation thingy where their son and his mates used to hang out ... that's why it's so roomy down here.'

'*Wow ... yes ... very* roomy.'

'So I thought you could have your bedroom down here if you like Belle.' Pointing to the left I said, 'Over there is a lovely shower room and separate toilet, so it would be like having your own ensuite,' I smiled. 'And there's still heaps of room for you to have a large table to do your painting. I thought we could put up a dividing wall to separate your bedroom and work area ... and build in some wardrobes of course.'

Belle was quite speechless for a moment, then she smiled, saying, 'Oh my goodness I love it. What a great room ... *and* a great idea.'

'Definitely!' Evie agreed.

Before anymore could be said I hustled them out, saying they *had* to see upstairs.

'Oh my ... this is *very* nice.'

'*Absolutely.*'

I couldn't stop grinning as I said, 'I just *knew* you'd both love it.'

We were standing at the top of the stairs which were situated to the right of a large open plan area. We could see that the lounge room took up the entire front end of the house, with large windows on the north and south side walls. Two tall windows flanked a brick wall on the eastern end, where a gas log fire was featured. This room flowed into the kitchen and dining area; the kitchen on the southern side, looking over the paved outdoor area, and the dining room on the opposite side, looking over the garden.

Belle and Evie then inspected the kitchen, exclaiming at

the size and layout, while I opened the drapes in the dining area, then unlocked a sliding door to reveal the wide verandah. We were all then immediately drawn to step outside; marveling at the gorgeous view.

A large lawn and colourful garden lay directly before us, with a variety of native trees and shrubs screening the fences. To the right we could see the blue of the ocean and a line of golden sand; the view being obstructed here and there by a couple of tall trees. We were drawn in that direction so, walking towards the eastern end, we then leant against the timber railing and watched a ship on the horizon heading towards Melbourne.

'Oh Liz … no wonder you bought this place.' Evie was shaking her head in disbelief. 'It's truly wonderful.'

'Absolutely,' Belle agreed once more.

'But wait … there's more,' I grinned wickedly. 'Come and see the bedrooms.'

Back inside we walked through a doorway situated centrally between the kitchen and dining room, into a passageway where four double bedrooms were located. The two on the right overlooked the garden and had spacious ensuite bathrooms, while the two on the left were separated by a large bathroom and a separate toilet. These two looked directly at the foliage of two gum trees, both of which had stunning flowers; one orange, the other a deep red. Each bedroom also had sliding door access to the encircling, covered verandah.

I couldn't stop smiling as I listened to Evie and Belle gush over everything they saw, making me *more* than hopeful they'd decide to live here with me. Thrilled at the prospect of us all sharing, I led them past the bedrooms towards the western end of the house.

My two friends were quite surprised to then enter another lounge room, smaller than the other but very cozy, having enough room for a T.V. and a couple of couches. Book shelves mostly covered the western wall; Evie commenting there was enough shelving to house her large collection of books. This room wasn't as wide as the other lounge room. It had been made smaller to enable wider deck spaces to be created on the north and south sides. Both these areas were quite spacious; one provided shade in the summer, the other was a perfect spot to catch the winter sun. Stairways were situated at the ends of both decks, one leading to the front garden, the other to the rear.

'Oh I love this room,' Belle exclaimed. 'It would be perfect if we wanted to watch different T.V. shows, or just for reading and relaxing.'

'And I love the *style* of the house,' Evie added. 'It has a Scandinavian feel … don't you think?'

'Yeah, that's exactly what I thought,' I nodded.

'Yes me too,' Belle agreed. 'I *love* the pale gold colour of the timber; it works so well in the kitchen, and those book shelves look so interesting the way the shelves are staggered for different size books or nick knacks.'

'And the colour scheme of neutrals and different shades

of blue would make it a very relaxing house to live in,' Evie added, nodding her head.

'Do you think it needs any Feng Shui remedies?'

'No, definitely not Liz,' Evie said emphatically. 'This place has a wonderful, flowing energy.'

We were all silent then as we walked back through the dining room, and out to the verandah again. Both Belle and Evie looked a bit stunned, while I looked extremely happy.

'So … who's moving in then?' I asked, smiling from one to the other.

'Liz … this place is *gorgeous* … I'd *love* to live here … but it's not that simple.' Belle frowned while she struggled to find the right words to say. 'I … I'll still have to think about it … thank you for thinking of *me* to share with you … but … well … how would it all work? You know I'm not overly financial, and if I sold my place I don't think I'd get enough to cover the cost of a share in *this* one.'

'Belle has a point,' Evie cut in, 'because Gabi's not very financial either, *and* she's renting. And Anna … well … who knows how she'll end up financially now that Jim's done what he's done. She might have to share her assets with that other woman. And as for me … well … I'm still not sure how I feel about sharing. But … after looking through the house I believe we *would* have plenty of room to do our own thing here. So … I'll definitely give it more thought, but in the meantime … what are you thinking Liz? Did you want us all to buy equal parts … or what?'

'Okay settle petal, everyone stop stressing,' I smiled at

them both. 'Come on, let's go downstairs and find some-where to sit outside and we'll talk it over. You really need to see the garden while you're here anyway. I know Anna will *love* it.'

After taking another admiring look at the marvelous view, we all filed downstairs … then outdoors. Walking across the expanse of lawn, we sat in another shady seating area beside a large banksia.

'Okay ladies, I don't want you to give up the thought of living here, because I have a plan which I think will suit everybody.'

CHAPTER SIX

'I give up. I damn well just give up.' Gabi was fuming as she strode back up the steps to her car. '*Men* … they can all go and … *grrrr* … I cannot even think of the words to say.'

Hopping into her car she wound down her window and endeavored to calm herself by breathing in the fresh air.

'Come on … deep breath in … and out … and again, in … and out. Okay … that is a bit better … I *think*.' Shaking her head again in disbelief, she suddenly started to laugh, then said, 'Oh my God … who the hell does he think he is? *George Clooney?*'

Driving off towards her home in Manifold Heights, still chuckling to herself, she felt she had to tell someone about this latest letdown. After nearing Anna's street in Newtown she tossed up whether to go there or to continue on to the other side of the river and see Belle in Highton. Suddenly deciding to do neither, she turned right at Shannon Avenue and drove another couple of minutes to her home.

With an *Enya* CD softly playing, Gabi was now completely relaxed; immersed in a hot bath scented with a selection of aromatherapy oils.

'Ahhhh … yes … this is perfect,' she thought to herself. Leaning her head back against her bath pillow, she closed her eyes, but couldn't stop herself from thinking about her dud date.

It had started well enough. Trevor had indeed looked like his profile photo, and had come across as being quite charming. They'd ended up having a late lunch and talked for a couple of hours before taking a leisurely walk around the promenade. After returning to sit at one of the café tables again, they'd enjoyed a coffee, before Trevor had suggested they have dinner together later. As they'd been getting along so well she'd agreed, so he'd phoned The Beach House Restaurant, which was situated right above where they'd been sitting, and had been happy to hear they'd had a table available. Laughing and joking about not having far to go, they'd later climbed the steps to the restaurant; sitting at an outdoor table so they could admire the view.

They'd been chatting while waiting for their meals to arrive - she just starting on her second glass of wine - when

Trevor had downed his second then asked the waiter for another one. She'd commented that he'd have to be careful as he still had to drive home, and was flabbergasted when he'd smiled and winked at her, saying he'd planned on them getting a taxi to her place later, as he'd assumed he was staying overnight!

'Ha … what a kretyn,' Gabi said, reverting to her native Polish as she opened her eyes and sat up. She laughed again as she remembered the look on his face as she'd said, 'No, you are not staying with me overnight. Who the hell do you think you are? I just met you today and you think I am going to do the sleeping together *tonight*? *Ha* … you have *got* to be *joking*.'

She'd stood up and laid twenty dollars on the table, saying 'this will cover the cost of my drinks … you can pay for the meals … enjoy.'

Smiling at the memory of his stunned expression, Gabi added more hot water to the old-fashioned, deep bath. When it was steaming and close to overflowing she slowly slid down, lying back so just her face was out of the water.

'Ahhhh … yes … I could stay in here forever. Well, maybe not *forever*,' she grinned again, 'but at least another twenty minutes.'

The sensation of floating in the hot water and the weirdly muffled sounds of the music in her ears had her thoughts drifting again … this time back several years.

Thinking back on her life she knew she'd been quite useless at choosing men. Tomasz, whom she'd once loved but who'd been a shocking flirt, had caused her a lot of grief. She'd married him at seventeen, wanting to get away from her large, impoverished family. The plan had been to work hard and save enough money so they could both get to America one day.

But eleven years later - only managing to get to Italy - she'd left him after catching him *in flagrante delicto* with another woman. Then, after becoming friends with Zofia, another Polish woman in a similar situation as herself, the two had made their way to France where Zofia had a cousin they could stay with for a while. It was there that she'd met Roger, a miner on holiday from Australia. She'd married him after divorcing Tomasz; moving to Australia and settling in Ravensthorpe with him.

Unfortunately she'd found out too late that Roger was a big drinker, and one who'd become more and more abusive towards her over time. After enduring it for ten years she'd finally had enough; packing a bag and hitching a ride with a truckie to Adelaide. After working in a vineyard for a couple of months she'd wanted to put as much distance as possible between herself and Roger, so had moved once more, this time to Geelong.

It was there that she'd met Eric, the love of her life. After divorcing Roger she and Eric had married and she'd thought she'd finally found her lifetime partner. Eric however had suffered a severe stroke six years later. She'd then been his care giver for more than five years until he'd died in her arms from pneumonia.

She hadn't been interested in men for quite a while after that, but these last couple of years she'd thought how lovely it would be to have that special person to share good times with again. Friends had encouraged her to 'go online' and find someone, and so she'd given it a go … to no avail so far. Sighing, she decided not to think about it anymore.

Suddenly jerking upwards, Gabi realised she must have dozed off. The water was now lukewarm, so grasping hold of the sides of the bath she managed to haul herself up enough to then become upright.

'That was *not* the graceful maneuver I must say,' she smiled as she stepped out of the bath. 'I am glad there is no man here to be witness to that.'

Happy with her now relaxed state of mind, she dried off and put on her pj's. Then, after making herself a cup of tea, she headed to the lounge and turned on her computer.

'Time to delete that moron … and will I see if someone else appeals?' Gabi sipped her tea as the online dating site loaded. As a new ensemble of male faces appeared, she smiled.

'Hmm … yes … no … ah okay … *why* not.'

CHAPTER SEVEN

Anna closed her eyes as the plane hurtled down the runway. Pushed back into her seat with the force of the plane lifting off, she couldn't seem to pinpoint the emotion she was feeling. There had been so many different ones over the last couple of weeks, and each one had left a small vestige of itself which now coloured her mood.

There had been the shock she'd felt at the cemetery followed by intense anger and a feeling of betrayal. Humiliation, depression and anxiety had all reared their heads, and then after seeing the house which Liz had bought for them to share, she'd felt wonder, gratitude and uncertainty. The most recent emotion she'd had to deal with was disbelief, after recently hearing the details of Jim's new will.

She hadn't *known* that he'd made a new will, but in the days leading up to the reading she'd imagined that he may have made a new one at some stage, to provide support for his daughter. Finding out that he'd actually left *that* woman total ownership of the Singapore apartment *and* half of his superannuation had just been too much for her to accept. Breaking down in tears, it was her solicitor who'd said he could challenge the superannuation bequest as he felt Anna should be entitled to more than half. After she'd managed to stop crying, a steely calm had come over her, and she'd said 'yes … challenge it. In fact challenge all of it.'

Her feelings towards Jim were now non-existent, but she'd still felt the need to go to Singapore and confront the woman with whom she'd been sharing her husband's affection. She had to know just what sort of a woman she was … a scheming home wrecker … or was she *really* someone who'd been lied to as well?

Even though she'd always been entitled to a reduced rate for air tickets - with Jim being a pilot – she'd never flown first class before, but when she found out there were no business seats available she decided to pay the extra … and was loving it.

After the plane had levelled off, she took a deep breath, opened her eyes, and decided to ditch all negative thoughts, deciding 'calm' would be her new focus. Accepting the proffered glass of wine from the attentive stewardess, she then relaxed and stretched, relishing all the room she had.

Fifteen minutes later, having finished her chardonnay, she put aside the magazine she'd been flicking through, and once more gazed out the window. The blanket of cotton wool clouds had finally obscured the occasional glimpses of terra firma, so she closed her eyes again and relaxed back into her seat. The email she'd received from Claire nearly two weeks ago then popped into her head, and she couldn't stop the words from floating through her mind again.

From *clairebaumann@yahoo.com.au*
To annanowiki@gmail.com

Hello Mum,
I have arrived home safely. I really can't say much now as I don't know what to say. But why would Dad do that? I just don't under-stand. I thought you were both happy.
I have to go now. Gunther says hello.
C

Knowing if she dwelt on it she'd feel miserable, she took a deep breath and pushed it to the back of her mind. She hoped one day her relationship with her daughter would be one of mutual love and respect, but as there was nothing she could do to achieve that right now, she chose to feel optimistic for the future and give more thought to Liz's proposal.

The day after the other three had looked at the house in Anglesea, they'd dropped in at her place again and insisted she and Gabi *had* to check it out as well. The five of them had fitted into Liz's Range Rover without too much difficulty - Evie in front with Liz; Gabi, Belle and herself in the back. She hadn't really felt like going, but couldn't be bothered arguing. So, having thought the outing might take her mind off things for a while she'd given in and gone … and how glad she was that she had.

Both she and Gabi had been as stunned as the others at the size and layout of the place, and she remembered how her spirit had been uplifted seeing the fabulous view and gorgeous garden. Afterwards they'd dropped into the Anglesea pub for lunch, and Liz had reiterated the plan she'd discussed with Evie and Belle the previous day.

They'd all been gob smacked at Liz's generous offer; being that the four of them would pay her a weekly rent of fifty dollars, with the utility bills being split equally between the five of them. Everyone would put in a certain amount for food each week, but that would be worked out as they went along. Liz said the rent money would total about ten thousand a year which would cover the cost of insurances, rates and maintenance.

Anna liked the idea in theory, but was unsure of actually sharing a house with *four* other people. After all, she'd lived most of her life by herself after Sam and Claire had left home. Jim had come and gone of course on a semi-regular basis, but she'd been alone more often than not.

Opening her eyes to look out the window again, she gave it some thought; deciding it was mainly the evenings she missed having some company. She often went out with friends to all manner of different entertainments, but for a couple of years now she'd been looking forward to Jim retiring so they could spend days and evenings together. Her musings were then interrupted by a voice from the aisle.

'Excuse me madam, would you like another glass of wine?'

'Yes, I would … thank you.'

'Lunch will be served in another half an hour.'

'Okay, thanks.'

After the stewardess had moved on down the narrow walkway, Anna put her mind to the question of whether or not she should move to Anglesea with the others. But she soon realised she couldn't concentrate, as thoughts of *that* woman kept intruding. After having initiated the planned meeting, Anna was now feeling unsettled thinking about it; never being one for confrontations.

After much discussion with her solicitor, she had agreed that the woman could keep the apartment, as long as she waived all rights to Jim's superannuation and life insurance. Otherwise she would go ahead with challenging the will, and as the apartment was part of her marital assets, she would insist it be sold. Even if the woman then received part of the money, she would still have to move and suffer the disruption of finding somewhere else to live.

Finding out the apartment was worth more than her

house in Newtown had made her stand her ground. She had no superannuation of her own as she'd only worked for one year before becoming pregnant. Then Jim had insisted she was to stay home to look after him and their child. So that's what she'd done. She *had* loved it though, and then when Sam was born two years later, she'd been in her element caring for her little family. But she'd always expected that Jim, and his superannuation, would be there to provide for her in her later years.

'At least I have quite a tidy sum saved in the bank, and with Jim's super and life insurance, I don't mind splurging some of it on this trip,' she thought contentedly. 'In fact I'm done with scrimping and saving. Time for me to live a little.'

As she finished her drink she saw the lunch trolley coming her way, so she sat up, smiled, and prepared to be waited on again.

CHAPTER EIGHT

Gazing out the train's window at the spectacular scenery, Evie felt happy. After tentatively thinking that she *might* move in with Liz and the others - at least to see if it could work out or not - she was now returning home to Terrigal. Getting off the plane in Sydney after sleeping the whole way, she'd then hopped on the next train to Gosford. She loved train travel, finding it really relaxing watching the country-side zooming past. This route was quite scenic, and as she gazed out the window her thoughts wandered to the short break she'd just had in Geelong, and then to Liz's generous proposal.

She'd really enjoyed staying with Liz, and actually thought all of them living together *could* be a viable plan. Her only uncertainties being whether she could adapt to having people around *all* the time.

'Hmmm … I think I'm a bit set in my ways now,' she mused, then grinned, deeming it something old people said. 'Oh well … I suppose I'm not a spring chicken any more,' which made her smile again. Shaking her head slightly and chuckling to herself she thought, 'Oh God, what's happening to me. I can't stop talking like an *old* person.'

Still grinning, she contemplated living with her four best friends on a daily basis, and felt a definite pang of apprehension. She was so used to having her own space, *and* being on her own to write, that she wasn't sure if it could work. Being bit of a loner by nature, writing suited her disposition perfectly. Creating stories by beavering away on her laptop for hours on end was right up her alley. She was lucky that her friends didn't mind when she was on a roll and loath to stop the flow of words; sometimes knocking back invitations. They'd just show up the next day announcing, 'I hope you've got the kettle on?' before staying for a while to have a coffee. She loved it when that happened as it gave her no choice but to stop writing and stretch her stiff muscles. Weather permitting they'd often go for a walk as well.

Even though Blue lived with her she was still usually on her own as her gregarious granddaughter was rarely at home. At Uni most days, or studying with friends, Blue was conscious of providing Evie with plenty of uninterrupted time to write. When she *was* home though, she would often have her friends around as well, which Evie loved. She'd cook for them all, or they'd have a barbeque and sit around talking 'girl talk' for hours. It being such a big house they often slept over as well; usually on the weekends.

Now nearing Gosford, Evie rang a taxi to ensure it would be waiting for her when she alighted the train. Her pangs of apprehension were still lurking, so even though she'd told Liz that she'd *probably* move in with her, she acknowledged it needed more thought.

'I could rent my house out for twelve months, then I could always move back if sharing with my crazy friends didn't work out,' she smiled. 'Hmm … what to do, what to do?'

The train was slowing as it approached the station so she decided to think about it later. Pulling her bag down from the overhead rack she then got ready to disembark.

After the twenty minute taxi ride to her address in Terrigal, she paid the fare, retrieved her bag from its boot, and then hurried along the winding pathway. Unlocking the front door she walked in, dropped the bag where she stood, and let out a loud sigh.

'Ahhh … yes … it's so good to be *home* again.'

Walking straight through the large family area, she opened the sliding glass doors and stepped out onto the huge verandah; her favourite place to be after a long day. She had an elevated view from there as the backyard sloped down-wards, enabling her to see over her neighbour's rooftops.

Breathing in deeply she savoured the tantalising smell of the ocean which was inherent in the area.

'I'd never get sick of this view,' she smiled, as her gaze took in the beachline through the stand of native trees. 'Hmm … but the view from the Angelsea house is just as good … maybe even *better*. Hmm … well I'd better unpack my stuff I suppose, and then see if I can track Blue down. We've got a *lot* to talk about.'

Now showered and holding a stubby in one hand, Evie was stretched out on the couch; mobile phone to her ear. After having a quick chat, ascertaining that her granddaughter would be home for dinner in an hour or so, she hung up and drank some of her beer. She smiled as she thought of the happy response she'd received from Blue upon hearing that she was home again.

'I'm so lucky to have that girl in my life,' she mused, '*and* Marley. I just can't imagine my life without them.' She smiled then, as she always did, when she thought of how Marley had named her red headed daughter. Marley's mum had wanted her to call the baby Ruby or Scarlet, but because Marley had been really annoyed with her mum at the time, she'd said, 'No … I'm calling her Blue.' Her granddaughter had always loved her name because it was different to everybody else's.

Her thoughts then went to Dash, thanking her lucky stars she'd married him, and in the process gained a daughter-in-law and granddaughter.

'Damn,' she then said, shaking her head, 'I can't believe it's been nearly eleven years since he's been gone. How can that be? It doesn't *seem* that long.'

They'd only had five years together before he'd died of the same type of brain aneurysm to which his mother had succumbed. Evie sat there for a while, lost in thoughts of the fun times they'd had, and of the all things they'd planned to do but now never would. Realising she'd finished her drink, she sighed, stood up, and headed to the kitchen.

'Oh well … that's the way life goes sometimes.' She stared out the kitchen window for a few moments, then gave herself a mental shake.

'Right … I'd better get some food organised I suppose. I wouldn't be surprised if Bluey shows up with a couple of her friends … she usually does!'

Smiling once more, she set about preparing enough food for half a dozen people.

'Gran … hi … I *missed* you.'

'I missed you too … but I was only gone ten days.'

'Well it seems longer than that,' Blue smiled as she hugged her grandmother.

Evie looked behind Blue and said, 'So … you're here by *yourself*? I was expecting a few of the girls to be with you as well.'

'Oh don't worry, they're on their way. They had to stop

and get petrol before they conked out, and then drop Jarrod off at the gym.'

'Ahh okay.'

'So how was your trip? No dramas?'

'No, no dramas. Jason and Simon came for a visit yesterday arvo so we ended up having *bit* of a late night. We went to the pub for dinner then had a couple of drinks at home.'

'A couple?'

'Mmm.'

Blue just smiled at that, then said, 'so I suppose they stayed over then.'

'Yes. It worked out well as they then dropped me at the airport. Saved Liz from having to do it.'

'Oh okay, so you had a good flight?'

'I think so … I slept the whole way. I was a tad tired,' she smiled.

'So how did it all go in Geelong? How's Anna? Was it a good funeral?'

'Well yes and no. Anna is … okay … but … come and sit down while I finish preparing this food and I'll tell you all about it. You won't believe me though.'

'*What* … I don't *believe* it! Poor Anna … what a *shock*. And *Jim* … how could he *do* something like that? What a *bastard*!'

'Yes, definite bastard,' Evie couldn't help but smile. 'But I'm so impressed with how she's dealt with it. I thought she'd be a mess for a long time, and understandably so, but it's like a switch was flicked on inside her and she's transformed into this strong, determined woman. You know what a quiet, sweet woman she's always been?'

Blue nodded.

'Well guess what she's doing?' Without waiting for an answer, Evie went on. 'She flying to Singapore to confront the woman … can you *believe* it?'

'Wow. I never thought she's do something like *that*.'

'I know. But good on her I say.'

Just then the doorbell rang.

'COME IN,' yelled Blue.

'I hope that's the girls and not an axe murderer,' Evie grinned.

'Hi Evie.'

'Hi Lauren.'

'Hi Evie.'

'Hi Chloe.'

'Hi Evie.'

'Hi Kim. I hope you're all ravenous because I've made a pile of food here.'

'Absolutely.'

'You bet.'

'I'm *starving*.'

'Okay great. Come on then … let's eat.'

It was nearly nine o'clock before Blue's friends left, and she and Evie were now curled up on the couch, each with a cup of tea. They'd caught up on all the comings and goings which they'd both had over the last seven days - except for Liz's proposal. Evie had decided to wait until they were alone to run it by her granddaughter to see what she thought of the idea. She took a deep breath and set forth to explain what her friend had proposed.

'So … that's it. Liz is being incredibly generous with her offer, and I actually think it *could* work … as long as I have my own space when I need it.

'Wow … that's an awesome idea … what do the others think? Are they moving in?'

'I *think* so. Everybody just needs to think about it a bit first. After all it's a life changing decision.'

'Yeah it is.'

'So, you already knew I was thinking about moving back to Geelong, well now I'm contemplating moving in with the others for twelve months. That way I can see if it'll work without making any final decisions about selling here.'

'Oh, okay Gran,' Blue said a little despondently. 'I think that's a good idea to try it out for twelve months.'

'Yes, but I was also wondering if you and a couple of your friends might like to stay in this house while I'm gone?'

'*What?* Oh *absolutely*. That would be *fantastic*. I was a bit worried I'd have to move out and find somewhere else to live. Umm … how much would the rent be? You know we're not very financial don't you?'

'You *are* a doofus. Of course I know that. I was thinking you could stay for free, but you split the utility bills between you … and you pay for any damages … which I'm *sure* won't be necessary,' she smiled.

'Oh that's *fantastic*. Thanks Gran.'

'That's okay. Just as long as you don't trash the place or burn it down,' she smiled.

'I promise we won't,' Blue grinned.

'Hmm … well I still need to think about it before I *definitely* decide though. I just wanted to know your thoughts on it first.'

'Well I would miss you *heaps* of course … but it would be so cool for me and the others to have our own place for a while.'

'Okay, I'll let you know what I decide soon. But for now I'm going to bed. What about you?'

'Yes me too … see you in the morning … I love you.'

'I love you too. Sleep well.'

CHAPTER NINE

Belle was feeling restless. She walked around the spare bedroom which she used as a studio, picking up brushes and putting them back down, then moving a canvas from a table to the floor, then putting it back again. Sighing heavily she sat down in an old recliner and put her feet up. As she looked around at her array of artworks hanging on the walls she sighed again.

'What to do, what to do, what to do? Move or stay, stay or move? I don't know … I *just* don't know.'

Deciding that she needed some fresh air and exercise, she put her runners on, grabbed a hat and headed outdoors. Knowing that a good walk always helped to clear her head, she set off on one of her usual routes.

Thirty minutes later she'd worked up a slight sweat as she crested the highest section of her circuit. Having been considering her dilemma since she'd left home, she now took a deep breath and slackened her pace slightly. She enjoyed this section of her walk as it was flat and the street was shaded by large, leafy trees.

'Okay … now … *focus*. What *feels* right? Hmmm … I absolutely *love* the house in Anglesea, but do I *really* want to move from where I am now? *And* share with the others, which is more to the point.'

Turning a corner she started the slightly downward, thirty minute walk back to her home. Thinking some more, she acknowledged that even though she was quite busy with her painting and different outings she went on with her assorted friends, there were many nights she'd wished someone was there to share a laugh over a romcom or a few tears over a sad movie. She and Tatiana often rang each other in the evening, but it wasn't the same as talking face-to-face.

'Yeah … I think that's what it is,' she nodded. 'I'd enjoy someone else actually *being* there of an evening.'

Smiling as she walked along, she was happy that she'd pinpointed the reason she'd even *considered* moving.

'But then again … I really like having my own space sometimes, or even *more* than sometimes,' she thought, causing her smile to disappear.

She knew her problem lay in the fact she was pretty comfortable with her own company, and didn't think she needed someone else there *all* the time.

'Still … that downstairs area could be perfect for me. It's

certainly big enough. In fact I'd have more room for my studio than what I have *now*.'

Her smile returned as she thought about the room's picturesque outlook and how the natural light flooded through the expansive windows. Plus, knowing she'd have her own bathroom was essential. She hadn't shared a bathroom in years, and didn't fancy starting again now.

Liz was unable to move for another three or four weeks, so Belle knew there was no urgency for her to decide right now. Never one to rush her decisions, she was wishing she'd been able to talk it over with Anna before she'd left for overseas. Anna however had said she couldn't think about it until she settled things with that woman in Singapore, which Belle had completely understood. She then contemplated Anna's decision to confront Jim's mistress; shaking her head with the realisation of how much her friend had changed. It wasn't something the old Anna would have even *thought* of doing.

They'd met on their first day at work when they'd both started as sales assistants at the now defunct Bright's, an upmarket department store in Geelong. They'd been close friends ever since. Feeling a bit impotent to help her friend after Jim's betrayal, Belle had gladly offered to drive her to the airport; hugging her tightly before she'd left.

Thinking about how Anna had been there for her after Grant had died, Belle smiled sadly. It had been a shocking time. Not truly knowing the actual circumstances of his death had made the whole horrible episode even harder to accept. The police had only been able to determine that he'd swerved before driving off the road and hitting a tree. He'd been killed instantly.

They'd asked her about his state of mind at the time, because he'd been driving on a straight stretch of road in good conditions. A lot of Vietnam Vets had committed suicide, and they'd thought this had been a distinct possibility. Nothing had been ascertained for sure though, so his death had been recorded as an accident.

Grant had been her first and only love. They'd married six months after he'd returned from his tour of duty. Even though he'd had a lot of issues settling into 'normal' life again, they'd both been thrilled when she'd become pregnant. She'd suffered a miscarriage though, and then over the next few years had three more.

When she'd finally gone full term carrying twins, they'd both been ecstatic, only to have their hearts torn apart again when one daughter, Annalise, had been stillborn. Grant had always blamed himself, positive that the chemicals which had been dropped on him, and his mates, in the jungles of Vietnam had been the reason for their baby's death and the multiple miscarriages.

In the following days, weeks and months they'd finally accepted that their precious little Tatiana was perfect in every way. This had been a miracle to Grant, and had gone a long way in aiding his healing process. He'd still suffered greatly at times though, often doing his best to obliterate his memories with alcohol. Whatever the reason though, four years later his life had come to an end.

Bringing herself back to the present, Belle smiled. She'd always felt that Grant was with her and often talked to him. But now she turned her thoughts to her daughter.

'I think I'll phone Tatiana and see what *she* thinks about me moving. No, *I* think I'll go for a visit. I feel like getting away for a while. I'll check out flights as soon as I get home.'

Belle had a new spring in her step as she picked up her pace again. Her restlessness had lifted to be replaced with a feeling of anticipation. She loved her daughter dearly and had come to love her partner, Naomi, as well. They all made time to visit each other at *least* three or four times a year.

Suddenly the image of the grandchildren that she would never have popped into her head. It actually made her stumble slightly; literally throwing her off balance. Taking several deep breaths to steady herself, she made a concerted effort to stop those thoughts and think of something else.

The one thing that had upset her when she'd found out that Tatiana was gay, was realising that she wouldn't have grandchildren. She'd actually been devastated, but had done her best to keep her feelings from her daughter, not wanting her to feel guilty in any way.

Seeing her friends with their grandchildren, and hearing them talk about babysitting, sleep-overs and tantrums was always difficult for her. She'd thought it would get easier over time, but if anything it had become harder. If she allowed her thoughts free reign to picture herself holding and loving a grandchild she would soon slip into a depression which could sideline her for days. It was something she was able to fully share with Anna, and it was one more reason as to why she treasured her friendship – it seemed neither of them would know the joy of being a grandparent.

More deep breathing helped her gain her equilibrium as she approached her driveway. Opening the small side gate she hurried up the pathway, unlocked her front door, then found and turned on her iPad. Five minutes later after making a cup of coffee she was sitting at the kitchen bench, checking out flight times to Alice Springs.

CHAPTER TEN

I had been undecided whether to sell my house at Eastern View, or keep it and rent it out. After talking it over last night with Evie, Simon and Jase I'd made my decision. I was going to sell. Either way, I hated the thought of other people living in the home which I'd shared with Hugh for nearly eighteen years. So out of the two options, I now felt that a complete break would be the easiest way to proceed. Otherwise, with renting it, I knew I'd still feel tied to the place.

The house had been noticeably quiet since my three friends had left this morning. Simon and Jason had offered to drop Evie at Avalon airport on their way back to Melbourne so that had saved me a trip, especially when I wasn't required to pick up Lisa and Libby from Tullamarine as I normally would have. They were flying in today but had *insisted* they'd get the Gull bus to Geelong this time, so I just had a relatively short drive to pick them up. Checking the time I calculated I had twenty minutes before I needed to leave.

Now sitting in one of my favoured spots - the rooftop terrace - I was endeavouring to make a list of things I wanted to take to the new house. I kept on being side tracked though by the squawking of rainbow lorikeets as they clamoured for position on the hanging bird-feeders. Standing up I strolled in that direction only to have the sweet smell of lemon scented gums fill my senses, immediately bringing to mind an image of my husband.

'Hmm … Hugh *loved* those trees. He said they were the first ones he planted when he built this place. I can't believe how *big* they've grown.'

Shaking my head in wonder I then walked over to the other side of the terrace. My gaze was soon transfixed on the scene over the sand dunes. Glassy, green waves were slowly rolling towards the nearly deserted beach. I watched as two surfers competed for the best spot on the curve of an exceptionally large swell, before one of them conceded; breaking off to the left. The other one rode the wave brilliantly, before maneuvering his board sharply to the right and was then lost to view behind the breaker.

Sighing, I shook my head again, knowing that I was going to miss this place … but also knowing I couldn't stay here without Hugh.

'How he changed my life,' I murmured to myself, 'and what a darling he was. The first man who'd truly loved me just the way I am.' My mind wandered back to when I'd first met him, and I couldn't help but smile.

I'd accompanied my ex-boyfriend, Jason, when he'd gone to tell his dad that he was gay. His dad was Hugh, and after the big 'revelation,' which Hugh had taken in his stride, he and I had talked and laughed and talked some more. He'd said that he'd love to take me out sometime, and after six months of dating we'd married.

Jason had been five years younger than I was, which had never been a problem, and Hugh had been fifteen years older, and that had also never been a problem. Being fit and very young at heart, Hugh had always been up for whatever I had proposed; dancing into the early hours, scuba diving, bush walking, or spending hours strolling around an art exhibition.

We'd had so much fun together, and the fact that he'd been quite wealthy meant we'd been able to spend a lot of time traveling. I remembered how grateful I'd been when he'd insisted we visit Lisa in England so I could be there for the birth of Libby. He'd been such a sweetheart, later arranging flights at least twice a year so we could catch up with them, and also paying for the two girls to visit *us* several times.

I'd spent the recent Christmas holidays with them in England; the first time I'd been there without Hugh. After I'd told them last week I was moving to Anglesea, they'd immediately arranged to come for a short holiday before the house was put into the hands of a real estate agent. It wasn't just to help me sort and pack my belongings; they'd wanted to come and say goodbye to Hugh one last time. They'd had so many good times here, accruing so many good memories of him, that the thought of the house being sold had them feeling quite sad. It was like they were losing the last physical link they'd had with the man whom we'd *all* adored. Thinking now of the girls' arrival had me checking the time again.

'Right, I'd better get going; can't have them getting there before me.'

Leaving my unfinished list on the kitchen bench, I locked the front door, walked through to the garage then climbed into my Range Rover. A beep on the remote had the roller door rising, and I was then driving down the steep driveway before turning left onto the Great Ocean Road. I had a huge smile on my face at the prospect of seeing 'my girls' again, and once more wished they lived closer to me. Letting out a big sigh, I slowly accelerated, knowing that life didn't always go the way you'd like it to.

After driving along the relatively flat section of the road at Eastern View, the road became more winding and undulating. I loved everything about the famous coastal road, and had allowed plenty of time so I could enjoy the magnificent scenery.

Gullies full of towering tree ferns gave off a delightful earthy odor which wafted through my open window, then, cresting a hill before turning left around a hairpin bend, I admired the royal blue of the ocean sparkling to the right.

I'd taken inspiration for designing several pieces of my jewellery from the ocean and rain forest in this area. It had started as a hobby after I'd married Hugh and resigned from my job at the real estate office. My best friends were all creative in some way … well, except for Gabi … and so after giving it lots of thought, I'd learnt how to make jewellery.

Using silver and semi-precious stones, my designs had sold quite well at the artisan's markets I frequented. I hadn't started my little business for the money, but I'd always received a real thrill when a piece sold.

Approaching Angelsea I slowed to the sixty kilometre speed limit and allowed my gaze to wander around what was soon to be my new neighborhood. I often had coffee with friends there, and regularly checked out the Sunday markets, but I was really keen to actually *live* there now; loving the idea of belonging to the diverse, arty community.

There was a multitude of people out and about enjoying the seaside town and the river which flowed through to the ocean. It didn't seem to matter what day of the week it was, *or* what the weather was like, there always seemed to be someone sitting outside with a coffee, or maneuvering a paddleboard along the waterway. All too soon though I was heading up the hill and out of the township; onwards towards Geelong.

Bypassing Torquay I arrived in Geelong forty minutes later. I was happy to get a parking spot close to the Gull depot, and also happy I had enough time to grab three coffees at the nearby Wintergarden café. After placing my order I had a quick squiz at the artwork lining the walls - making a mental note to come back soon for a better look – before returning to wait for the imminent arrival of the girls.

'Thanks Mum, I really needed this.'

'Yeah, thanks Gran, this is the best coffee.'

After hugs and kisses they'd loaded their bags into the back of the Range Rover and were now settled in their seats; coffees in hand.

'That's okay darlings … now sit back, relax and enjoy. I can't believe you're finally here. It's so good to see you both again.'

I merged into the traffic, did a U-turn to take us back to LaTrobe Terrace, and then turned left towards home.

'Now … fill me in on what's been happening. How's school Libby? Are you still enjoying it? And how's work Lisa? How's your love life …'

'Mum! Take a breath. We've got the whole week to talk about everything. How about you talk while we sit and listen?'

'Yeah Gran … I hope you don't mind … but I'm feeling a bit too tired to talk much, and I know that's a first for me,' Libby said from the back seat.

'Sorry darlings … I should have realised that you'd be tired.'

'But I'd love to hear more about the house you've found

in Angelsea Gran. Is it really better than the one you have now?'

'Well … *better*? I'm not sure if its better … but I think it's just as good … but in a different way. If you like we can stop by on our way home and you can check it out?'

'Yeah absolutely.'

'Ooh yes … I can't wait to see it.'

'Okay … sounds like we have a plan then. Now … how about when you've finished your coffee I put on some soft music and you shut your eyes for a while. I can wake you when we reach Anglesea.'

'Mmm … that sounds perfect Mum. I'm definitely feeling a bit weary.'

'Yes same here Gran. I don't think this coffee will keep me awake long.'

A couple of minutes later they were both asleep. I smiled, thrilled to have my girls with me again.

CHAPTER ELEVEN

Anna arrived at her hotel at six o'clock. She immediately stripped off her travelling clothes, had a long hot shower then donned the complimentary dressing gown. After giving Sam a quick call, letting him know she'd arrived safely, she then hung a few of her clothes on hangers before checking out what beverages there were in the bar fridge.

Now relaxing on her balcony with a glass of wine, she was remembering how much she used to love this city. "Used to" being the operative words. She'd been here many times over the past fifteen or so years, but its allure was now tainted forever.

As she admired the sunset and the lights of the metropolis as they twinkled into life, she couldn't help but also remember how much Jim had loved Singapore. He'd surprised her when he'd bought the apartment, saying it would be an investment and somewhere they could holiday each year. He'd told her he'd put it in the hands of a holiday rental company to ensure they'd receive a regular income; first blocking out a couple of weeks each year for their own use.

'Hmmm … probably another one of Jim's lies. He was most likely 'entertaining' women here from the beginning. Oh well … plenty more cities in the world for me to visit,' she said, a wry smile on her face.

She had tonight to rest up and relax as her solicitor had arranged the meeting with her dead husband's mistress, Pamela Koh, for tomorrow morning. Deciding she should eat something, even though she had no appetite, she perused the in-room menu, then rang room service and ordered a meal. While she waited for it to arrive she re-filled her glass and decided to email Claire.

From *annanowiki@gmail.com*
To *clairebaumann@yahoo.com.au*

Hello Claire,
Just a quick note to let you know I've arrived safely in Singapore.
I'll be leaving again tomorrow and will be in London for all of the following week. I hope you're feeling ok and you're not working too hard. Say Hi to Gunther for me … love to you both.
Mum xx

After eating her meal, which she'd really enjoyed – her appetite being enticed back by the smell of the spicy dish – she'd then stood under the shower again, allowing the steaming water to once more work it's magic on her stiff limbs. The wine had briefly lifted her spirits, but she now realised the alcohol had contributed to her tiredness.

The softness of the expensive sheets felt wonderful against her skin as she stretched out in bed; it being the last thought she had before dropping into a very deep sleep. It was the first time she'd slept without the aid of sleeping tablets since the funeral.

She arose early feeling wonderfully refreshed, then a little surprised at her lack of unease regarding her intended meeting. After giving it some thought while enjoying her breakfast *al fresco* under a sunny sky, she realised her expected feeling of apprehension had been overridden by her anger, which simmered below the surface of her outwardly calm appearance.

'Ha … this might be the best thing that's ever happened to me,' she joked to herself, before realising that it might actually be true. Standing up from the small table, she picked up her cup of tea then relocated to a very comfortable reclining deckchair; positioned in the shade but still giving a glorious view of the city.

Sipping her earl grey she acknowledged she was now a very different person to what she was before Jim's death. She'd always been quite happy to be in the background a little; always ready to give a hand, to help out, to accommodate other people's needs. But where had it gotten her? She'd ended up with a cheating husband who obviously hadn't put her wants and needs first, *and* a daughter who didn't seem to appreciate or value her in any way.

After checking her emails, and finding no reply, she closed her tablet and stowed it into her onboard carry-all. Thinking of Claire she shook her head, knowing how dysfunctional their relationship had become.

She was her first-born and had been so cherished, the thought brought a tear to Anna's eye. These days Claire lived in Dusseldorf with her husband, also a pilot, and had maintained that as neither of them were fussed about procreating they weren't going to have any children.

'Hmm … not sure what I did wrong there,' Anna sniffed and wiped away the tear. 'I used to love the way she and Jim had such a strong bond. We were all so proud when she followed him into aviation and became a pilot.'

Giving her nose a quick blow she then smiled. 'Thank goodness for Sam … I really don't know what I'd do without him.'

Two years younger than his sister, Sam had always doted on his mum. Tall, dark-haired and good-looking, Anna had lost count of the number of girlfriends he'd had over the years. Whenever she'd subtly suggested settling down with one to give her grandbabies he'd always laughed and then hugged her, saying he was in no hurry to do that.

And then there was that terrible day last year when he'd casually declared that he'd decided not to have any kids, as he didn't want the responsibility of raising a child. Anna sighed at the memory and wiped away the last of her tears.

'No good dwelling on all that,' she decided. 'They're both healthy and happy and I should be grateful for that. Now … what time is it? I should start getting ready to go.'

Taking a deep breath Anna knocked firmly on the door at precisely 11am. Her solicitor had notified Pamela of the day and time of her intended visit before Anna had left Australia, and had promptly received confirmation that she would be expected.

As she waited, Anna gave another 'thank you' in her mind to her very zealous solicitor who had taken it upon himself to organise all her flight and hotel requirements. He'd been recently widowed and Anna had an inkling that he fancied her, but although he was an attractive man she had no intention of being in another relationship … not now, and probably never.

The door opened and the two women locked eyes for a moment before Pamela dropped her gaze, stepped back, and quietly asked Anna to enter. Walking into her own apartment like this felt quite surreal, and Anna suddenly lost some of her composure. However Pamela immediately indicated for her to sit down on a couch in the lounge area, where a long, teak coffee table displayed an ornate tea service and a variety of cakes.

'Please, make yourself comfortable. Would you like a cup of tea? Or would you prefer coffee?'

'Tea would be fine … thank you.'

The woman poured the freshly brewed tea, and Anna watched the steam rise gently from both of the gold rimmed cups. After replying that she didn't need milk or sugar, she accepted the proffered cup and saucer and sat it down before her. Before she could begin her rehearsed speech though, Pamela spoke.

'I am so glad you have come to see me. I have wanted to apologize to you ever since I've known of Jim's lies to me. I didn't think you would ever want to see *me* though. My daughter too has been very, very sad knowing what her father has done, and she too has wanted to see you. But first I have to say … I am so sorry. Yes it is true that I knew he was married, but when I first met him he said his wife was dying and probably wouldn't live more than a few months. I foolishly believed him.'

Anna opened her mouth to say something but Pamela went on.

'And yes, I should have doubted him or questioned him more as time went on, but every couple of months he said you didn't have long to live, and he always looked so sad that I didn't like to question him further. And then I became pregnant.' Pamela lowered her eyes again, as if in shame. 'I was worried at first, but he was happy and said he would marry me as soon as … well as soon as you were no longer with us.'

Again Anna went to speak, but Pamela rushed on.

'Then when my daughter was born I could no longer go home. My parents would not have me there if I was not married. So I stayed with Jim thinking that soon, soon we would be married. And I loved him. And he loved our daughter. And she loved him.' Pamela suddenly seemed to run out of momentum and slumped slightly in her chair.

Once more, just as Anna went to speak she was distracted as a door slowly opened and she saw a young girl peeking around the doorframe.

'This is Jim's daughter,' she thought as she stared at the child slowly making her way to her mother's side. 'She's beautiful,' she couldn't help but think.

'Anna … is it okay if I call you Anna?' Pamela asked.

Anna could only nod.

'Anna, I'd like you to meet my daughter, Grace. Grace this is Anna.'

'Hello Anna,' Grace spoke softly, 'I'm very pleased to meet you.'

'Hello Grace, I'm very pleased to meet you as well,' Anna replied, slightly astonished at herself.

The young girl looked down, then up again, then looked directly into Anna's eyes and said, 'I am very sorry for what my daddy did. It was very wrong of him. I hope you don't hate me and my mummy.'

Anna could not stop the tears from welling in her eyes, then spilling over to run down her cheeks.

'No … of course I don't hate you or your mummy. None of this was your fault.' Then to her surprise the youngster ran over and gave her a hug … which brought more tears to her eyes. She hugged Grace for a moment then looked towards Pamela and saw that she too was crying.

Later, after fresh tea was made, cakes were eaten, and Grace was dispatched to her bedroom, she and Pamela sat and talked. Pamela was quite happy, and very thankful, to know that the apartment would be put in her name, and was also very happy for Anna to retain all of Jim's superannuation and life insurance. She said that she had been working in the I.T. industry for many years and had her own Central Provident Fund, which was similar to an Australian Superannuation Fund.

'So you see … you don't have to give me any money. Knowing that I can stay here in this apartment has taken a big worry from me, and I am very grateful to you for that.'

She then asked after Sam, saying what an honorable young man she thought he was, adding that she'd told Grace that he was her half-brother, and that Grace was hoping to meet him again one day.

'Well Sam travels a lot so there's always a chance he may be in Singapore sometime,' Anna replied. 'But talking of travelling … I have to go now as I fly out to England this afternoon and I still have to pack my things.'

'Oh okay. I would love to have you stay longer but I understand. And truly I am so glad to have met you Anna. You are a very special person. Thank you for being so understanding of my situation. Grace and I will always keep you in our prayers.'

With that they both stood and hugged. Then Pamela called Grace, and they all hugged again.

Walking through the door, Anna turned to wave, and Grace called out, 'Bye Anna, I love you.'

Anna stopped for a second, smiled, and said, 'Bye Grace, I love you too,' before walking down the hallway towards the elevators, the smile still on her face.

'Okay … well … that went differently to what I was expecting,' she thought as she hailed a taxi to take her back to her hotel. Hopping into the back seat she then gazed out the window as the driver wended his way through the traffic. Her thoughts were not focusing on what she saw though, they were still lingering over the events of the last hour.

'Hmm … what an interesting and surprisingly pleasant morning.' Nodding to herself she realised how good she was feeling, as though all negativity had been erased from her body and mind, leaving her feeling lighter and ready for anything.

She was now looking forward to the flight to London. After giving her sisters a quick phone call before leaving to meet Pamela, Anna knew they'd be waiting at Heathrow for her, ready to hear all about todays 'confrontation'.

CHAPTER TWELVE

'Mum! There you are! We were beginning to think you'd missed your flight.'

'No way,' Belle laughed, 'I was just one of the last ones off the plane. But … I'm here now, so … how are you both?'

Tatiana hugged her mum tightly. 'I'm okay, and *you're* looking wonderful.' Then, holding her out at arm's length she said, 'doesn't she look wonderful Nomi?'

'Hi Belle. Yes she does look wonderful,' Naomi replied as she also gave Belle a big hug. 'It seems like ages since we saw you. Come on, give me your bag and let's get out of here.'

'Thanks Naomi. Whew … it's certainly hot enough. I think a nice cold beer's on the cards if I'm not wrong.'

'You are certainly not wrong Mum. Okay,' she winked at Naomi, 'lead on McDuff'.

Driving into Alice Springs always gave Belle a thrill. She absolutely loved the colour of the desert and the hills, the massive sky and the *brightness* of everything. Twenty minutes later they'd parked the car and were walking into Monte's.

'Okay my shout,' grinned Naomi, 'what would you two lovely ladies like to drink?'

'A stubby of Pure Blond for me please.'

'Yeah … I'll have the same as Mum, thanks Nomi.' Tatiana smiled as her lover and best friend made her way to the crowded bar. 'Ahh … I love that woman Mum. I'm so happy with her. I can't wait 'til we're able to get married legally. The ceremony we had last year was fantastic, but it still wasn't *legal.*' Sighing, she went on, 'I just don't see what the problem is. We love each other and want to get married … simple.'

'I know love, it's crazy, but I'm sure things will change in the near future.'

'Hmmm … I hope so.'

They sat and chatted about Tatiana's work until Naomi reappeared with the beers, then after Belle proposed a toast to her two favourite people, they drank their beers and then got another. They were on their third when they decided to stay there and have a meal, so they all ordered steaks and then found a table to sit at outside.

It was *slightly* cooler now that the sun had passed its peak, but still quite hot … and Belle loved it.

'Hmmm … I'm sometimes tempted to live here … I love this dry heat.'

'Yeah, but I don't think you'd like it in the winter. It drops below zero some nights.'

'Oh no bugger that!' she grinned. 'Perhaps I'll stay where I am. Actually, one of the things I like about living in the Geelong area is the weather because we usually have four distinct seasons ... sometimes in the one day,' she laughed.

After chatting and catching up on the latest gossip, their meals arrived so talking became a bit sporadic. Afterwards Belle and Tatiana had another beer, while Naomi said she's better have a coffee as she was driving.

'So ... as I was talking about moving before,' Belle started, 'well ... I might just be doing that.'

'What ... *moving*? But I thought you loved your home, *and* where you live?'

'Yeah I do, but Liz has come up with this idea where a few of us could share a house which she's just bought. And I have to say I'm seriously thinking about it as the house is *fabulous*. Huge. Roomy. Awesome views. And it *could* quite possibly work.'

Belle spent the next half hour telling them all about the house, and the proposition which Liz had put forward.

'Hmm ... well it does *sound* good,' Tatiana said, 'and Anglesea is a *beautiful* area. And I suppose if you sold or rented your house out you'd have more spending money. Hmmm ... yeah it really *could* work. You'd have some company too with your friends there ... as long as you have your own space as well.'

'Oh yeah absolutely. With my room being downstairs, I could *really* separate myself if I felt the need.'

'So when do you have to decide by?'

'Well there's no real rush. Liz said she'll probably move in a couple of weeks after her other house is on the market, and if Evie *does* decide to give it a go, it wouldn't be for a few weeks either. Gabi's pretty thrilled with the idea, but she leaves on Monday for an eleven day cruise to New Caledonia and Vanuatu, and Anna … well I'm not sure about Anna. She left for Singapore two days ago to confront the woman who'd been having an affair with Jim for the last ten years.'

'WHAT!'

'Yeah … I haven't told you about *that* yet.'

The next morning was brilliantly sunny and delightfully hot. Belle had slept like the proverbial log and woke feeling totally refreshed. She had the house to herself as both girls had left for work, but being Friday they had the upcoming weekend to spend more time together.

After showering and having breakfast, she donned some loose cotton pants, a tank top and hat, then set off to find the new art gallery which Naomi had told her about. She'd been to Alice Springs many times since the girls had moved there, and was happy using the local bus service to get around. Now knowing the area reasonably well, she was eager to look through the new gallery which was totally run by the local indigenous community.

Belle *loved* Aboriginal art and usually incorporated dots into her own paintings. She had never done it to copy that particular style, it was just something she felt compelled to do. She'd once had a past life hypnosis session which revealed that her most recent past life had been spent as an aboriginal woman, so she felt that her depiction of dot work stemmed from that lifetime.

Finding the gallery without too much trouble, she then spent a blissful couple of hours checking out the art works while talking to the artists and watching them at work; marvelling at the intricate designs they created. Eventually feeling hungry, she realised it was early afternoon so wandered off to have lunch and a coffee.

That night after they'd had dinner at home and were relaxing next to the pool, Belle revealed her plan to paint a portrait to submit to the Archibald Prize.

'*What*! That's *fantastic*. Who are you going to paint?'

'Well I was talking to a very talented artist today by the name of Aunty Betty. She's lived in the area her whole life and is a very well-respected elder of the community. After chatting to her for a while I found out her artwork sells extremely well; she's quite well-known here *and* internationally. She also has the most wonderfully expressive face, and the idea just popped into my head. So I asked her if she'd be willing to sit for me … she said yes … so I think that's what I'm going to do.'

'Wow, that sounds stupendous,' Tatiana grinned.

'Super stupendous,' nodded Naomi.

Belle laughed then said, 'Yeah well, just because I submit one doesn't mean it will be on show at the main event, but I thought I'd like to give it a go.'

'Mum that's a really awesome idea. I can't wait to see the finished painting.'

They spent the next hour or so before bedtime going over the submission details, and looking online at last year's winning portraits. All of them preferred the People's Choice award for the portrait of Asher Keddie to the actual winner; a portrait of Hugo Weaving. Belle really didn't think she had *any* chance of winning, but thought that just having one of her painting short listed for such an iconic art prize would be fantastic enough.

The weekend arrived bringing more scorching heat. They all agreed it was a day to hang around the pool and relax. Naomi rang a few friends, saying that a barbeque was planned for lunch, and so it wasn't long before several people arrived bearing salads or deserts, plus their beverages of choice.

Belle was told she had to stay out of the kitchen as she was on holiday, so she alternated her time between catching up with the girl's friends, and cooling off in the pool. Most stayed for another barbeque that evening, which soon became quite a party, with the music, fun and laughter continuing well into the early hours.

They all slept in the next morning, not rising 'til lunch time. Again they stayed home, preferring to have a quiet day. They had a rehash of the latest gossip they'd heard during the party, then after more swimming and nibbling of left-over food they decided to go indoors and watch a couple of movies. By ten o'clock they were all yawning so decided to call it a night.

Next day after the girls had gone to work, Belle found an art supply shop and bought black lead pencils, sticks of charcoal and a large sketch pad. She then set off to find Aunty Betty, locating her at the gallery. After checking it was still okay to do her portrait, she then asked if she could take a few photos. That all being okay, Belle set about taking several shots, then did as many sketches as possible. She was leaving for home tomorrow but would come back in a month or so when, hopefully, she had a good start on the painting.

'Bye Mum, have a great trip home and come and see us again soon.'

'Yeah don't worry, I'll be back again soon enough,' she smiled. 'Thanks for helping me decide whether to move or not. I really appreciated your and Naomi's input. And thanks again for dropping me at the airport. I could have rung a taxi you know.'

'Yes I know, but it was no drama to take a quick break. We weren't that busy and the boss didn't mind at all.'

'Okay … well … see you then … give Naomi another hug for me as well.'

'Okay I will. Bye Mum.'

'Bye love.'

After one last hug Belle walked through the gate and out towards the waiting plane for her journey home.

CHAPTER THIRTEEN

Gabi had always planned to go on a cruise one day, thinking it would be a fun holiday, but had never been able to arrange it … until now. She'd joined a local Probus group last year, thinking that there might be some interesting, *available* men there. However she'd soon discovered that the men were either married, or too old for her liking. She had though, made a couple of really good friends amongst the female members.

Then last month, Carmel, one of her new friends, had mentioned she'd like to go on a cruise sometime. One thing had led to another, with the result that Gabi, Carmel and two other friends had set sail yesterday. They'd booked inter-connecting rooms, both with twin beds and balconies, and had been pleasantly surprised to see how roomy they were. They'd left the dividing door open, and there had been plenty of laughter and threats regarding anyone who snored, but the first night had passed without anyone having to throw a pillow at a snoring head.

They were now sitting in the area of the ship called The Pantry, where a wide variety of meal options were always available. The four women had tried several different dishes, finishing with desert, and were now entranced by the rolling ocean waves, visible through the large windows.

'Oh I am so full,' Gabi groaned, 'I think I will have to go for the walk around the deck. Anyone want to come?'

'Yes I'll come,' nodded Josine. 'I really think I've eaten too much as well. But it all looked so tasty it was hard to resist.'

Marlene and Carmel had shown a bit of restraint, so didn't feel the need for a walk. Instead, they both said they'd get another cup of tea then find a spot near the pool to people-watch. Standing up with another little groan, Gabi nodded. 'Okay, we will track you down later.'

The two of them made their way outside and then slowly strolled past the swimming pool area. There was quite a throng of variously shaped bodies stretched out on sun lounges, all hoping to get the perfect tan while on their holiday. Several were yet to find out just how painful sunburn can be.

Now back inside waiting at a bank of elevators, they were admiring some of the quirky artwork adorning the walls when they heard the 'ding' signaling the arrival of their lift.

'Well I am promising I am not eating so much next time,'

Gabi sighed as she stepped through the open doors, 'I do *not* like this bloated feeling at all.'

'Same here,' Josine nodded, 'but I *do* like not having to cook ... *and* no dishes to wash.'

As they travelled down to level eight where they intended to walk along the deck encircling the ship, they continued discussing the wide selection of food which was available. When the doors opened Gabi stepped out and straight into the back of a man who was talking to a few other people.

'Oh I am so sorry,' Gabi said, but before she could say anything else, the man turned and smiled at her.

'That's okay, I was probably standing too close to the doors. Are you alright?'

'Yes ... yes thank you, I am fine. I should have looked where I was going.'

'No harm done,' he smiled at her again before entering the elevator and pushing the relevant button for his floor.

Gabi and Josine both smiled at each other before making their way towards the outer deck area. Stepping out onto the deck and into a stiff breeze, they turned to have their backs to the wind and began their walk.

'Well that's one way to meet men I suppose,' Josine grinned. 'Just plough straight into them.'

'Yes,' Gabi laughed. 'That will be my new tactic I think. He looked quite nice too, yes?'

'Yes he did ... but probably has a wife here somewhere.'

'Yes probably.'

Putting the man out of her mind, Gabi looked out

towards the horizon. She was hoping to see a whale while on the cruise, or at least some dolphins. After walking two laps of the ship they both decided that was enough for now, so went inside to find their other two friends.

That evening, as they were waiting to be seated in the Waterfront Restaurant, Carmel said, 'Umm ... does anyone know that guy over there? He seems to be staring at us.'

'What guy?' both Gabi and Marlene said simultaneously.

Carmel nodded slightly towards the rear of the restaurant. 'That guy down the back.'

'Oh that's the man Gabi pounced on earlier,' Josine grinned.

'What?'

'*Pounced* on?'

Carmel and Marlene looked quizzically at Gabi and smiled.

'Gabi ... what *have* you been up too?' Marlene tried to look stern but failed. 'We let you out of our sight for half an hour and you're accosting strange *men?*'

Before Gabi could explain, their waiter came up to escort them to their table ... which was right next to the one where the 'strange man' was sitting with a small group of other people.

'Oh my God,' Gabi said under her breath, 'this is bit of the embarrassment.' But after sitting down she decided to take the initiative and say hello.

Later, after they'd all introduced themselves – laughing at how their friends had bumped into each other – they'd asked the waiter to join their tables together to make conversing easier. After a wonderful meal and lively conversation, they'd all decided to take a stroll around the deck. Somehow Gabi and the 'strange man', who's name she'd found out was David, were paired off and they'd walked and talked long after the others headed back indoors. Now sitting together at one of the many bars on board, David was laughing at a story she had just related.

'Gabi you are hilarious,' he grinned, 'and you tell a great story.'

'Thank you, and you also tell the great story,' she smiled. Thinking that she hadn't had as much fun in a long time, she wondered if he was already 'taken'. Deciding to just ask him she took a big breath first.

'So … David … I have really enjoyed talking to you tonight. It has been fun. So … are you married … or do you have a partner?'

Before she even had time to blush at being so forward, David replied. 'Good heavens no. I wouldn't be sitting here with you now if I was already in any sort of relationship. What sort of a person do you take me for?' he said in mock horror.

'Oh I am still deciding what sort of a person you are. I do not rush into anything these days.'

'Ha … well that's probably a good thing.' Then gazing

straight into her eyes he said, 'But I must say I haven't enjoyed myself this much for a very long time.'

She did blush then, and felt completely stupid for doing so. Trying to cover her discomfort she offered to buy the next round of drinks.

'No way. I'll buy the drinks when you're out with me. I believe in looking after the lady I'm socialising with. So … Gabi … would you like another drink?' he said with a dazzling smile.

'Yes please David … that would be lovely.'

After breakfast the next morning they met for a coffee and immediately seemed to click again. Gabi had wondered if it had just been the alcohol which had made the conversation flow between them last night. But he was so attentive, really listening to whatever she was talking about, she felt she was being swept off her feet; relishing the lovely feeling it gave her.

They had arrived at Noumea early that morning - it being the first of the five islands they were to visit - so she soon excused herself saying her friends would be waiting for her. He was totally agreeable, saying hopefully they'd talk again another time, then wished her a wonderful day.

Friends who'd previously done the same cruise had advised the women to do their shopping in Port Vila, so today was reserved for swimming, trying the local cuisine, and taking in some of the sights. So, after disembarking and having several photos taken with the friendly welcoming party - a ritual they would encounter on each island - they got their passports stamped, then bought tickets to travel on the hop-on, hop-off bus … known locally as the ho-ho bus. It drove in a circuit around the island and allowed them to hop on and off at any stop. They'd decided to do a complete circuit first to get the lay of the land, and then they'd hop off at the Aquarium as they'd been told it was a 'must see.'

It was now early afternoon; quite hot and humid, with only a couple of clouds occasionally obscuring the glare of the sun. The four women had hopped off the bus again and were now sitting in the shade at a beachside bar, waiting for the cocktails they'd just ordered. Loving the relaxed vibe of the place, they marveled at the variety of palm trees and the bright colours of the tropical flowers. When their drinks arrived they proposed a toast to their first overseas port-of-call.

Later, after having a light lunch and a second cocktail each, they wandered over the road to the beach and swam in the gloriously warm but refreshing water. After a fun-filled and relaxing day they returned to the ship, then took turns in the bathrooms; showering off the salt and sand.

That night after they'd set sail for their next destination, they had dinner at Angelo's, the Italian restaurant, and saw David with the same group of people, but this time he and Gabi just waved as he was seated over the other side of the room.

'Hmmm … he's not stalking you is he Gabi?' Carmel asked with a smile.

'Ha-ha … no I do not think so. Because he came on this trip alone, the staff matched him up with other singles so they have the company. I think they take the turns to choose where they will eat.'

'Hmmm … okay then.'

Changing the subject, Gabi spoke excitedly about their next destination. 'I hear that Lifou has some amazing spots for the snorkeling. I am so looking forward to getting there.'

'Yes me too,' Marlene agreed. 'I haven't snorkeled since I was a kid, but I'm hoping I'll get the hang of it again okay.'

'Yes same here,' Josine smiled. 'Fingers crossed.'

'Hmm … well I've *never* done it, and I *hate* getting my hair wet, but I'm willing to give it a go,' Carmel stated. 'I just hope I don't sink and drown trying'.

By the time they finished their deserts and coffees they'd decided to have an early night. They'd also decided that drinking cocktails in the afternoon may not be the best of ideas if they wanted stamina in the evening.

On their way out of the restaurant Gabi glanced over to where David was still sitting and saw that he was looking her way. They both smiled and gave a little wave, and she felt a happy thrill course through her body. She was tempted to stay and meet him for a drink again, but tiredness won over so decided to head back to the cabin with her friends.

Standing in a group waiting for the elevator Gabi felt a tap on her shoulder. Turning, she saw a smiling David standing behind her, so as the elevator doors opened, she indicated to her friends that she'd follow them shortly.

'Hi Gabi. Sorry for interrupting your evening, but I was wondering if you'd like to have dinner with me tomorrow night. I thought I'd better ask you now in case I don't see you tomorrow.'

'Oh … um … yes, that would be lovely.'

'*Terrific*.' David was really smiling now, 'how about we try out Luke Mangan's restaurant? I hear it's pretty good.'

'Okay.'

'Great. Does six o'clock suit you?'

'Um … yes I think so.'

'Terrific. Well I'll meet you there at six then.'

'Okay … see you then.'

Just then the elevator doors opened again so she stepped inside, pressed the button and gave him a smile as the doors closed.

'Oh he is so *nice*. Well, more than nice really,' she was thinking to herself. 'Oh I feel the funny feeling inside,' she smiled, loving the sensation. Her thoughts then flew forward to six o'clock the following night, as she contemplated what she would wear.

The next morning the four women were up early as they'd planned to disembark before the crowds. They'd been told that as the ship was too big to dock at Lifou, the passengers would be ferried across to the island in tender boats, a process which could apparently take a while if there were long queues. So, after a quick breakfast they put on their bathers, filled their tote bags with everything they thought they may need for the day, then went downstairs to stand in line; ready to hop on the first boat.

Now on board – all slightly squashed together - they were rapidly approaching the thickly treed, tropical island, mesmerised by the colour of the seawater visible through the open doorway.

'Oh … look at the colour of that *water*,' Carmel exclaimed. 'It looks absolutely *gorgeous*.'

'Yes it certainly does.'

'I've never *seen* water that colour blue before.'

'Me neither … is it aqua or turquoise?'

They couldn't decide on which shade of blue it was, so settled on 'gorgeous' instead. A couple of minutes later they pulled up at the jetty, and were soon walking towards the welcoming party of Islanders and photographers. They'd all decided they were going to do the whole touristy thing and have their hair braided while on holiday, so they soon set off up the hill to where several local women were waiting, ready to waylay any tourist who seemed interested in having the intricate braiding done.

Half an hour later they were all laughing at each other's new hairstyles; taking lots of photos before continuing on towards a market selling a wide range of interesting goods. They'd decided to forgo any tours of the island, as they wanted to check out a church they'd seen from the ship. It was white, so stood out amongst the greenery, and was perched on top of a hill at the left-hand end of the island.

An hour later, all feeling ready for a rest after the steep walk to the church and back, they were completely happy to 'make camp' at the first beach area they came across. The wonderfully warm water was just what they needed and they were soon marvelling at the variety of fish they could see as they snorkeled.

They were all a bit tired as they were ferried back to the ship after their day on Lifou, *and* a little sunburnt, even though they'd all 'slip slop slapped'. As they'd been among the first onto the island that morning, they'd been ready to leave by mid-afternoon, so arrived back on board before the usual crowds. They all showered and dressed – Gabi taking extra time to choose her outfit – then went to a bar for a drink before dinner.

'Hmm … I'm definitely feeling a bit yawny,' Marlene said, after stifling one behind her hand. 'I think all that swimming has tired me out.'

'Oh no … now you've set me off,' Josine said as she yawned as well.

That set the other two off, Gabi saying, 'Stop it everyone, I have to stay awake to meet David later.'

After having bit of a laugh about old age creeping up on them, it was decided they'd go and have an early dinner in The Pantry, then later watch a magic show … if they could stay awake that long. Gabi decided to stay with them 'til she met David at six, in another hours' time.

After polishing off lemon chicken and salad, followed by a variety of fresh fruit, they were now sitting out on the deck enjoying their cups of tea … Gabi feeling decidedly hungry after watching them eat.

'Hmm … I'm going to sleep well tonight.'

'Yes, me too. But what a great day, yes?'

'Yes absolutely,' Josine agreed. 'But I'm just hoping I'll be able to sleep with these beads in my hair.'

'Yeah me too,' Carmel laughed. 'I'm not so sure it was the best idea now.'

After all having bit of a chuckle they became aware of a kaleidoscope of colour spreading across the western sky as the sun slowly slid below the horizon. They were drawn to the ships railing to maximise their view of the spectacular sunset as a nearby door swung open and a few people walked out on deck.

'Well hello there. How are you ladies this evening? This is a lovely surprise Gabi. I was just about to go and wait for you at the restaurant.'

'Oh hello David, we are all very good thank you,' Gabi replied smiling. 'Yes, I was soon to leave to meet you also. And how are you. Are you good also?'

'Yes very good thanks.'

They continued to admire the sunset for a couple of

minutes before David looked at the women's new hairstyles and smiled, saying, 'I must say I think you're all very brave getting your hair braided. Did it hurt?'

The women laughed, assuring him that it hadn't hurt getting it done … but they weren't sure how comfortable it would be for sleeping. He chuckled at that, and then looked again at how intricate the designs were. They all assured him they'd only had it done as it was their first cruise to the Islands, and they'd wanted to do something that was fun and memorable.

'I did not see you on the island today David. Did you go over there?'

'Oh yes, I went with Paul, the guy I'm sharing my cabin with. You met him the other night at dinner.'

'Oh yes, I remember Paul. So did you also do the snorkeling? We went to the lovely little beach to the left of the jetty. There were so many fishes, it was beautiful.'

'Ahhh … so that's why we didn't see each other. We went to a great snorkeling spot to the *right* of the jetty. Then later we walked up a very steep hill to that little church. Quite a trek but a terrific view from there.'

'Oh we did that also, but we went there first,' Gabi exclaimed.

David checked his watch, then asked Gabi if she was ready to go for dinner. She smiled and said she was, so after wishing the others an enjoyable evening they headed inside. On their way she mentioned that her friends planned to see a show later, but as they were all feeling so tired they may not end up going.

'Yes, I'm feeling a little tired myself … all that swimming and walking I suppose,' David smiled.

'Yes, and me too. But it does not matter. Perhaps we could see the show together tomorrow night?'

'Now that sounds like a terrific idea.'

With that thought in mind they were both smiling as they arrived at the restaurant, right on six o'clock, and were then shown to their table.

CHAPTER FOURTEEN

Evie stretched her shoulders forward and back, then stood up. She'd been on a roll with her writing for hours but was now vacillating … unsure if she should kill off one of her characters or not.

'Hmmm … I think I need a break … a walk should help me decide.' Nodding her head as she entered her bedroom she knew it was also time she made a final decision regarding moving, selling and sharing.

She usually went for a five kilometre walk most days, both for exercise and for thinking through plot lines, so after changing her sandals for runners she donned a 'Save the Sharks' hat and headed off into the sunshine.

Turning left at the first corner she set off on one of her usual routes – towards the beach. She inhaled the mingled scent of eucalyptus and sea spray as she strode along, and once more appreciated living in such a beautiful location. Previous to Liz's suggestion of sharing a house in Angelsea, Evie had given a lot of thought towards whether she should stay in Terrigal or move back to Geelong. The knowledge that her house would be too big for her on her own had sat heavily on her mind.

Marley and Blue had continued living with her after Dash had died which had been great for all of them. Then, after Marley had married Zac and moved to Perth with him two years ago, Blue had chosen to stay and finish her degree where she'd been studying for the past three years; the University of Newcastle in nearby Ourimbah.

Evie had loved sharing the house with Blue. They'd had so many great times together, but knew her granddaughter planned to travel overseas for a year after finishing Uni, and would most likely settle in Perth on her return.

Knowing the time was approaching for her to downsize, the question *now* was whether to buy a smaller house in Terrigal, the place she'd grown to love; buy one in the Geelong area where she'd grown up, or … share a house with her four best friends.

Increasing her pace a little as the path led slightly upwards, she pondered the pros and cons of her situation. Whenever she had difficulty making a decision, she'd compile lists – good and bad points of each option. Whichever option had more good points than the others would be the one she'd go with. After a bit of mental list making though, she soon realised it was pretty even between buying a smaller house in Geelong somewhere, and sharing a house with the others.

'Hmm … okay then … which choice makes me feel best inside?' Walking on towards the summit of the small rise she concentrated on her feelings, and after a moment she grinned.

'Must be something about getting older, but I *would* like to spend more time with those crazy ladies,' she nodded, thinking that old friends were the best friends. They'd shared so many ups and downs and knew they could *totally* rely on each other … not to mention all the fun they had together.

'Right … I've made my decision,' she nodded again as she paused for a moment to look at the view. 'I'll move in with others, but I'll keep my house so Blue and her mates can live here for now. If sharing doesn't work out I'll sell it and buy my *own* place in Angelsea.'

Happy with having that problem settled she continued her walk, smiling at the image she'd conjured of Liz reacting to her decision. Two minutes later she was at her destination and all thoughts dropped away.

Savouring her favourite view of Terrigal beach, she was momentarily transfixed by the sun's rays as they glittered and danced across the rolling waves. A cluster of youngsters were building sandcastles and frolicking in the shallows while several surfers were waiting patiently to catch just the right wave. Multi-coloured umbrellas dotted the sand, and a few older folk were walking along the high tide mark; heads bent, scanning for shells.

Evie breathed in deeply … then let it out again.

'Ahhh … yes. I *love* the smell of the beach, and I know I'll love living in Anglesea; it's such a beautiful place. Trust Liz to find such a fantastic house.'

Smiling with contentment she began to make her way homewards along the shoreline. The gritty crunch, crunch of the sand as she walked, combined with the crash of the waves as they endlessly broke on the beach was quite mesmerising, and it took her a while to refocus her thoughts back to her writing dilemma.

By the time she reached her street she'd decided that she would indeed bump off one of her characters. This was her second novel, but the first time she'd ever considered eradicating a character. Unsure of the best way to go about it, she was nonetheless impatient to get into it again as soon as she got home.

After writing into the early evening, Evie then curled up on the couch to watch an old black and white movie. Her granddaughter had gone to see 'Grand Piano' with a few friends at the movie theatre in Erina. Expecting Blue to be home soon, she then smiled in anticipation of Marley's arrival in the morning.

Her step-daughter had been living in Perth for a couple of years now, but made the trip back at least three times a year - for Evie's and Blue's birthdays, and for Christmas. She was coming for a quick visit this time after Evie had mentioned she was considering moving. The sound of the front door opening then heralded Blue's return.

'Hi Gran, I'm back. The movie was excellent, but I won't tell you what happens because you should see it yourself some time.'

'Okay, I might go next week. Have you got a minute? I wanted to tell you something.'

'Oh okay. What is it … have you decided if you're going to move or not?'

'Yes I have. I've decided to move in with Liz and the others, and you can stay here with your friends until you take off overseas.'

'Okay. *Wow* … that should be awesome for you. I'm sure you'll *love* having their company. You're all such good friends.'

'Yes, well I hope so.'

'I've already mentioned it to Chloe, Kim and Lauren and they're rapt at the thought of living here, so I'll phone them now and let them know it's all systems go,' she grinned. 'Oh Gran, as much as I'll miss you, I'm *so* excited about sharing with *my* friends. And I promise again we won't trash the place *or* burn it down,' she laughed.

Giving Evie a big hug first, Blue then ran off towards her bedroom, squealing in delight.

'Hmm … that went well,' Evie grinned, 'now … I feel completely knackered … I'm off to bed.'

Evie was up in time to wave at Blue as she rushed out the front door, her long red hair still wet from her shower.

'Remember we're going out for dinner tonight with your mum,' Evie called after the retreating figure.

'Oh yes thanks Gran … I'd almost forgotten. Okay see you tonight,' she called as she pulled the door shut behind her.

Listening as Blue's car reversed down the driveway, then took off down the road, Evie smiled and shook her head before putting the kettle on. As she reached for a cup from the overhead cupboard she calculated her daughter-in-law's plane would have landed an hour ago, and she'd now be on the train to Gosford.

'Okay … a cup of tea first, then a shower, then the train station. I'm so looking forward to seeing Marley again.'

Turning up the stereo when a Chrissy Amphlett song came on, she sang along until the kettle boiled, thinking how good she was feeling this morning. Taking her hot cuppa out to the verandah, she then leant against the railing and watched several birds darting here and there; catching bugs as well as deterring other birds from their territory.

Evie though autumn was the best time of year. She'd preferred summer when she was younger, but now had more appreciation for the varying nuances of the current season. Crisp chilly mornings, pleasantly warm days and cold clear nights were now more appealing to her than stifling hot days and sweaty humid nights. She also enjoyed it when the green of her neighbour's deciduous tree was transformed into red and gold before creating a rustling, crunching blanket underfoot. She smiled then, thinking of the times she'd seen the dog next door running around crazily amongst a pile of brittle fallen leaves.

Sighing deeply she straightened up, then leant backwards in an attempt to alleviate some annoying tightness in her back. Taking one more appreciative look at her wonderful view, she then took her now empty cup indoors, popped it in the sink and headed for the shower.

Marley had dropped her bags in her old bedroom and was now sitting in a deck chair next to Evie. They both held a beer and said 'cheers' as they clinked them together.

'Ahh … this is lovely,' Marley smiled after having a mouthful. 'Very relaxing.'

Evie grinned, taking a sip herself. 'It's so good to have you here again. Probably for the last time too, unless you come back to see Blue after I'm gone. But I know you'll love the Anglesea house when you see it, and you can visit anytime you like … there's plenty of room.'

'Yeah from what you've said it sounds terrific. So you've definitely decided to move then?'

'Yes I've decided to give it a go and see if we can all coexist without blood being spilt,' she grinned.

'Ha … I don't think that will happen, you've been friends for too long now.'

'Yes, I think it'll be okay. I've just got to decide what to take with me, and what to buy when I get there. I think I'll leave the bed and get a new one. Time to move on from those memories I think. Not that I'll ever forget your dad of course … but you know what I mean I hope?'

'Yes I know what you mean. And I think that's a good idea. It's probably cheaper to buy a new one rather than take the old one all that way anyway.'

'Yes probably.'

'And if Blue and her friends are going to be living here they'll need beds.'

'Yes they will.'

'So that will work out good then.'

'Yes. It *will* feel strange though, leaving after all this time. Your dad and I had so many good times here … we *all* did.'

'Yeah absolutely. But … time moves on and we have to move with it. It's exciting in a way … a new chapter in your life beginning. I felt the same when Zac and I moved to Perth.'

'Yes you must have. So tell me … how's everything going in Perth? I bet Zac enjoys working closer to home these days. And you … how are you liking your new boss?'

They sat and caught up on all their latest comings and goings before having lunch. Later, after walking down to the beach, they soon had their sandals off; relishing the coolness of the water as it rippled over their feet. It was then that Marley decided to tell Evie her other bit of news.

'Now I don't want you to say no before you hear me out,' she started, which made Evie look at her and grin.

'*Oh* … what now? Please don't tell me you've hooked me up on another blind date.' When Marley didn't immediately reply, Evie went on, 'Oh my God … you *have* haven't you? And after last time when I said it *was* the last time.'

'Yes but that wasn't my fault. Remember it was Lauren who arranged that date with her neighbour's dad. And you have to admit he *looked* okay. She didn't know that his first love was playing the pokies.'

They both had bit of a chuckle then, thinking of Evie's disastrous date, where she'd sat and watched him playing 'his favourite machine' for an hour, before she'd excused herself and took herself home.

Still smiling she shook her head and said, 'No. No more blind dates for me. Thanks anyway … but *no*.'

'Hang on, just let me tell you about him first. I actually met him years ago; he's lovely,' she added smiling.

'But I'm not looking for a man now. I mean, I wasn't looking for one *anyway*, but I'm moving in a few weeks, so there's really no *point* in meeting someone here.'

'Ah yes, but apparently he travels a lot and is in Melbourne regularly, so he's quite able to see you in Geelong … or Anglesea.'

'So … you've already told him about *me*?'

'No *I* haven't, but Adrian … remember Adrian? We

worked together when I got my first job here. Well it's *his* dad.'

'Um … yes I remember Adrian. I thought you had bit of a thing for him back then?'

'Well yeah I *did* like him, but he already had a girlfriend. Anyway … I met his dad when Adrian had a few pool parties. He would always come and say hello to all of us, then go and leave us to it. Their pool was great; we always had a ball.'

'Yes I remember.'

'So … I just happened to run into Adrian last week. Did I mention he lives in Perth now too?'

'Um … no you didn't.'

'Well we got talking about stuff and I said I was coming here for a visit. Then Adrian said he was also coming here for a few days as he's going to be best man at a mate's wedding. And then somehow the conversation got onto how you and his dad are both single, and how we both thought you'd suit each other. *And then* … you won't believe it … we realised we were going to be on the *same* flight coming here. Spooky huh? Sort of seems like it was meant to be.'

'Um … not sure if it's spooky, but it *is* bit of a coincidence.'

'*Ha* … you always say there *are* no coincidences,' Marley grinned, 'so it *must* be meant to be.'

'*Marley* … what am I going to do with you. I don't know whether to laugh … or cut you out of my will.'

'Ooh I'm in your *will*?'

'Yes but not for much longer.' Evie couldn't help but

laugh before saying, 'But you haven't actually set up a day to meet him yet have you?'

'Well … not a *day*, no. The thing is … his dad is also only here for a few days before he leaves for another job in Darwin. So, because he flies out in two days we thought we could all catch up for a drink tonight after dinner.'

'*Tonight*. Bloody hell … you don't waste any time do you.'

'Ha … no I don't. But look, this is perfect. Blue, Adrian and I will be there so it won't be like a date. It'll just be some people having a couple of drinks together, and if you like each other you can decide to meet again … or not.'

Sighing, Evie knew there was no way out. 'Okay, I suppose it won't hurt to go out and have a couple of drinks.'

'Brilliant!'

'So … tell me a bit about him then.'

'So … tell me a bit about him then,' I prodded, holding my mobile to my ear. Evie had just finished her account of her proposed blind date, and I was wanting more info.

'Well I only know the basics Liz, but I have to say he *sounds* alright.'

'Oh, in what way?'

'Well he's sixty three, been widowed for about fifteen years, and he's supposed to be quite good looking.'

'Well that's always a plus, the good looking bit I mean.'

'Yes, doesn't hurt,' Evie smiled. 'He's also some sort of engineer and needs to travel a lot, so he'd be able to drop in and see me wherever I lived.'

'Oh … well that sounds promising.'

'Hmmm … it's just that I hadn't planned on starting a new relationship *now*. Actually, I'm not sure if I *ever* want to get into all that again. I just don't know if I can be bothered with the whole thing. You know … any guys I've gone out with in the last couple of years have all turned out to be drop kicks in one way or another.'

'Yeah you *have* had your fair share of wankers,' I laughed, which set Evie off as well.

'Yes you're not wrong there. And I've also got packing to do, and stuff to sort out before I move … I'm not sure it's a good idea to be meeting a guy now.'

'Well look, my advice is to meet him for drinks like Marley suggested, have a chat, and that could be the end of it. You're not obligated to go out with him again … so just leave it at that.'

'Yes that *does* make sense. I think because she dropped it on me so unexpectedly it freaked me out a bit. But you're right, *as usual*. Okay, I'll let you go and *I'll* go and decide what I'm going to wear … not that I'm going to get all glammed up or anything. I'll fill you in tomorrow with all the gory details.'

'Okay … oh, what's his name? Do you know?'

'Yes, it's Ross. Marley didn't mention his last name, and I can't remember what Adrian's is.'

'Hmm … Ross, I like that name. Okay, break a leg; I'll call you tomorrow … bye.'

'Bye.'

Evie, Marley and Blue were now ensconced in a booth in one

of Terrigal's trendy restaurants, having just finished their meal.

'Well that was *very* tasty. How was yours Bluey?'

'Mmm … mine was yummy too. Thanks Gran.'

'Yes so was mine,' Marley agreed. Thanks Evie.'

'My pleasure. It's not often that I get to take out my two favourite people.'

They sat and continued discussing a variety of things as the waitress removed their desert dishes. Asking if they'd like another drink or coffee, they declined, saying they were leaving shortly to meet up with friends.

'Are you excited Gran? It's been ages since you went out with a man.'

Evie smiled at her granddaughter. 'Well, no I can't say I'm excited. I suppose I'm slightly interested to see what he's like, but I'm not thinking that it will turn into anything. In fact I'll probably never see him again.'

'Yes, well you just never know,' grinned Marley as she checked the time on her mobile. 'Come on, let's get out of here. The Sand Bar is just in the next block so we can walk if that's okay with everybody. Adrian and his dad will be there by now.'

Evie felt flutters in her tummy, something she hadn't felt for a very long time. She was doing her best to appear relaxed and interested in what Ross was saying, but the immediate attraction she'd felt towards him was playing havoc with her composure.

After the initial introductions they all sat at a corner table where it was a bit quieter. Now with drinks in hand they talked about the subjects which Blue was studying at Uni, and then about Adrian's new job as an intern at the Perth hospital. After discussing Marley's new job and how she was liking Perth, Ross turned to Evie and asked about her imminent departure.

'Well I'm not going for another couple of weeks, so it's not *too* imminent,' she smiled. 'I still need to sort out a few things here and decide what to take and what to buy when I get there. My friend Liz, who's bought the house I'm moving into, also can't move for a couple of weeks as she wants to have her other house on the market first.'

Evie noticed that Ross appeared to be really interested in what she had to say, and when talk turned to the novel she'd self-published the previous year, he wanted to know all about it. She realised she was feeling really relaxed in his company, so when the younger ones said they were going to catch up with friends they'd seen at another table, she wasn't fazed at all.

The conversation swung easily between them. Evie found the stories he told about the different engineering jobs he'd overseen to be fascinating, and he seemed to enjoy the stories she told him about her Feng Shui clients.

It didn't seem long before Blue, Marley and Adrian were back, saying they had to get going as they had to be up early in the morning. When Ross suggested that he could take Evie home if she'd like to stay and have another drink she only pretended to hesitate.

'Um ... yes, that sounds okay. Marley you take my car and you can drop Adrian off on the way. I'll see you a little later; I won't be long.'

The next morning Evie was on her phone to me once more, enthusiastically describing the previous night's date.

'... and he's so nice ... well more than nice actually ... he's really easy to talk to and was genuinely interested in whatever I had to say.'

I was on the rooftop terrace again, my mobile on speaker, grinning while I waited for a break in the conversation to say something.

'And he *is* rather good looking; tall, dark and handsome. And dark is the operative word. His dad was English but his mum was Mauritian so he has this beautiful brownish coloured skin, green eyes, and black hair with a little bit of grey in it. '

'Ooh sounds gorgeous.'

'Yes, and he's quite intelligent; we covered heaps of different topics. I think it's the most I've ever enjoyed talking with a guy.' Evie stopped to take a deep breath before continuing. 'And, he seems to like me too because he wants to meet for lunch before he flies out tomorrow.'

'Wow ... this is sounding serious already.'

'Well I wouldn't say *serious* … but I have to say that I *do* like him … so far anyway. But who knows, he could collect shrunken heads or something gross like that.'

'*Shrunken heads?*'

'Haha … well I don't know, or he might have some other weird habit or hobby. What if he loves zombie movies … or ferret racing or …'

'*Ferret racing* … Evie, you do realise that *you're* the weird one here?' I couldn't help but laugh though. 'Listen girl, from what you've said about your night with him he definitely sounds like a 'potential', so stop stressing and just see where it goes. If it fizzles out because he collects his belly button fluff, then so be it.'

'Eww … and I thought *I* had a weird imagination.'

'Yeah well I've never claimed to be normal.'

'Hmm … yes that's true. Okay then, I'll meet him for lunch and ask him what his hobbies are and take it from there.'

'Good girl. Now I've got to go as I have the woman from the real estate agency arriving shortly. Phone me tonight though okay?'

'Okay. Hey which real estate people did you end up going with? Not the one where you used to work I hope?'

'No way. I decided on Sally Gilleece Real Estate. They're located in Anglesea, and Sally said she was happy to handle the sale herself.'

'Oh okay, that sounds good then. Alright, talk later … bye.'

'Bye you crazy woman.'

I smiled and shook my head as I wandered back inside. I was happy at the thought of my friend finding a nice guy, even though I had no intention of doing the same. Before I could think any more about it the doorbell rang.

After welcoming Sally inside, I took her for a tour of the house and garden; the agent being very impressed with the entire property and quite excited to prepare a sales campaign. Her estimate of a selling price tallied with mine, so after having a coffee and discussing viewing times, I walked her to the door.

'I'll be in touch soon Liz. I already have people who are interested in buying in this area, and I know they'll just *love* this place. I think I can guarantee a quick sale at a good price.'

'Great, thanks Sally. I'll leave it with you then.'

'Okay, bye for now then.'

'Bye.'

I wandered back into the kitchen and stacked the coffee cups into the dishwasher; happy in the knowledge that Sally seemed to be a very professional sales agent. I then sighed and sat at the dining table again. Letting my eyes wander around the room I suddenly felt a bit flat, and knew it was because of my impending departure.

'Oh, this is *so* hard. I feel like I'm leaving Hugh behind.' Shaking my head I knew I was doing the right thing ... I just wished that Hugh was still with me.

'Oh babe, why did you have to die?' I really seemed to feel

his presence then, and it made me smile and brought tears to my eyes at the same time.

'I love you, you gorgeous man,' I said, 'and you know what? It doesn't matter where I live, you'll always be with me.' I pictured him wrapping his arms around me then, and I shut my eyes and savoured the moment.

Sighing again, but now feeling better, I stood up and made my way upstairs. I knew my clothes were due for a cull – I'd been putting it off for a while now – but once Lisa and Libby were back from the supermarket I was sure the three of us could have it done in no time. We'd planned a drive to Apollo Bay tomorrow so would donate my superfluous garments to the op shop in Lorne on our way through the picturesque town.

We were now on the terrace having a late afternoon tea break, after spending most of the day indoors.

'I wish we could stay 'til the house is sold Mum, but Libby has school and you know I could only get one week off work.'

'That's okay darling, I know you would if you could. But I'll be alright. You've really helped me be ruthless with deciding what to keep and what to donate, especially with my assortment of nick-nacky things. Now there's just the big items of furniture to decide about. Luckily I have a lot of storage space in the garage at Anglesea for anything that won't fit in the house.'

'So what furniture do you think you'll take Gran?'

'Well I've decided to take my bed. It's not very old … and I feel close to Hugh when I'm in it … so it's a keeper. Plus *this* lounge suite because it's sooo comfy. I know the others will have couches and armchairs they love, so we'll just have to sort out what goes where when we've all moved in.'

'What about your big fridge/freezer and washing machine Mum? They're not very old either are they?'

'No, not very old. I'm not sure yet, I'll talk to the others and see what they have. We can always store some in the garage and then when something packs up we can just wheel out another one.'

'Hey yeah that's a good idea. You won't have to actually buy any new appliances for *years*.'

'No hopefully not,' I smiled. 'Well you know what? I think I'll just leave everything else for now. The real estate woman said the house will look better for sale if it's furnished, so I think I'll decide on the other things after it's sold. After all there's no real rush.'

'Yep that's a good idea Mum. So … I think it's time we had a break. How about I drive us to the pub for a counter meal and a couple of drinks … my shout.'

'Cool,' grinned Libby.

'Ha … soft drink for you my girl,' Lisa replied.

I smiled at my granddaughter, linked arms, and said, 'Yeah very cool. Come on, let's get out of here.'

'Ahhh ... that fish was yummy, and I just *loved* the garlic prawns. They're not that good back home are they Mum?'

'No way ... unfortunately,' grinned Lisa.

'Well that's one more thing which might entice you to move back here one day,' I smiled.

Lisa and Libby looked at each other and smiled, then I saw Lisa give Libby a small nod of her head.

'Okay ... what's going on?'

'Well ... Gran ... *guess what, guess what, guess what?* We didn't want to say anything until we had your house sorted, but I can tell you now ... *we're going to move back to Australia at the end of this year!*'

'*What ... really?* Oh my God that's *fantastic.* Oh I can't believe it ... *really?*'

'Yes Mum, really. We really miss the summer weather and beaches, and we *really* miss *you*. And since Finn and I are no longer together it's the perfect time to come back home. I figured it was best for Libby to finish this school year where she is now, and then I'll enroll her in a school in Geelong for the next two years.'

Through all this I just sat with the biggest smile on my face and with tears forming in my eyes.

'I ... I'm feeling a bit speechless,' I finally said. 'I'd always hoped you'd be back sometime, but didn't know if you ever would.'

'Yeah. Well I think I've stayed there long enough. It's been nineteen years ... and all of Libby's life!'

'Yeah, our little Pommie will have to become an Aussie now.'

Libby smiled and said, 'Yeah … bring it on.'

'Come on, let's go home,' I stood up. 'This news deserves champagne … and you can have a small glass too Libby … just this once.'

'Yes!'

CHAPTER SIXTEEN

APRIL 2014

'I just do not think I can go through all that again.' Gabi spoke quietly while slowly shaking her head. 'I cared for my Eric more than the five years before he died, and it was terrible. I loved him so much, and watching him die … I just do not think I can do that again.'

'Well … you don't *have* to Gabi. You've only just met this guy about four weeks ago. You're not *obligated* in any way.'

'I know this Anna, but he seems so *perfect* for me. I feel I have *finally* met the right man. Then he tells me he may only have a few more years before he becomes the invalid. God, why is this life so *unfair*?'

They were sitting outside on the deck of Gabi's unit, both with a cup of herbal tea in their hands. It was a warm afternoon; sunny with a collage of clouds slowly drifting towards the horizon. A slight breeze rustled through a Virginia creeper which clung tenaciously to the overhead timber verandah. Every now and then a golden leaf would fall, but neither Gabi nor Anna were aware of its descent.

'His daughter told him he *had* to tell me about his illness. I am not sure if I am happy about that, because I am now thinking it would be better if I did not know.'

'Well…'

But before Anna could reply, Gabi went on, 'But he said he wanted to be completely honest with me because he loves me. He *loves me* Anna, and I love him too. Oh I am so *angry* about this now. Why is life like this? It really is very so unfair.'

'Well…'

'What time is it? He will be here soon to hear what I have decided. And I still do not know.'

'It's four-thirty.'

'Okay, we still have the time. So tell me Anna, what should I do?'

'Well … I can't tell you what to do, but if you love him, and he loves you, then maybe just go for it. No one knows how long they have with their loved ones, so maybe just enjoy each other as you would if you *didn't* know.'

'Yes, yes I could do that … but I am just not sure if I can do the whole *caring* thing again. It is *so* hard seeing the person you love suffer in any way. That is my biggest worry … being his caregiver and watching him suffer.'

'Well you don't know what breakthroughs in treatments there might be in the meantime. I think there's a lot of research into Motor Neuron Disease these days, and they're coming up with cures for different things all the time. Who knows, something could happen which could completely change the situation for both of you.'

'Yes … yes I can see that maybe that could happen. Oh he is just *so* perfect for me … and he *loves* me Anna. It feels *so* lovely to be *loved* again.'

'Hmmm … well I think you've made your decision. What do *you* think?'

Gabi released a big sigh, then nodded. 'Yes … yes I think I have. I know I would rather be with him than with anybody else … and we will have the few good years before he becomes too unwell. So … I think I will just do the dealing with that when it happens.' She smiled at Anna then, saying 'Thank you so much my friend, for listening to me and helping me sort this out.'

'That's okay, happy to be of help. You two can go into the future as a couple and do all that travelling you were telling me he wants to do.'

'Oh yes, he wants to take me to so many different places. He even said we could visit where I grew up in Poland if I would like too.'

'Oh that could be good.'

'Yes. But I do not think I want to go back there now as all my family have died. I would actually like to see more of *this* beautiful country. Did you know that I have not yet seen Uluru? Or Kakadu or Darwin. Now they are *real* Australian places which I *must* see.'

'Absolutely. And you'll have to go to Alice Springs first before you see Uluru, and then you can visit Sam while he's there … and Tatiana.'

'Oh, Sam is back from Canada?'

'Yes, he arrived the week before last. I'm hoping to visit him after my house sells and I've got myself organised in Anglesea.'

'Oh Anna, you must be *so* happy to have him back in Australia again, yes?'

'Yes very happy. I'm not sure what I'd do without him. I hate it when he's living overseas. Well, I'd better get going now so you can get ready for your man,' Anna grinned.

Gabi laughed, saying, 'Yes … okay. Oh I feel so much better now, like the new life is starting for me. I am so very excited inside, so I know I have made the right decisions. And I *know* we will have the fun together, like we did on the cruise, and also since we have been back. Now I will make the time for all of you to meet him too,' she smiled.

'That sounds terrific. He could also help you move all your stuff to Anglesea.'

'Yes I have been thinking about that too. I think that now I have decided to be together with him, I will wait to move to Anglesea. If I stay here we will have more of the privacy to get to know each other, and he could then also stay over. I think this would be good, yes?' she grinned.

'Yes, I'm sure that would be good,' Anna grinned too.

'So I will let Liz know what I have decided. Hopefully her offer will still stand at some time in the future for me.'

'I'm sure that will be okay. Hey … did you hear that Evie's met a guy as well?'

'*What* … no I did not hear that. Who is he? When did this happen?'

'Well Marley set it up …'

But before she could get any further they heard the doorbell ring.

'Ooh he is here,' Gabi smiled. 'Damn … I wanted to hear about Evie's new man; how exciting for her.'

'Yes it is, but early days yet. Okay my friend I'm getting out of here. Hey … would you like me to tell the others about you and David and what's happening? I'm just thinking that you will be a bit distracted for a while now,' she grinned again, 'and I know they will be either phoning you, or asking me if I know what you're up to. It will save you from going over it again with each of them.'

'Oh … yes … that is the good idea. And tell them I will make the time soon so they can meet him. Thank you Anna.'

Gabi then opened the door for Anna to leave, and for David to enter.

'Anna, this is my friend David. David, this is my friend Anna.'

'Hi David.'

'Hi Anna, very nice to meet you.'

'Yes, same here. Anyway, see you some other time … I have to go now so … bye.'

'Bye.'

Anna was surprised that she actually had a happy feeling

inside as she walked towards her car. Since Jim's funeral she'd often struggled to appear happy so as not to worry her friends. But the joy on Gabi's face when she saw David at the door instantly transferred to herself; putting a genuine smile on her face.

'Ahh … new love,' she sighed. 'There's nothing better.' Getting in her car and fastening the seat belt, she then sat for a moment, thinking about how two of her friend's lives had changed recently because of a man.

'Hmmm … well I'm happy for them, but it's certainly not for me. There's no way I could ever trust a man again,' she thought.

Starting the car she then headed towards Belle's place where she'd been invited for dinner. It was their first opportunity for a proper catch-up since her trip overseas, having been busy with estate agents and maintenance men getting her house ready for sale.

'Come in Anna,' Belle called, noticing her friend through the kitchen window, walking towards the back door. 'I thought you'd be here soon so I've just poured us both a glass of wine.'

'Oh thanks. I've bought my overnight bag as I thought if we have a couple of drinks I'm ready to stay the night,' she smiled, dropping it down near the dining table.

'That sounds like a good plan. Did you think to bring your swimming gear with you?'

'Yes I did … I'm prepared for every eventuality.'

'Good thinking ninety-nine,' Belle grinned. 'So … cheers,' she held out her glass towards Anna.

'Yes … cheers,' Anna clinked her glass against her friend's. 'Mmmm … something smells good … can I help you with anything?"

'No, all good, sit down and relax. I've got the roast in the oven so now you can tell me all about your trip. You've told me the basics of your encounter with that woman, but I'd love to hear all the nitty-gritty's.'

'Okay. But first … have you spoken to Gabi about her new man yet?'

'Um … she rang and told me all about how she and David had met, but I haven't actually seen her to catch up properly. I've dropped round a couple of times but she hadn't been home. I thought she may have been out and about with him somewhere. Why, what's happening?'

'Well I actually just met him briefly before I came here. I'll tell you about them first, then I'll fill you in on my trip. Gabi thought it was a good idea for me to tell you and the others,' she smiled, 'because she's going to be a bit busy in the near future.'

The roast was eaten and the dishes done, and they were now settled in Belle's cozy lounge room. An old Moody Blues CD was playing; turned down low enough so they could continue talking.

'Another wine, or a cup of tea?'

'Well seeming though I'm staying here tonight, I will have another. I'll certainly sleep well later,' she smiled.

'Yeah me too,' Belle smiled as she retrieved the bottle from the fridge. Passing over the refilled glass, she went on, 'I've got to say that I really admire the way you went to Singapore and confronted Pamela. Not many women would have done that. So … *well done you*,' Belle said, raising her glass to her friend.

'Oh … thanks. Yes it's not something I thought I would've done either, but … it's a bit hard to explain … but I really feel like I'm a different woman now. It's like the pain and the *anger* I felt towards Jim just stripped off my outer layer and revealed another me underneath.'

'Yeah you're such a different person now … a new and improved model,' Belle grinned, raising her glass again.

'Yes, I am. I was happy to be meek and mild before … but not anymore. Remember that Helen Reddy song? "I am woman, hear me roar …" Well that's me now. Well, sort of, anyway,' she grinned.

'Ha … that's one of my favourites. Hey it must have been good to catch-up with your sisters. It was a shame they couldn't get here for the funeral.'

'Yes. Neither of them could afford it though, not that I minded.'

'So, did you like it over there?'

'Well, yes, it was lovely seeing *them* again. But I'm not a fan of London, it was really cold and grey. But I had a good time while I was there … caught up with their kids and grandkids … went and saw a couple of shows. I have to say I was happy to get on the plane when I was leaving though, knowing I was heading back to sunny Australia.'

'Hmm … have you heard from Claire since you've been back?

'Yes, I finally received an email a couple of days before I left London. Not that it said much. Just that she was feeling okay and not working too hard. I *know* both she and Gunther lead busy lives but it doesn't seem to matter if I send her a long or short email, I always just receive the bare minimum in reply.'

'Hmm … not much else you can do though is there?'

'Well I'd prefer to phone her, but when I do she doesn't answer. So if things don't improve over time, I'll visit and try and sort things out. But I think she still needs time to process her dad's death first.'

'Hmm … yeah. Well if you *do* go I could probably go with you and keep you company,' Belle said before taking a sip of her drink. 'I'd enjoy a week or so in Dusseldorf.'

'Me too, so we might have to do that sometime anyway.'

'Sounds good,' she smiled, then went on, 'but you know what? I can't stop thinking about Gabi lately. She certainly hasn't had an easy life has she? Remember how devastated she was when Eric died? She'd thought 'third time lucky' with that marriage. He was such a lovely man and they were so suited. It really wrecked her for a long time; caring for him until he died. I can so understand that she had doubts about getting into a relationship where that may happen again.'

'Yes, she was pretty upset thinking about it, but I think she's done the right thing. She said how excited she feels now, and I believe that gut feeling is always right.'

'Yeah I believe that too. So … I suppose we won't be seeing her much now if they're going to be travelling to who knows where.'

'No probably not. But she wants us all to meet him soon, so maybe we could have a party in the new house … like a housewarming … and meet him then?'

'Yeah that's a brilliant idea,' Belle smiled. 'I'll run it by Liz tomorrow. I think she should have most of her stuff moved in by now. How fantastic that her other house sold so fast. She didn't actually say for how *much*, but I know she was really happy with the price.'

'Yes she was very happy. So are you still moving at the end of the week?'

'Yeah I am, and the woman who's going to rent this place is ready to move straight in which is good. I've organised a removal van for Friday, so … it looks like all systems go. What about you? Are you still going to wait until your place sells?'

Anna thought for a moment before replying. 'Yes I think I will. As much as I'd love to be out of there now, I know the house looks better with furniture in it. My agent thinks it will sell pretty quickly anyway, so I don't mind waiting a little while. At least all those small maintenance jobs have been done, so it can actually go on the market this weekend.'

'Oh that's good then. So are you going to take most of your furniture or get new stuff?'

'Ha … definitely getting new stuff. There's one or two of my favourite things I'll take, like that recliner I bought last year, but there are too many memories attached to most of the other stuff. So, I'm planning on having a big garage sale and hopefully selling most of it that way.'

'Good idea.'

'Yes. My washing machine is fairly new, so I'll probably take that, *and* my T.V. Liz said we can store a fair bit of stuff in the garage at the new house so that's good as we'll probably double up on a few things. Have you heard when Evie's moving?'

'Yeah, her furniture's leaving on Monday but she's not leaving 'til Tuesday. She's staying the extra day as Blue's friends can't move 'til then and Evie didn't want to leave her there on her own. So, she reckons she'll get to Anglesea on Thursday.'

'Good, that's not long then. I'm wanting to hear more about her new fella when she gets here … I don't know what's going on … first Gabi has a new man, and now Evie. Maybe you'll be next Belle,' Anna teased.

'Ha, no way. What about you … maybe *you're* next?'

'No, I have *no* intention *whatsoever* in being with another man. But I *am* happy for Gabi and Evie.'

'Yeah me too. Okay … how about we watch a movie

before we call it a night? Sonya lent me 'Gravity' on DVD the other day. She liked it, and it has George Clooney in it,' Belle grinned.

'Sounds good to me. I'll watch anything with George in it. You get that organised and I'll make us a pot of tea.'

CHAPTER SEVENTEEN

It felt hot and humid to Anna and Belle as they walked into the Leisurelink pool complex the next day. Fortunately for them, there weren't *too* many kids there so it wasn't overly noisy. They strove to do a water aerobics class at least twice a week, often doing three, and sometimes fitted in a fourth.

Passing the Hydro pool on their left, they waved to a couple of friends who were just beginning *their* class. Most of the participants were intent on copying the fit instructor on the side of the pool, but several were *more* intent on talking and socialising.

'Come on you ladies up the back, stop talking and get into it … two in, two out …' the instructor called while demonstrating the move with her arms and legs.

Continuing on their way towards the rear of the complex, they were both anticipating their Deep Water class, believing it was more of a workout for the time they put in. Neither of them wore flotation devices as they both preferred treading water; hopefully burning off a few more calories with the extra exertion.

An hour later after finishing the class, they'd roughly dried off and were now walking towards the changing rooms, chatting to a couple of friends as they went.

'Oh wow, look what we've just avoided,' Judy said as she pointed towards the carpark area.

They all looked in that direction and saw a stream of kids disgorging from a school bus, and another bus pulling in behind it.

'Talk about good timing,' Maureen grinned.

They all nodded, glad to be missing out on all the noise that a multitude of kids added to the indoor pool.

'So who's staying for coffee today?' Judy then asked.

'I am,' replied Maureen.

'Me too,' agreed Ingrid, 'although I can't stay *too* long … babysitting duties are called for.'

'Neither of us can stay today,' Belle quickly cut in, indicating herself and Anna. 'I've still got things to pack and Anna's helping me.'

Anna nodded, saying, 'Yes, and I'm doing the usual and having a shower at home.'

'Yeah same here,' Belle agreed.

After a chorus of 'see you next time,' Anna and Belle each

popped into a changing cubicle while the others headed for the showers.

Anna was driving along South Valley Road, nattering away about some plant cuttings she was planning to take to Angelsea, when she realised that Belle was noticeably quiet.

'Are you okay? You seem a bit quiet. Is there something wrong?'

'Oh … it was just hearing Ingrid say she has babysitting duties … it just makes me feel so sad. It doesn't look like *either* of us are going to have grandkids does it?' Without waiting for a reply, Belle went on. 'Tatiana has *never once* told me she'd like to have kids, and after all the chats I've had with Naomi, she's never mentioned it either. And anyway, how would they go about *conceiving* a child?'

'Hmm … I'm not sure what that would entail.'

'Yeah … but I'm sure she would have talked to me about it if they'd been thinking of something like that.'

'Hmm … yes, probably. I know how you feel though. I wish things were different … but I think we just have to accept it.'

'Yeah … I know.'

A couple of minutes later, Anna pulled over and parked in front of Belle's house. Declining the offer of a cuppa, Anna said she'd go home and shower, and would be back shortly with the boxes that would be perfect for the last of Belle's bits and pieces.

Driving off, Anna sighed, feeling a bit depressed about the situation as well, but didn't want to bring her friend down any more than she already was. She was actually pretty good at hiding her low spirits these days, after all, she'd had several years of practice. Sighing again she shook her head as she parked in her driveway and turned off the car.

'Oh well, at least Belle can relate … I don't know how I'd manage without her being in the same boat. The same *crappy* boat,' she managed a small smile.

Knowing there was no point in dwelling on it she made her way indoors, dumped her wet towel and bathers straight into the washing machine, turned it on, and then headed for the bathroom.

Now showered and dressed, Anna went outside to peg her swimming gear onto the clothes line. Then after making a cuppa she wandered back outside to sit for a while in the leafy surroundings. After previously feeling a bit down, it wasn't long before she felt her spirit lifting.

'Hmmm … I have to say the garden *does* look marvelous. But I'm still looking forward to getting stuck into the garden at Anglesea. I love that it's been a bit neglected … it'll give me more to do.'

Anna actually smiled as she thought about it. She loved nothing better than dressing in her old gardening clothes and getting her hands dirty. Weeding, digging, planting, watering … she loved it all. Suddenly wondering if she'd 'let herself go' and that was why Jim had looked elsewhere, her mood dropped once more.

Her emotions had been fluctuating wildly these last few months. Now making an effort to suppress the dark ones, Anna turned her thoughts to the love she'd felt from Grace and Pamela in Singapore. It had been so unexpected it had thrown her a bit; not knowing how to handle it at first. She'd still been smiling about it on the plane to London.

But it had been Liz's offer to share the house in Anglesea which had truly saved her. Knowing she'd soon be living with her best friends in that wonderful house had eliminated a large part of her depression. She knew she would have sold this house and bought another one somewhere in the Geelong area, but that would've meant spending a lot of evenings on her own again.

'Ahhh … not much longer and I'll be out of this house forever,' she thought, nodding her head. 'And I won't miss this garden *too* much as I'll be busy whipping the new one into shape,' she managed to smile.

Finishing her cuppa, she went and retrieved the boxes from the garage; folded them, and stowed them in her car. A few minutes later she was driving back to Belle's place to help her complete the last of her packing.

CHAPTER EIGHTEEN

Evie stood and watched as the removal van drove away with her possessions. She suddenly felt a bit displaced and it felt slightly unsettling. Having moved many times in her life she thought she'd be used to it, but suspected it felt different this time because of the memories she'd made here with Dash.

'You look sad Gran … are you sure you're doing the right thing?' Blue put her arm around Evie's shoulders and gave her a hug.

'Haha … well … it's a bit late to think about that … unless I run after the truck,' Evie managed to laugh. 'But no … it's okay Bluey, if it doesn't work out I can always come back here.'

'Yeah you can,' Bluey smiled. 'Okay, I think we can just make it in time to have a counter meal at the pub if we hurry. What do you think? Are you hungry? I'm starving.'

'You're always starving,' Evie grinned, 'but yes, I *am* hungry now. I only had a coffee for breakfast.'

'Excellent. Then after lunch I think we should have one last swim at the beach. I mean, what's with this *weather*? It's so *hot* today.'

'Sounds good to me,' Evie agreed. 'A swim should help me sleep really well tonight, and I'll be bright-eyed and bushy tailed in the morning for my big drive down south.'

'*Bushy tailed?*' Blue raised her eyes.

'Yes, bushy tailed,' Evie grinned. 'It's an old-timers saying.'

'Ahh … okay. So … let's get going or meals will have finished. Can we go in your car? I'm nearly out of petrol.'

Evie smiled and said, 'Are you sure you're going to be able to manage here without me?'

'Of course Gran, it'll be good for me. I *am* twenty-two now, so it's time I became more responsible.'

'Yes that's true. Okay, let's get going … I'll drive.'

The next day after a breakfast of pancakes which Bluey made for everyone – her mates having arrived early that morning - and then after lots of hugs and a few tears, Evie finally drove out of Terrigal. She had to admit that it did feel strange to be leaving, but she was also quite excited about beginning a new chapter of her life. The fact that it was going to be with her best friends made her smile even more.

'Okay Anglesea, here I come.'

She loved driving, and also loved the new Honda Accord

she'd bought herself for Christmas, so was eager to see how it would perform on a long trip. Her plan was to drive about five hours to Gundagai, stay overnight at a motel, then drive another three hours the following day to her friend's home in Porepunkah. She hadn't seen Jenny and Nick for quite a while so was anticipating a good catch up. Then the next day she'd have a four hours' drive to Angelsea.

By the time she got to Gundagai, she was more than ready to stop at the motel she'd booked. She'd had a few short stops on the way to stretch her legs, replenish her caffeine levels and have a light lunch, but had decided to press on while she'd felt relatively fresh.

After a hot shower – which did wonders for her stiff muscles - then a tasty meal at the adjoining restaurant and she was ready for bed. She was rather surprised at how tired she felt; accepting that, yes, she *was* getting a little older. With a smile and a sigh, she turned off the bedside light and was asleep within minutes.

On the road again the next day by nine, Evie arrived at her friend's house just in time for lunch. After a lovely time hearing about their recent trip to China, she then filled Jenny in regarding how she'd met Ross; Nick having left them to their 'girl talk.' That evening after dinner they had 'a couple' of Baileys, and it ended up being quite late before they called it a night.

They were all up by eight the following morning though,

but as no one felt like rushing, they enjoyed a leisurely breakfast outside on the balcony. Bright rays of sunlight streaked through the hovering clouds every chance they got, and the conjecture was it would end up being another lovely sunny day. Evie sipped her coffee and admired the extraordinarily beautiful mountain range which encircled the area, noting pockets of white cloud still hugging the thickly forested gullies. It was extremely peaceful, with just some noisy cockatoos making their presence known every now and then. Later, after extracting a promise from her friend to visit her soon, Evie began the last leg of her trip.

By one thirty that afternoon she was definitely getting excited as she drew closer to her destination, but also felt her body starting to protest at being in a sitting position for so long. The last fifty kilometers seemed to fly past though, and it seemed to be no time at all 'til she was pulling into the driveway of her new home, tooting the horn a couple of times as she came to a stop.

CHAPTER NINETEEN

It was just after two o'clock when I heard a car horn tooting. Stopping what I was doing I stepped out onto the front balcony and saw Evie had finally arrived. As she got out of the car and started stretching, I called out to her from above.

'*Yay! You're here!* Oh *finally* … I can't believe you're *actually* here. I'm *so* excited. *Come up, come up* … I'm going to open a bottle of champers. We *have* to celebrate.'

After hugs, kisses and two glasses of bubbly each, we were chatting and nibbling the assortment of food which I'd prepared earlier, when we heard a truck pull up in the drive-way. Looking through one of the front windows we saw the large furniture van had arrived with Evie's 'stuff'.

'What good timing,' I exclaimed.

'Perfect,' Evie agreed.

We spent the next hour and a half directing the removal

men as to which things to bring indoors, and which to put in the garage.

'Well I certainly won't get much of this unpacked today, but I don't suppose there's any rush,' Evie sighed, surveying the array of boxes.

'No, absolutely no rush,' I concurred.

'But one thing I *do* want to get organised is a bed,' she stated. 'I've already looked online at the bedding stores so I'm pretty sure which one I'd like to get. How about we finish eating, then you drive me to Waurn Ponds so I can check it out before I buy it. I think *I've* done enough driving to last me *quite* a while,' she smiled.

'Okay, no problemo. Hey if we have time we can drop in and see Anna, Belle or Gabi … or maybe *all* of them. I don't know what they're up to today so I don't know who's home or not.'

'Okay, I'll ring them when we're on our way, but first, let's finish eating so we can get to the store before closing time.'

We looked at each other again and hugged once more. Making our way to the kitchen bench, we sat on the comfy barstools, then proceeded to work our way through the remaining food; catching up on a bit of gossip as we did so.

We got to the bedding store just in time. By half past five we'd arranged to have the bed that Evie had bought to be delivered the next day, then fifteen minutes later we were ringing the doorbell at Anna's house. Gabi and David had driven to Daylesford to spend a few days at a spa retreat, and Belle was in Melbourne checking out an art gallery with some friends, so we'd arranged to catch up with them another time.

'Come in you two … it's great to see you again Evie. How was the drive? All good I hope?'

'Yes, all pretty uneventful, which is definitely good.'

'Yes. Uneventful is usually best for driving. Now, who wants what? Tea, coffee or a glass of wine?'

I sat on a swiveling bar stool at the kitchen bench, replying that as we'd already had champagne earlier, that I'd have a coffee.

'Yes me too,' Evie nodded, as she sat down beside me, 'otherwise we'll be staying *here* the night.'

'Well that can be arranged,' smiled Anna.

'Thanks anyway,' Evie grinned, 'but we have to be back when my new bed arrives. The guy said he'd deliver it first thing in the morning.'

Chatting about this and that while Anna made the coffees, we then followed her outside to check out her re-vamped outdoor area. She'd explained that when she'd been clearing out the garage she'd come across a box of un-used garden lights, so when her handyman had finished the work she'd employed him to do, she asked him to string them up somewhere.

'Wow, Anna, the lights look fabulous … in fact your whole garden appears to be extremely manicured. You *have* been busy.'

'Yes, thanks Evie. Actually hiring the handyman was one of the best things I've done. He cleaned out the guttering, and cut back a few branches on that tree over there. He even brought round one of those pressure wash machines and cleaned off the paving stones. I hadn't realised how dirty they were 'til he cleaned them.'

'Yes, well it all looks fantastic. I suppose you'll miss it a bit when you move? Are you taking any plants with you?'

'Yes, that azalea over there in that pot, and a few cuttings from some plants Sam bought me over the years. But no, I don't think I'll miss it,' she shook her head. 'I'm actually looking forward to moving now. I don't feel connected to here at all anymore.'

I could see Anna was feeling low, so as we wandered back indoors I suggested she and I visit the large plant nursery on the Colac road tomorrow.

'Oh ... that would have been lovely Liz. My real estate agent is bringing some people through tomorrow, and I'm not supposed to be here. But, I've already promised Belle that I'd help her move tomorrow.'

'Oh ... of course ... I'm such a nong,' I exclaimed. 'I've been waiting so long for all of you to move in with me, and now I can't keep up with who's doing what. Okay, so how about I pick you up and we'll *both* go to Belle's? What time suits you?'

'I'll be ready any time after ten.'

'Okay, well I'll ring you when I'm leaving Anglesea.'

That night as I made up a bed for Evie on the couch, I commented on how worried I was about Anna. 'I'm surprised she didn't take up Belle's offer to go to Melbourne with her. She usually loves checking out an art exhibition.'

'Yes I know,' Evie nodded. 'But you know what? I reckon once she's out of that house and moved in here she'll pick up again. She's had a lot to contend with lately.'

'Yeah that's true.'

Evie yawned, setting me off, which prompted me to ask why yawns are contagious.

'I don't know, but I once heard someone say that a yawn is a silent scream for coffee.'

'Ha … that's a good one.'

'Yes, but all I know right now is I'm completely knack- ered. I'm getting on that couch and hopefully sleeping all night.'

'Okay sleepyhead … see you in the morning.'

'Yes see you then.'

We were woken at eight by the delivery man ringing the doorbell. Having slept like logs, we woke relatively quickly and made our way downstairs. The man had his off-sider with him so it didn't take long for them to manoeuvre each piece of the bed frame, and the mattress, up the stairs and into the bedroom which Evie had chosen.

'Thanks again,' Evie smiled at the men as they headed back out to their truck.

'No worries love … see ya.'

'Hmmm,' Evie pondered for a moment. 'Do you have a tool kit or some spanners?'

'Yeah, I actually kept Hugh's toolkit, it's in the garage. Hang on and I'll go out and get it.'

'Great. I'm sure we'll be able to put this bed together ourselves.'

'Yeah … I'm sure we can,' I slowly nodded as I headed downstairs, not quite as certain as she was.

An hour later we stood back and admired our handy work. The mattress had been rather awkward to move, but we eventually managed to manhandle it into position onto the newly assembled bed base. Getting the bedlinen on had been the finishing touch, both of us loving the turquoise and coral colours of Evie's new doona cover and pillowcases.

'Whew … I'm glad that's done.' Evie stood with her hands on her hips for a moment surveying her new bedroom. 'Come on, time for coffee.'

'Yeah okay. I'll pop some croissants in the oven to heat up while you get the coffee organised. I bought the most wonderful blend at a coffee roasters in Geelong last week; just wait 'til you taste it.'

'Mmm … sounds good.'

'*Woo hoo* … I've just remembered that Belle will be moving in here later today too. Oh happy days,' I grinned. 'I can't wait 'til were all here. Such a shame that Gabi's not moving in now though.'

'Yes, but she probably will later … you know … when David's no longer with us.'

'Yeah. I'm so looking forward to meeting him. Anna said he seems really lovely.'

'Yes she did. Okay, we'd better get a move on or you'll be late picking up Anna.'

'Okay, okay,' I grinned at my friend. 'Oh it's *so* good to finally have you here.'

CHAPTER TWENTY

Belle was surprised but happy to see Liz arrive with Anna, not knowing she'd decided to come as well. The removal men had been busy loading her furniture into the truck for a while now, and there was just a couple of heavy boxes and some pot plants to go. She was experiencing a mix of emotions – apprehension, excitement, worry, anticipation – and didn't know which one to settle on. Waving at her friends she relaxed a little; letting out a big breath.

'Hi Anna, hi Liz, thanks for coming. I was just starting to feel a bit frazzled.'

'Hi Belle,' I grinned. 'No need to worry about anything now because *we* are here. Now … what needs doing?'

'Well, nothing much really. The men got here early so they've nearly finished.'

'Oh, okay. Sorry we couldn't get here sooner; my fault.

Evie's new bed was delivered this morning and it took us a while to assemble it. I picked Anna up a bit later than originally planned.'

'No that's okay Liz. I had everything pretty much organised anyway. I just need to put my laptop in the car, and a couple of my smaller paintings. The larger ones are in the truck after I nearly bubble wrapped the life out of them,' she grinned. 'Wow, so Evie's moved in then. I can't believe it's all happening. Just you now Anna. Hopefully your agent will have good news for you later today.'

Anna nodded and smiled, but before she could say anything one of the men strode over and spoke to Belle.

'Well I think that's it, so if there's nothing else we'll get going. I have the address in Anglesea, but will there be someone there to let us in? I'm assuming you'd like the furniture put inside,' he grinned.

'Yeah there's someone there now, and we'll also be there shortly. I just have to lock up here first.'

We watched as the big truck slowly drove off, then we walked inside and looked around. There was still a large bookcase in the lounge room, and another smaller one in the dining room, but the other rooms were now bare; Belle's personality no longer evident.

'Kaye, the woman I'm renting to, said she could use the bookcases if I didn't need them straight away. I wasn't sure how much was going to fit in the house and garage at Anglesea, so thought I may as well leave them here for now.'

'Yeah, we'll work that out as we go,' I nodded. 'But first

things first … come on, let's go and get you settled. I am *so* excited. I had the dividing wall and the wardrobes installed last week so your room is all ready for you.'

'Oh *really*. How fantastic. Thanks so much Liz.'

'Don't mention it. Now it would have been good if we could all drive back together, but of course you need to bring your car Belle. Hey Anna, how about if you come too and stay the night. I can always bring you back tomorrow. That way we can all have a couple of drinks and relax.'

'Um …'

'No um. Say yes, it'll be fun.'

'Well …' Anna still hesitated a little. 'I don't have a change of clothes for tomorrow though.'

'No problem. I'm sure between the three of us we can find something for you to wear. And I have a couple of new toothbrushes at home as well … so what do you say?'

'Well … okay then. With a bit of luck the people inspecting my house today will decide to buy it. Hopefully we can celebrate that as well.'

'Yes, hopefully … okay let's hit the road then.'

The delivery men had left a while ago after unloading Belle's furniture, assorted boxes and accoutrements; some things going in the house, the rest in the garage. The four women were now solely concentrating on getting her bed assembled. It took them nearly an hour – after a few laughs and a bit of swearing - but they eventually had it in one piece. Belle then retrieved the bed linen from a box marked 'linen', and it was finally 'sleepable'.

'Okay ladies, me thinks it's time to celebrate,' I smiled. 'I suggest we just have one drink now, then have something to eat. What do you all think? I could go and get us a pile of fish and chips?'

'Ok sounds good to me,' Evie grinned. 'I'll go with you.'

'Yep sounds good to me too,' Belle nodded.

'Yes me too,' Anna smiled. 'How about if we all go? I wouldn't mind having another quick look at our selection of local shops.'

'Okay we'll all go then,' I laughed, as I headed to the fridge to get the champagne. 'Oh I *love* this … I just *love* us all being here … we're going to have a lot fun together, I can just *feel* it.'

'Well, I haven't had a phone call,' Anna sighed. 'I suppose it was a bit much to ask, that the first people to look would buy the house.'

'Yes, never mind … they might get back to you tomorrow though.'

'You're always so positive Liz,' Anna smiled at me, 'but yes, you never know.'

We were sitting on two couches in the lounge room; one was the extra big one which I'd brought, and the other one was Belle's.

'Anyone for another glass of champers?'

'Not for me thanks Liz, I think I'll have a cup of tea. I can't remember when I've had so much champagne,' Evie smiled. 'I might end up growing accustomed to it at this rate.'

'Yeah me too,' Belle agreed.

'Me three,' grinned Anna.

'Ha … well that's all good. We'll have some more when Anna moves in officially then. But actually a cup of tea sounds good.'

'I'll make them,' Anna offered. 'Are you having one too Belle?'

'Yes please.' She sat for a moment then added, 'Wow, what a day. I'm actually *here*, I can't believe it.'

'Yes, I feel the same,' agreed Evie. 'I think it'll take a day or two for it to really sink in.'

'Yeah,' I nodded. 'I've been here all week on my own which was a bit weird, so now it feels perfect having you all here.'

After converting the couch into a bed again, this time for Anna, they all had showers and then decided it was time to hit the hay. Evie went to her room to sleep for the first time in her new bed, and Belle headed downstairs to *her* new room.

'Ahh … I just love this room,' Belle thought as she checked out the new wardrobes and shelves again, 'but I am *sooo* tired, I've got to get into bed.' She was asleep within ten minutes of her head hitting the pillow, and didn't wake 'til nine-thirty the next morning.

After a yawn and a good stretch she continued to lay in bed for a while; contentedly savouring her new surroundings. Then, becoming aware of the muffled drone of a distant lawnmower she smiled, picturing the person pushing the noisy machine around their lawn. Thinking of how industrious they were, she decided it was time she was up and into the day as well.

Pulling the curtains open she caught a glimpse of a kookaburra as it took flight from the branch of a nearby tree. She opened the sliding door and breathed in deeply. The smell of freshly cut grass wafted in the breeze and it produced an extremely satisfied smile on her face.

'Mmm … what a perfect start to the morning.'

Leaving the glass door open but the screen door shut to keep out any bugs and insects, she headed for her bathroom. Stifling a huge yawn, she decided a shower was the best way to become fully functional for the day ahead. It wasn't long before she was standing under streams of steaming water.

'Ahhh … yes … one of life's luxuries … a lovely, hot shower.'

Ten minutes later she was dressed and walking up the stairs; her hair loose and still damp. It seemed rather quiet up there so she assumed the others were still asleep, but after feeling the kettle was warm she knew that someone had to be up. Pulling aside the dining room curtain, she slid open the door and found Evie and Liz lying in the sun on a couple of banana lounges.

'Good morning ladies.'

'Good morning yourself.'

'How did you sleep?' Evie asked.

'Like a dead person. What about you two?'

'Yes us too. And it looks like Anna is the same.'

'Okay, I'm making a coffee … would either of you like another one?'

'Yes please.'

'Me too please.'

'Oh, did I hear someone say *coffee*,' Anna smiled as she made her way out to where the others were talking. 'Oh my goodness I had the best sleep I've had for ages. It's wonderfully quiet here, all I could hear were some birds … quite delightful.'

Belle made everyone a cuppa then said she was just going to ring Tatiana. She'd promised her daughter a phone call after she moved in, so taking her coffee back to her room she dialed her number.

'Hi mum, how's it all going? Did you move everything okay? Are you settled in yet?'

'Hi love, yes everything's here and I'm reasonably settled in. I still have heaps to unpack of course, but there's no rush. We had a few glasses of champagne last night so we've all had bit of a sleep in this morning.'

'So who's "all"? You told me yesterday that Evie's there, but is Anna there as well? Has her house sold *already*?'

'No her house hasn't sold yet, but yes she *is* here. Liz picked her up yesterday to get her out of her house for a while, and we then talked her into staying here overnight. She was just saying how good she'd slept, so hopefully it won't be long before she's living here too.'

'Well that all sounds great. I'm definitely coming for a visit in the not too distant future. But look … I've got to go now, we're pretty busy here for a change. I'll call you tonight and you can fill me in on all the gossip.'

'Okay love. Take care, talk soon, bye.'

'Bye mum.'

Belle was smiling as she walked back up the stairs, confident that whenever her daughter was able to visit, she'd love her new home as well.

CHAPTER TWENTY-ONE

MAY 2014

Gabi and David were laughing so hard they had to lie back on their picnic rug to try and calm down. Holding hands as they lay side by side, each time they looked at each other they started laughing again.

'Oh no … I have to stop … my side is hurting,' Gabi moaned.

'Yes … mine too,' David groaned loudly, which set them both off again.

After slowly getting their laughter under control they watched a large flock of birds flying in a v-formation; high up through the unblemished sky. Sighing with contentment they sat up and surveyed their surroundings again.

A towering pine plantation soared skywards on two sides; tree ferns and native plants flourishing everywhere else. A small creek flowed to their right, and the melodious sound of water rippling over rocks could just be heard. As they let their eyes wander they both inhaled the invigorating scent of pine, mixed with the inherent earthiness of the rain-forest. Their attention was suddenly drawn to the other side of the creek when they caught sight of something moving. A small, grey wallaby then appeared at the water's edge; Gabi and David both holding their breath as it lowered its head to drink. Gazing in wonder at the furry marsupial, time seemed to stop for a moment.

They'd driven to Beech Forest as Gabi had never been there before, and David had enthused how beautiful the area was. After driving along many winding roads where massive ferns had dominated the scenery, they'd parked in a clearing, then walked down a steep track to admire an incredibly beautiful waterfall.

The crystal clear water had tumbled downwards before crashing onto large boulders causing the water to spray in all directions. This had produced a fine mist which had rendered them slightly damp. A variety of thick foliage had towered above, and they'd marveled at how refreshingly cool the magical spot had been. Later, after eventually making their way back to the car, they'd driven on, soon discovering the grassy glade where they'd decided to stop and have their picnic.

Now finished drinking, the wallaby quickly darted back into the undergrowth and was hidden from view within seconds.

'Oh David, that was amazing. Thank you for bringing me here. I *love* it.'

'My pleasure. There are lots of other places I want to show you as well … but first … how about we pack up this stuff and get going.' Checking the time on his watch he said, 'It's just after two o'clock. Check in time at the Tall Trees Retreat is at three. It'll probably be about an hour's drive, so we should be able to check in as soon as we get there. You're going to love it, it's really peaceful.'

'Yes and the spa sounds good,' Gabi grinned.

'Yes … *and* it has an indoor fire. I wonder if it will have a bearskin rug we can lie on?'

'Ahh you are so funny,' Gabi laughed, 'but yes, let us go now. I am so wanting to relax in the spa.'

'And tomorrow it will just be a short drive to Apollo Bay where we can have lunch and a walk along the beach.'

'You are so organised David, I am impressed,' she grinned.

'Ahh well … my mission is completed then. I have *impressed* the woman I love … there is nothing left for me to do.'

Gabi smiled and threw a small towel at him, saying, 'Ha … no there is still plenty for you to do. We have to get all this stuff back into the car yet.'

Twenty minutes later they were back on the sealed road which led to the coast. They talked, laughed, and talked some more, always delighting in each others company.

Since Gabi had told David that she *would* be in a relationship with him they had been virtually inseparable. She had stayed at his place in Mount Waverley a few times, but mainly they preferred to stay in Geelong as it was so close to fantastic beaches, bush walks, and the rainforest they were enjoying today. They had also been busy planning some longer trips; several within Australia, and a couple of overseas ones.

It took a little less than an hour to reach their destination, and they both loved the cottage at first sight. After booking in and completing the formalities, they wandered around the large property before deciding that a glass of wine in the spa was calling them.

Twenty minutes later they were laying back in the steamy, bubbling water sipping their drinks.

'Ahhh … this is the life,' David grinned. 'I wonder what the peasants are doing today.'

'*Peasants? What* peasants?'

He laughed a little before hugging her, saying, 'No … sorry Gabi, it's just a saying. It means … um … that we are living like royalty, and everyone else is a peasant.'

'Oh … yes … I see that. Yes that *is* a bit funny.'

After talking about all the fun they'd had today, David said once again how much he liked Gabi's friends. He'd ended up meeting them when he and Gabi had driven Anna to Angelsea the day she'd moved.

Anna's car's battery had been flat as she'd failed to fully close the rear door, allowing the interior light to burn all that night. She'd phoned Gabi, hoping for a lift from her, and was happy to hear that she and David had just arrived in Geelong from Mount Waverly so were able to pick her up. They'd *all* then been able to have a glass of champagne together to celebrate Anna's arrival in Anglesea.

'Yes I am very lucky to have such good friends. And it was so good that Anna's house sold so quickly. I cannot believe it only took *one week*. She was *so* happy to move in with the others. I think she won't be so depressed anymore.'

'Yes, I think it's the best thing for her too. It wouldn't have been good for her to be on her own every night. I'm actually very glad to know that you'll move in there one day too,' he smiled.

'*Hey*, we said we are not going to talk about that, *okay*?'

'Okay.'

After pouring the last of the wine into their glasses, David asked Gabi how she came to know her friends.

'Well … after I got to Geelong I rented the small flat, and it was just up the road from Belle's … not that I was to know that then of course.'

'Of course,' David smiled.

'I used to go for the walk most evenings after work … it was summer then and did not get dark until late … and I had often seen her walking, and we had sometimes said hello. Then one time I saw her trip and hurt her foot, so I stopped and asked her if she was okay. I ended up helping her back to her place, and said I lived just four houses down the street. She asked me in for a coffee, we got talking some more, and just became friends.'

'Ahhh … I see …and what about the others. How did you meet them?'

'Well I was working at the plant nursery, and Belle said her friend Anna was *mad* about the gardening, and so they would come and see me at work sometimes. I found Anna to be very lovely as well, and we became friends also. Then one day they said they were going to visit their friend Liz at her house at Eastern View, and would I like to come. So of course I said yes.'

'Of course,' David smiled again.

'I had not been on that coast road before and I could not believe the beauty of it. And when we got to the house of Liz and Hugh … my God it was gorgeous … and so big with the beautiful views … I thought that these people would not want to know *me*. But they were both so welcoming to me. I felt very happy.'

'Well of course they would like you, you silly thing.'

'But I did not meet Evie for another month or so after that. She came from her house in Terrigal to stay for a week with Liz and Hugh when it was the fortieth birthday for Liz. They had a big party and I was invited too and I met her then. We have all been friends ever since.'

David nodded, saying it was terrific how that had all

worked out. Finishing their drinks they thought it was time to eat, so got out of the spa and dried each other off. Deciding to drive the short distance to Apollo Bay to have dinner, they quickly dressed, then David ate the leftovers from their picnic to counteract his alcohol consumption, before driving.

'Mm, mm … you do make a delicious quiche Gabi.'

'Thank you. The tomatoes are from my garden, and also the spring onions.'

'Hopefully your neighbour can water your garden when we go on our trip.'

'Oh yes she said she would be happy to do that. I said she can eat as much as she likes of whatever is ripe. So it will be good to know that nothing is being wasted.'

'That's great then. Okay, enough about gardens … let's get going.'

They covered many topics over the course of their dinner, and after starting on their deserts they were both happy to re-live some of the wonderful times they'd had on the cruise where they'd met.

'I just loved the water taxis in Port Vila … what a great way to get around.'

'Yes, and it was also the great place to buy the souvenirs. But I still think Isle of Pines had the best snorkeling, yes?'

'Yes. We had a terrific day there didn't we? I'm so glad I

suggested we all go together. I think our whole group had a wonderful time.'

'Oh yes. My friends also said that. And the next day we had the same wonderful day at Mystery Island. What a cute little island it was,' she smiled.

David grinned, saying, 'Yes it was. I was just a bit sad as it was our last stop. Knowing we just had a few days left of our cruise made me realise I wanted to keep you in my life. I was so glad you agreed to see me when we were home again.'

'I was so very happy that you wanted to see *me* again. I already liked you very much.' Pushing her now empty desert bowl aside, she asked if he'd done much travelling when he'd worked for the bank.

'A little. I sometimes had to attend a conference somewhere, but I never had a lot of time to sightsee unfortunately.' He chuckled then saying, 'I have to admit that on some of those flights I daydreamed I was heading off to explore some exotic destination. Those conferences could often be very boring.'

'You must be *so* glad you are not working for the bank anymore … everyone hates the banks, yes?'

David had a laugh at that before saying, 'Yes. Everyone *does* hate the banks. Oh Gabi … I love your honesty and how you just say what you think. It's very refreshing.'

'Thank you David. You too are very honest which I love as well.'

'So … if we are finished here I think we should head back.

That big bed looked quite inviting, don't you think? Unless you would like coffee first?'

'No, I don't need the coffee first, as I also think the bed looked quite inviting.'

Smiling at each other David paid the bill and they left, walking arm in arm out to the car.

CHAPTER TWENTY-TWO

Anna could not get enough of the new garden. Since she'd moved to Angelsea she'd virtually spent all her time there. It was a lot larger than her old one, and because it had been unattended since the previous owners had moved out, there had been plenty to keep her occupied. She'd been surprised to see there'd been no vegetable garden so that had been her first mission. The ground had been easy to dig so it hadn't been long before she'd had an area dug and vegies and herbs planted. Everything had grown remarkably well, so she'd decided to extend the plot and plant more edibles, which was her mission for today. Now slowly straightening her back as she stood upright, she then arched back a little in an attempt to stretch out some tightness.

'Hmm … I think I need a break. I'll regret it tonight if I overdo things.'

Pulling off her gardening gloves and dropping them into the now empty wheelbarrow, she stood for a moment and appraised the work she's done so far that morning. Just then she heard a voice call out to her from upstairs.

'Hey Anna, are you ready for a cuppa? I'm making some lunch too if you're hungry?'

'Okay, thanks Liz, I won't be long … just have to wash up first.'

'It's looking fab out there Anna,' I smiled. 'A huge improvement to when I moved in. I would have had to hire a gardener if you weren't here.'

'Thanks Liz … but you know how much I love it … I actually haven't missed my old garden at all.'

'Good … I'm glad to hear it. Now, I have to go into Geelong later. Would you like to come with me, or is there anything I can get for you?'

'Umm … no, there's nothing I'm needing. So thanks, but I think I'll stay here. I want to cut back that bottlebrush outside the laundry before it flowers again, and then finish preparing the next section of the vegie garden.'

'No worries. There's no stopping you is there?'

'No there's not. I'm really in my element out there,' Anna replied, a smile on her face, 'although I *am* feeling rather stiff now that I've stopped. I'll have to see if there's a good massage lady in the area soon.'

'Oh, yes there is. I have a massage every two weeks. My

back and knee give me hell otherwise. I'll give you her number later.'

'Ok thanks.' As Anna finished the last of her lunch I returned some leftovers to the fridge, smiling when I saw what was in there.

'Hey there's two chocolate eclairs still here … how about we finish them off?'

'Ooh yes, to hell with my figure. If the others complain we can say we were saving *them* from putting on weight.'

'Yes … that we *sacrificed* ourselves for their own good,' I grinned.

We both laughed as Anna then made a fresh pot of tea before we sat and ate the delectable pastries.

'Hmm … that was more filling than I was expecting,' Anna said as she sat back and licked some sticky chocolate icing off her fingers.

'Yeah, you're not kidding,' I agreed. 'We probably should have gone halves in one.'

'Yes … too late now though,' Anna smiled. 'Oh well, they *were* rather yummy.'

'Mmm … yeah.'

'Just as well I'm keeping active in the garden or I'll be the size of a house soon,' Anna sighed. 'Which reminds me that I have to get back into my water aerobics soon too. I haven't been since I moved here; Belle hasn't either. We've both been a bit slack about it.'

'Yeah but you've both been busy unpacking and sorting your stuff. *And* just relaxing after moving. It was a bit stressful for *all* of us, deciding what we wanted to take, then packing and leaving our homes.'

'Yes you're right. It *was* rather stressful ... *and* everything else in the last few months. But ... that's all done now, so I think it's time for me to get into a new routine. I really enjoy water aerobics, so when Belle's back from Alice Springs I'll see if she's ready to get back into it too.'

'Sounds like a plan,' I smiled. 'I might even go with you. I could certainly do with losing a kilo or two.'

'Oh that would be great if you came with us. We have a lot of fun there. I'm sure you'd enjoy it.'

'Yeah okay,' I smiled and nodded. 'You know ... it's *really* good to see you happy these days Anna.'

'Yes, I *am* happier now,' she smiled again. 'But how could I *not* be, living here with all of you?'

'Well yeah, that's true,' I grinned.

'I'd still love to see more of Sam and Claire, but ... life goes on doesn't it?'

'Yeah, it certainly does. Have you heard from Claire recently?'

'Well I sent her a long email a couple of days ago, and attached a several photos of the house and garden, but I haven't heard back yet.'

'Hmm ... I suppose she's busy flying somewhere.'

'Yes, I suppose so. Right ... I think I'll waddle off back to the garden again.'

I chuckled at that replying, 'Yeah ... and I'll waddle to my work room before I head into Geelong.'

Both smiling, we went our separate ways.

'Okay, I think I'll do the pruning first, *then* finish the vegie patch. I can't wait to get more vegies and herbs planted but that bottlebrush looks shocking.'

Fifteen minutes later Liz called out her goodbyes from the balcony, then offered to bring home Chinese food later as it would just be the two of them for dinner; Belle being in Alice Springs and Evie in Melbourne. Anna soon heard Liz's car reversing out of the driveway and heading off down the road. Continuing her pruning, she thought again how thoughtful her friend was. Stopping the rising thoughts of how she'd be feeling if she was living alone, she made the effort to maintain her positive attitude.

'I am *not* going to think depressing thoughts,' she reminded herself. 'There is only *now*, and *now* I'm feeling happy.' She continued cutting off the old, knobby remains of the bottlebrush flowers, disturbing the resident ants and causing them to scurry to and fro.

After digging for a while and savouring the smell of the fresh soil, Anna thought a cold drink was on the cards. Leaving the gardening implements where they lay, she again pulled off her gardening gloves, dropped them in the wheelbarrow then wandered inside via the laundry door.

After dabbing some more lavender oil onto an ant bite

she'd received earlier, she was now sitting with a large glass of chilled water in the shade of the verandah. Thinking of her two absent friends, *and* her two absent cffspring, she placed her glass on a small table next to her chair then checked her phone for messages.

'Hmm … no messages, but I think Belle should be in Alice Springs by now,' she thought, noticing the time. Anna had been disappointed she hadn't accompanied Belle as originally planned, but Sam had phoned last week saying he had to go to Manila so wouldn't be there. He'd suggested waiting until he was back in a few weeks and coming for a visit then.

Sipping more water her thoughts went to Evie; wondering how her lunch with Ross had gone. It was their first date since Evie had moved, and Anna knew she'd been a bit nervous. None of them had met him yet; Evie saying she'd wait and see how things progressed before organising a get-together.

Apparently when Ross had rung for a chat earlier in the week, Evie had mentioned she was taking Belle to Tullamarine today. He'd then suggested they have lunch together since he was going to be in Melbourne, so she'd dropped Belle at the airport before meeting him in Carlton. She'd also said he'd offered to pay for a room so she could stay overnight at the motel where he was staying, but she'd declined. Not wanting to move too fast with the relationship, she'd told him her friend Gayle lived in Seaford, and that she was going to stay with her and have a catch up.

'I *hope* it works out for Evie, she's been on her own for a long time now,' Anna thought. 'It'll be interesting to hear all the details when she gets home tomorrow. Hmm … *home* … it's still a bit hard to believe that this is now home for all of us.' Smiling, she spoke out loud. '*Home* … yes that feels good.'

Still smiling she made her way to the vegie patch, ready to finish it off; automatically checking her mobile once more before replacing it in her pocket. Seeing an email which had just arrived from Claire, she stopped where she was and opened it, not realising she was holding her breath.

From *clairebaumann@yahoo.com.au*
To *annanowiki@gmail.com*

Hello Mum,
Glad you have settled in to new home. The pics look lovely. I'm flat out as usual. Just arrived home from L.A. Have to go now. Gunther says hello.
Bye
C x

Anna exhaled and sighed. 'Hmm … oh well, at least she replied.' Determined not to let her daughters' meagre response put a dampener on her day, Anna dropped the phone in her pocket and concentrated on the task at hand.

CHAPTER TWENTY-THREE

Lunchtime in Lygon Street had been extremely busy, but Evie had managed to find the restaurant without too many dramas. She'd had to park a couple of streets away and then walk, but she hadn't minded as it had given her time for her nerves to settle a bit.

Later she didn't know why she'd been so nervous, because as soon as she'd seen Ross waiting out the front of the restaurant, she'd smiled in anticipation. He'd seen her at the same time; walking towards her, a grin on his face. He'd kissed her on her cheek and commented how wonderful she looked, before they entered the eatery and were escorted to their table.

Two hours later after enjoying a delectable Italian meal - talking pretty much non-stop - Ross walked Evie back to her car, kissed her on her lips and said he'd call soon.

'Another glass of wine?' Gayle looked at her enquiringly, 'or would you prefer a cuppa?'

'A cup of tea thanks. I think I've had enough wine for today.'

'No problem. If you put the kettle on I'll get the cups and teapot ready.' As Gayle headed for the kitchen with Evie following, she added, 'I have some homemade lamingtons too if you'd like one?'

'Yum … yes *please*. I *love* homemade lamingtons.'

'Yes me too. One of my neighbours made them … look, they're *huge*.'

'Mmm … yes … one will definitely be enough for me thanks.'

After popping two of the cakes onto a plate, Gayle spooned tea leaves into the pot. 'This is great, having you here … it's been ages since I've seen you.'

'Yes it has been a while.'

'I wish I'd been able to help you with all your unpacking. I'm thinking it would have taken you a while.'

'Yes, well if you hadn't been gallivanting around India you could have,' Evie replied smiling.

'Yes, bad timing on my part, but it *was* planned for nearly a year.'

'Yes I know … I'm only stirring you.'

They both had bit of a laugh before Gayle asked to hear more about her and Ross.

'Well I think I've told you everything. The food and wine were delicious, Ross was interesting to talk to - he always really *listens* to what I'm saying - and I think the coffee was the best I've ever had.'

'Okay, but I meant what's happening with *you* two? Do you think this could become serious?'

'Well … I don't want to moz things by talking about it … but … yes … I think things *could* become serious. We really seem suited … so far anyway. I think the next step is for him to meet my friends to see what *they* think.'

'Oh good. Let me know when you can bring him here then.'

'Okay. *Actually* … now that I'm thinking about it … Anna's birthday is coming up soon, so I think we should combine it with the housewarming party and make a real night of it,' she grinned. 'I'm sure the others will agree so I'll phone Ross later to make sure he can come, and that way everyone can meet him at the same time. You can stay the night if you like, there's heaps of room.'

'Yes I definitely like. I can't wait to meet Ross, *and* David, and I've been wanting to see your new home too so that sounds like a terrific idea.'

'Great. Well I've really been wanting to hear all about your trip to India … I hope you've got lots of photos.'

'Yes I have actually, but I've had the best ones printed off so you won't be bored looking through *all* of them,' Gayle smiled. 'Okay … let's take our tea and cakes into the lounge room and get comfy.'

Evie was driving home the next morning and had just merged onto the ring road on the outskirts of Geelong. She *had* planned to catch up with Gabi today, but after phoning her last night she discovered that she and David were in Port Douglas. They'd apparently flown there on impulse five days ago, and were now in the process of deciding where they'd go next.

After Evie had updated them on the plan to combine Anna's birthday with the housewarming, and making it an opportunity to meet Ross, both Gabi and David said they would *definitely* be back in time to attend; Evie hearing Gabi squeal at the mention of meeting Ross. Just thinking about it made her grin.

She'd phoned Ross before phoning Gabi; inviting him to the celebratory weekend. He was generally pretty busy with work and meetings, so she'd wanted to give him enough time to hopefully schedule it in. To her delight he'd said he wouldn't miss it, as he'd been wanting to meet her friends for some time.

Forty-five minutes later she parked her car under the carport behind Anna's. Walking past Belle's and Liz's cars, Evie at first thought they were *all* home, before remembering that Belle was in Alice Springs.

I was in the kitchen with my head in the fridge when Evie returned from her overnight stay in Seaford.

'Hi honey, I'm *home,*' I heard her call as she walked up the stairs.

'Hi, you're just in time for lunch,' I replied, sitting a large bowl of salad on the bench.

'Hi Evie, how was your date? Tell us all the juicy details. Do you want a cuppa first? I'm just making one,' Anna offered.

'It was good … no juicy details to tell … and yes I'd love a cuppa,' she grinned.

'Ha, not so fast,' I said. 'Have you asked Ross what his hobbies are yet?'

'Yes Liz I have.'

'Hobbies?' Anna looked at both of us quizzically.

I quickly explained Evie's initial concern that although she and Ross seemed suited, he might have some weird hobby which would rule him out as a 'potential'.

'So, I actually slipped it into the conversation a while ago. He said he hasn't had time for hobbies as he's too busy with work, but he enjoys reading biographies or a good mystery, and he also enjoys doing crossword puzzles when he's flying or waiting in airports.'

'Oh, that sounds alright. Looks like he passes muster then.'

'Yes, that's what I thought,' Evie smiled.

I'd made a frittata and salad for lunch which we'd eaten inside to avoid the annoying flies, but we were now sitting in a spot we all favoured … at the long table on the deck. I'd also bought some more tasty treats, and we'd each chosen one to have with our cuppa.

'Hmm … thanks for lunch Liz, it was delicious.'

'Mmm … yes quite delicious,' Anna agreed.

'My pleasure ladies. I'm actually really enjoying having people to cook for again. After Hugh died I'd thought I wouldn't have *anyone* to cook for - not on a regular basis anyway - and then I wouldn't get to utilize those gourmet cooking classes I did years ago,' I grinned.

'Well Anna,' Evie smiled, 'I think the kindest thing we can do is let Liz cook any time she wants. I mean just so she can enjoy herself … what do you think?'

'Oh yes, I agree. I'd *hate* for her not to be enjoying herself.'

'Oh you two are just *so* funny,' I replied, rolling my eyes, then smiling.

'Mmm … this is the tastiest peach tart I think I've ever had,' Anna said just before she popped the last bit into her mouth.

'Yes, and I'm loving this apple turnover … it's quite delish. Where did you buy them Liz?'

'Well I found a new bakery when I was in Torquay this morning. It hasn't been open long … but guess who owns it?' Without waiting for them to answer, I went on, 'Deb Kairn.'

'Deb Kairn?' asked Anna.

'Oh, wow I haven't seen Deb for years,' Evie smiled. 'She

lived near Liz and me when we were teenagers. We used to go swimming in the river together.'

'Yeah I remember that,' I grinned. 'I'm thinking her *last* name might be different now if she's married, but she's called her place *Deb's Delights*.'

'Oh, okay. So did she make these *delightful* treats herself?'

'Yeah apparently so. The bakery was really busy when I was there so I couldn't talk for long, but I'd say she's on a real winner.'

'Hmmm … I must drop in and see her soon, although I suspect we'll *all* put on weight if we drop in there *too* often.'

After Anna had returned to the garden, Evie and I talked about who we'd invite to the birthday party and housewarming. We decided we'd like to try and keep it a secret from Anna, as it would be fun to give her a surprise.

'I have Sam's number so I'll ring him later to see if he can get here too,' I said. 'I'm not sure if he'll be back from Manila in time, but I know he'll come if he can.'

'Okay. And I'll phone the pool girls. I know they'll come too if they don't already have plans.'

'Great. Once we have a list of people I'll start organizing the food. I'll order a heap of finger food from that catering place in Highton, but we'll need something a bit more substantial later. Do you think we should have a barbeque? Or maybe it would be easier to have some pizzas delivered?'

'Hmm ... I'm not sure. I think I'll leave that to you. I'll concentrate on doing some salads and buying the drinks.'

'Yeah okay ... I think we have a plan then.' I grinned, adding, 'And no doubt you'll have to spend a lot of time on yourself, seeming though your man will be here ... deciding what you're going to *wear* ... what colour *lipstick* ... which *shoes* ...'

'Oh ha ha ... you know me better than that,' Evie grinned. 'But I *am* looking forward to all of you meeting him, and more importantly, hearing your opinions.'

'Yeah, well we're all looking forward to checking him out, although I'm sure he's as nice as you've said.'

'Yes, he *is* pretty nice.'

'Okay, well I'll go and ring Sam now while I think of it,' I said. 'No time like the present.'

'Righto. I've got some clothes to wash first, then I'll call the pool girls. Oh and I must remember to drop past her old house soon and ask the next door neighbours. I reckon they'd like to come too.'

'Yeah good idea.'

But before we could make a move, Evie's phone rang. After checking the screen she said, 'Oh it's Belle,' before swiping the green button. 'Hi Belle, how's everything going in the Alice?'

'Hi Evie, everything's good here, and there too I hope?'

'Yes all good. Hey Liz is here so I'll put you on speaker.'

'Hi Belle,' I called out.

'Hi Liz,' Belle responded. 'Hey guess who's just arrived

here?' Without giving us time to think about it, Belle went on, *'Gabi and David!'*

'What, *really*? They were just in Port *Douglas*,' Evie said, smiling. 'I suppose they're going to see Uluru. I know Gabi's been wanting to go there for ages.'

'Yeah that's fantastic,' I cut in. 'I can't keep up with those two, they're certainly getting around.'

'Yeah, they rang me as soon as they landed, then came straight round to Tatiana's, but they couldn't stay long as they're off to see the rock today, then after that they're off to Darwin on the *Ghan*.'

Anna had come back inside to get a drink and hearing Bell's voice, joined in the conversation.

'Hi Belle … oh the *Ghan* … I've always wanted to go on that,' sighed Anna.

'Hi Anna … yeah me too,' said Belle.

'Me three,' grinned Evie.

'I've been on it but would love to do it again,' I added.

'Well we might have to organise that … maybe next year … what do you reckon?'

We all agreed that it sounded like an excellent idea. Belle then asked Evie how her date with Ross went so Evie took it off speaker and wandered into her bedroom to relay the details, as Anna and I had already heard all about it.

Later after getting off the phone, Evie returned to the verandah to find me there on my own; Anna just visible through some foliage at the end of the garden.

'Okay, Belle will be back the day before the party,' Evie

said quietly. 'She's going to get the Gull to Geelong and I'll pick her up from there, so if there's any last minute things we need to buy I can get them then.'

'Sounds like a plan,' I smiled. 'I'm getting quite excited about it all, and I'm sure Anna has no idea about it.'

'Yes I'm getting excited about it too. Hey I'll ring Gabi later and see what time they're landing at Tulla'. If they could catch the same Gull bus as Belle I could pick them all up.'

'Hmm … yeah well I doubt that the stars will align enough for *that* to happen. And anyway, Gabi and David might stay overnight at his place in Mount Waverly.'

'Oh yes, I didn't think of that,' Evie nodded. 'Oh well, it was just a thought,' she grinned.

CHAPTER TWENTY-FOUR

'Hold that thought,' Belle smiled at Naomi, before diving into the deep end of the pool. 'Ahh … that's better,' she said after swimming to the end and climbing out. 'I love being able to get in and out of the pool whenever I feel hot.' Not worrying about toweling herself off before sitting back down, she continued on with her conversation. 'Now … Naomi, you were saying you've lost a bit of weight since you've given up alcohol.'

'Yes well I've lost a kilo, which is a kilo more than Tat,' she grinned.

'Ha. So how long are you planning to stick with it for?'

'Well …' Tatiana and Naomi looked at each other, before Tatiana answered, 'we're not sure yet. We've just decided that we really needed a break. Everyone drinks heaps here; it just seems to become a way of life. But we had to acknowledge we'd both chubbied up a bit.'

'Well I'm going to stick with it too if I can. It *is* rather fattening, and I'd like to lose a couple of kilos as well.'

'Good on you mum.'

'Yes, good on you Belle.'

'I'm not sure how successful I'll be at Anna's birthday party though,' she smiled.

'Yeah, you'll have to have a couple to celebrate,' her daughter laughed. 'So how are the preparations going?'

'All good by the sound of things. Gabi is usually our event planner, but she of course is otherwise engaged,' Belle grinned.

'Yes she sure is. David seems really nice doesn't he? And he seems to really dote on her.'

'Yeah, she'd certainly been due to meet a nice man.' Belle then stood up and began clearing up their lunch dishes causing Naomi to protest, saying, 'Hey leave that, I'll do it.'

'No it's okay, I don't mind helping. I wouldn't mind another cuppa though if you'd like to put the kettle on again.'

'Coming right up.'

'I'll have one too thanks Nomi. What time did you say you were seeing Aunty Betty again Mum?'

'Four o'clock. Do either of you want to come?'

Tatiana and Naomi looked at each other and both nodded.

'Okay that's great. I'm sure you'll find her as fascinating as I do. And just *wait* 'til you see her artwork … it's amazing.'

It wasn't long before they'd finished their cups of tea, changed out of their swimwear, and were on their way to the gallery where Belle and Aunty Betty had agreed was the best place to finalise the sitting process.

They spent an enjoyable hour and a half at the gallery; Tatiana and Naomi checking out the extensive exhibition, while Belle did several more sketches of her subject. Later at home they were once more talking about the intricate designs featured in the artworks they'd seen.

'Oh I loved *so many* of those paintings,' Naomi was saying. 'I'm going to have to buy one but I can't decide which one.'

'Yes, me too,' Tatiana agreed. 'I'm thinking that one we saw as we first walked in … I think it was called *Yam Dreaming*.'

'Ooh yes … or that black and white one that looked like lightning … I *loved* that one too.'

'Yes that was my favourite,' Belle agreed.

Having decided to stay home for the evening, the women were now sitting outdoors discussing a variety of topics. The sun was swiftly descending towards the horizon producing a glorious display of peach, pink, blue and mauve which completely filled the western sky. Several bats could just be heard flapping overhead, and were then momentarily silhouetted against the sunset before disappearing in the dusk.

'It's a shame Anna had to cancel her trip.' Tatiana's voice seemed surprisingly loud in the stillness. 'She must have been pretty disappointed her son had to go to Manila.'

'Yes she *was* disappointed. I'm happy to come back with her though, when she does come to see him. So, you can expect another visit from me in the near future.'

'Well that's good. We love having you here, and we'd like to meet Sam too, wouldn't we Nomi?'

'Yeah sure. Any excuse for a get together,' she grinned. 'Okay who'd like a juice?'

'Mmm … yes please Naomi. I love that juice, what have you put in it?'

'Pineapple, pear, banana and Passionfruit.'

'Yum.'

'I'll have one too thanks Nomi.'

'Oky doke.'

'Actually I think I'll head inside,' Belle shivered a bit. 'It's become a little chilly now, don't you think?'

'Yeah it *can* get chilly once the sun sets,' Naomi agreed.

'Okay let's all head inside then,' Tatiana nodded. 'It's time we ate something anyway, then we can watch a movie before bedtime.'

Belle was only staying four nights this time, as her primary reason for visiting was to complete the second of the two sittings which were required as part of the Archibald submission process. The second sitting also gave her the chance to make sure she had really captured the essence of the woman's creativity and humour. Now feeling confident she could complete the portrait back at home, she was wanting to get back to Angelsea to help out with the last of the party preparations.

That evening they had Indian food delivered, then after watching 'My Big Fat Greek Wedding' on DVD - laughing themselves silly in the process - they were all pretty tired so headed to bed.

Belle had a window seat again on her return journey home. She was gazing in amazement at the vast red earth below, never tiring of the view, until it was eventually concealed under a layer of cloud. Sighing with contentment, she sat back and closed her eyes; contemplating the lovely time she'd had during her visit.

She knew she was fortunate to have such a thoughtful daughter, and felt blessed that Tatiana and her lovely partner wanted to spend time with her. Then, for some inexplicable reason, the notion of grandchildren popped into her thoughts, causing her mood to drop a little. Determined not to go down that track she opened her eyes and rummaged around in her bag to find the small paperback she'd bought with her.

She'd read half a dozen pages when she came across a new character ... called Annalise. Images of the baby she'd lost all those years ago immediately flooded her mind and she quickly stuffed the book back into her bag.

Sighing, Belle shook her head. She'd come to accept the death of her little one many years ago. These days her thoughts tended to imagine what she'd be like now … smart, funny, creative … *hetro?*

'Oh … why even think about that,' she said to herself, staring out the window. She couldn't help it though, thinking that maybe her other daughter might have given her grand-children.

'Right … that's it,' she thought angrily. 'I have a beautiful, healthy daughter and I'm very blessed. Not everything in life goes the way you might like … but that's life. Now snap out of it.'

The drinks trolley was heading her way, so throwing to the wind her undertaking to give up alcohol for a while, she ended up ordering a scotch and coke. It wasn't long before she'd refocused her mind, knowing there was absolutely no benefit in going over 'what if's'.

Two and a half hours later she landed at Tullamarine airport. After the long walk to get out of the terminal building, she only had a fifteen minute wait 'til she was picked up by the Gull bus. The hour twenty ride to Geelong was a bit boring, so when she saw Evie waiting - two coffees in hand - she felt relieved to be nearly home again.

CHAPTER TWENTY-FIVE

The next morning, after some surreptitious talk between Evie, Belle and myself while Anna was in the shower, it was decided that Belle would take Anna to the pool for a swim. That way Evie and I could make the side dishes which would accompany the barbeque I'd decided to have for the party tomorrow. Hopefully I'd also have time to make and decorate the birthday cake.

'I hadn't planned on going to the pool today,' Anna replied to Belle's suggestion as she looked in the fridge for milk. 'I've just had a shower. I would have waited and had one afterward if I was going to the pool.'

'Oh I know, sorry Anna, but I'm really needing a swim,' Belle groaned. 'I'm feeling *so* stiff after yesterday's flight and I reckon a few laps will really loosen me up. We could stay and have a sauna too. You love a sauna.'

'Well ...'

'Come on ... come with me. I don't feel like going on my own. I'll even shout you a coffee.'

'Alright then, if you really want me to I'll go. Just give me time to have a cuppa and some breakfast first.'

Half an hour later they were gone, and Evie and I began our separate tasks. Having turned on the extra fridges in the garage last night - putting all the meat and drinks in one already - we were ready to store whatever food we prepared today. We hoped it would all be finished before Anna and Belle returned so it would be a surprise for her tomorrow.

Just over three hours later I'd made and decorated the cake, and the two of us had finally finished preparing the different rice, pasta and potatoe dishes, leaving just the green salads to do tomorrow. We'd made several treks to the garage carrying a variety of food containers when I mentioned I hadn't yet finished making Anna's birthday present. Thankfully Evie offered to clean up all evidence of our labours in the kitchen to give me time to finish my project.

Having retreated to the sunroom - now my workroom - I found the garnets I wanted to set into the earrings I was making. As I beheld my new working space I sighed happily;

thrilled with how good it all looked. I'd employed a local handyman to build a long bench, and then install my jewellery making equipment which I'd bought from Eastern View. A kettle, coffee making necessities and a mini fridge completed the setup, saving my knee from negotiating the stairs every time I fancied a cuppa.

My chair had been positioned so I could look at the garden whenever I liked, and I now relaxed as I watched dragonflies and bees darting here and there amongst the flowers. Making jewellery is an extremely pleasurable pastime for me; even more so in my new workspace. I'd lost my creative urge after Hugh had died, but felt good knowing that I'd managed to resurrect it again.

Checking what I'd done so far I knew I'd have the fiddly work done soon, so putting my head down I was soon totally absorbed in completing Anna's gift.

'Hmm … yeah … they look good,' I smiled half an hour later. I held the finished earrings at arm's length; the purplish-red of the garnets glowing brilliantly in the shafts of sunlight which were streaking through the window. 'Yeah … I think they'll really suit Anna's colouring.'

Pleased with my finished work I popped them into one of my specially made, small cloth gift bags and pulled the draw-strings closed. Admiring the wording stenciled on the bag - **Jewellery by Liz** - I then stood up, stretched my neck and shoulders, and began putting my tools away.

As I methodically tidied my work area, I allowed my thoughts to dwell on my friends, and how fantastic it was they'd all accepted my unexpected proposal. I knew they thought me extremely generous in having them move in here for minimal cost, but it was actually me who was extremely grateful they'd agreed. I'd told them I'd been lonely living by myself, but I don't think they'd really comprehended just *how* lonely I'd felt.

After I'd married Hugh a lot of my 'friends' had dropped out of my life. It seemed they'd been jealous of my new life-style - having married a very wealthy man. At first the women I'd worked with at the real estate agency had seemed genuinely excited for me when I'd become engaged, but I'd noticed how their interactions with me had changed over the ensuing months, especially after I'd said I'd be resigning as Hugh wanted to take me around the world. They had, of course, accepted their invitations to attend the wedding, and had smiled and wished me well at the reception, but not one of them had contacted me since.

Hugh, knowing how much it had upset me, had encouraged me to not worry about it, saying I would make new friends in no time. And I *had* made new friends. Several among the people who lived in our area, and a few others at the Anglesea golf club who also 'had money'. But having grown up in a working class family which had sometimes struggled financially, I'd always felt just a little out of place with those people.

I *had* loved how Hugh and I had spent a lot of time travelling; making friends with people from all walks of life, but it hadn't always been easy to stay in contact. After a couple of weeks back home after each trip, life seemed to overtake all good intentions, and it had eventuated that contact had only been maintained with a handful of people. The fact that they lived overseas had of course limited their ability to lessen my feelings of loneliness after Hugh had died. A phone call – although appreciated – had been no substitute for a face-to-face get-together.

I'd gradually slipped deeper into depression a couple of months later, after my genuinely well-meaning friends had become enmeshed in their own lives and were no longer visiting regularly. Living at Eastern View hadn't made it easy for them to drop in either. It could be an hour's drive from Geelong on a sunny weekend when everyone was keen to head for the coast, and even slower driving home when everyone seemed to leave at the same time. Evie had stayed with me for a month after the funeral – which I'd massively appreciated – but she'd of course been limited in the number of times she could visit as she'd lived interstate.

After finally deciding to move to Anglesea I'd felt my spirit lift, so knew I'd made the right decision. Then, after committing to house hunting and everything that it entailed, I'd felt a little better every day. I'd also begun my early morning walks along the beach again, consciously absorbing the positive energy which Mother Nature produced, when one day I'd met up with George and Iris on *their* daily walk. They'd mentioned they were selling their house and moving to France, so after they'd revealed the price they'd be willing to accept for a quick sale, I'd bought it on the spot.

Having come to truly appreciate my 'old' friends, I had no hesitation in sharing my financial security with them. Living with people who know me – and my foibles – and still love me, means more to me than any amount of money. I can't help but smile when my thoughts go to Jason and Simon; feeling totally blessed to have them in my life. I'm so glad they're coming to the party as I don't see them as much as I'd like since they moved from Torquay to Melbourne. They'd *also* stayed with me following Hugh's death, and a couple more times since, including the weekend when I'd decided to sell the house.

'I bet at the party Jase calls me his evil step-mother again,' I thought, still smiling. 'He never seems tire of it and *always* thinks it's funny.'

It was then that I heard Anna and Belle arrive home, so after stashing the earrings out of sight I scanned the room one last time before shutting the door. Chuckling to myself as I slowly mounted the stairs, I was wondering how Belle had managed to keep Anna away for so long.

CHAPTER TWENTY-SIX

The next morning Anna woke as usual, delighting in the dulcet warbling of birdsong outside her bedroom window. Glancing to her right she saw the time on her clock/radio had just hit eight o'clock. Having a quick stretch before sitting up, she then headed for the loo before adjusting the shower taps to her preferred temperature. It was then she remembered that today was her birthday. Her sixty third.

'Hmm ... well ... *happy birthday to me*', she said, as she stepped into the cubicle. 'I wonder what the day will bring.'

Hoping to hear from Sam and Claire at some stage, she then wondered for a moment if her new housemates would remember; not expecting that they would. Taking her time under the hot water, she decided to visit the plant nursery later to buy herself something special.

'What to buy? Hmmm … maybe a Daphne … I love the scent of Daphne.'

Fifteen minutes later she was dry, dressed and headed towards the kitchen, not concerned that her hair was still damp. She usually just left it to dry on its own, fluffing it up with her fingers now and then. As soon as she opened the door separating the bedroom wing from the living area, she was greeted with birthday wishes.

'*Happy birthday Anna.*'

'Yes, *happy birthday.*'

'*Happy birthday, Birthday Girl.*'

'Thank you, thank you, and thank you.' Anna had a huge smile on her face as she looked at her friends. 'I wasn't sure if you'd even remember.'

'Of course we remembered, and …' I looked at my friends, 'we've decided that we have to tell you something now.'

'Oh … what?' Anna asked with a quizzical expression on her face. 'Should I be worried?'

'No, nothing to worry about,' I laughed.

'Yes, it's all good,' Evie nodded.

'Yep completely all good,' grinned Belle, then went on. 'Later we're having a combined birthday party for you, *and* a housewarming party for *all* of us. People have been invited to come from three o'clock onwards. We just have to put up the decorations so we thought we'd better tell you now.'

'Oh wow … *really?*' Anna had a completely surprised

expression on her face. 'That sounds *fabulous*. Who's coming?'

'Well, come and sit out on the balcony and we can fill you in on the details. I heard your shower running and knew you wouldn't be long, so there's a pot of tea waiting, and Liz is going to cook us all omelettes. We know they're one of your favourite brekkies.'

'Oh that was all *so* delicious Liz, but I think I've eaten too much.' Anna sat back and groaned slightly.

'Mmm … me too,' agreed Evie, pushing her empty plate forward.

'Yeah,' nodded Belle, 'you make the best omelettes Liz; I couldn't stop eating either.'

I grinned, saying, 'So I'm assuming no one wants croissants then?'

'You're right … no one wants croissants,' Anna replied while the other two nodded in agreement, 'but I could possibly fit in another cup of tea.'

'I'll make another pot,' Belle offered, but before she even stood up they heard a familiar voice calling out.

'*Hello, hello … is there somebody having the birthday here today?*'

We all peered over the railing and saw Gabi and David smiling up at us.

'Hello you two … you're here nice and early. Come up and have a cuppa. Have you had brekky yet?'

The new arrivals made their way up the outdoor stairs to where we were seated, replying that 'yes they'd had breakfast but would certainly love a cuppa'. After more birthday wishes, hugs and kisses, extra chairs were added and we were soon all settled with our hot drinks.

'I said to David last night we *had* to be here early so I could help with the preparation of the party … so … what is there for me to do? I hope there is *something*?' Gabi looked at each of us expectantly.

'Oh yes, there's lots of decorations to go up yet Gabi, and I know that's one of your specialties. And having *you* here David will be a bonus, as all the decorations are in a heap of boxes stored in the garage. Any chance you could get them down off the shelves for us?'

'Not a problem Liz, consider it done,' he replied. 'I can be you're official fetcher and carrier for the day if you like.'

'Fab, thanks David. Hey … I have a present for you Anna,' I then said. 'Would you like it now or tonight?'

'And I also have the present for you,' Gabi added.

'Me too.'

'Me three.'

David laughed and shook his head. 'You ladies definitely make my day.'

'Yes we are a *bit* crazy, but in a *good* way,' Anna joked. 'And yes I'd love them now please,' she smiled at each of us. After opening her presents Anna was a bit overwhelmed. 'Oh my goodness … thank you all again … I love everything. You have all really spoiled me.'

'No, we haven't spoiled you,' Belle smiled 'You deserve to have it all. You're a special person and a really good friend.'

We all nodded in agreement before giving her more hugs. Evie then said she'd clear up the breakfast dishes, and Belle said she'd help seeming though I'd cooked. I smiled, loving that I didn't have to do it, and instead offered to show David my workroom. He'd admired the earrings I'd made for Anna, so I thought he might like to see where I'd made them. The previous time he and Gabi had visited, the workroom hadn't been finished, so the three of us headed downstairs while Evie and Belle stacked dishes into the dishwasher.

Anna, being banned from the kitchen today, wandered down to the garden. Smiling, then sighing, she couldn't remember when she'd had such a lovely birthday. She'd been awed by the earrings which Liz had made for her, and was now wearing them, along with the gorgeous silk scarf from Evie, and the stylishly trendy necklace which Gabi had bought at the Port Douglas market. Belle had thoughtfully bought her a new overnight bag as her old one had definitely seen better days.

She was now really excited thinking about the party later, especially after Belle mentioned that several of her old neighbours were coming, as she hadn't seen them since moving. Seeing a few deck chairs which had already been placed around the garden, she chose one and sat down. Stretching out her legs, she leant back and gauged the sky, wondering if the afternoon and evening would remain rain free. It was overcast, but patches of blue were visible through the grey, and she felt there was a good chance the storm clouds in the west would blow out to sea in an hour or so. Sighing again she shook her head; thinking how her life had changed, going from the worst time, to one which was now wonderful.

'You just never know *what* life has in store,' she said softly to herself, then smiled as she heard her friends laughing about something upstairs. It was then she decided to check her phone for emails. She'd been hoping for a phone call from Claire, seeming though it was her birthday, so was slightly disappointed to see her email.

From *clairebaumann@yahoo.com.au*
To *annanowiki@gmail.com*

Hi Mum,
Happy Birthday. I hope you have a nice day. Do you have
anything special planned? All ok here. Gunther says hello and
Happy Birthday. Got to go, running late.
Bye.
C x

'Hmm … Oh well, better than nothing I suppose.'

They'd been corresponding solely by email since Jim's funeral. The many times she'd phoned her daughter had been met with a recorded message, and no return call, so she continued emailing. Anna wasn't prepared to let Claire ignore her completely, and didn't want a bigger rift to develop than already had. Longing for a better mother/daughter relationship, she hoped that one day they could have a proper conversation regarding her father, and clear the air between them.

'Oh well, at least Sam will phone me sometime today. Actually … I'm surprised he hasn't already. He *must* be busy.'

Sighing once more, she put the phone in her pocket and headed towards the stairs, determined to thoroughly enjoy her birthday, her friends *and* the housewarming party.

CHAPTER TWENTY-SEVEN

The party was a huge success. Nearly everybody who'd been invited showed up, many bringing gifts either for Anna, or for the housewarming. Several people had offered to bring food, so they'd been encouraged to bring deserts, of which there was now a scrumptious selection in one of the garage fridges.

Simon and Jason had arrived early afternoon with the intention of helping, so had been delegated to carry the barbeque down from the upstairs dining area. They'd just positioned it near a tall crepe myrtle bearing a swathe of glorious pink flowers, when David announced he'd be happy to be chef for the day.

'I've cooked more barbeques than I can count,' he'd said to Simon, who was delighted to let him take on the cooking responsibilities.

When Evie heard that Simon was off the hook regarding cooking, she roped him in to light the many mosquito coils she'd placed around the garden. As he hated the little blood suckers, he was happy to light them, and replace any that burnt out over the course of the party.

It was now early evening of what had been a magnificent autumn day; the pending storm clouds having cleared by midday to reveal a clear azure sky. Everyone had enjoyed the warmth of the afternoon sun, but its current descent now produced a coolness which crept across the grass. Jason noted the rapidly lengthening shadows and decided it was time to light the outdoor fires.

Evie had sourced three, old washing machine drums which made excellent receptacles for the pine kindling and split red gum which she'd recently bought. Earlier in the day she'd expertly stacked the wood over scrunched up newspaper, so all that was needed now was a lit match to ignite each warming blaze.

As Jason finished this task, Simon flipped the switch to turn on the fairy lights which Gabi had strung from trees all around the garden. Everyone oohed and ahhed at the sight of the twinkling lights, many saying it looked quite magical. The theme for the music was hits of the 70's, an era the five women loved, and as Carol King's *Tapestry* album finished, Marvin Gaye kicked in with *What's Goin' On*.

The mouthwatering selection of finger food had been

polished off a while ago, so Belle gave David the okay to light the huge barbeque in readiness to start cooking. Liz had bought steaks, gourmet sausages and a variety of kebabs to go with two big baking dishes of scalloped potatoes she'd made yesterday; now heating in the oven.

It was extremely handy that they'd had extra tables and chairs stored in the garage, as these were now strategically set around the garden. Evie's culinary contribution of a spicy rice dish, two pasta salads and a tasty coleslaw were placed on a long table next to Belle's garden salads, while all the meat was placed next to David and the barbeque.

Anna was speechless when she saw how much food preparation had been done, asking Evie how they'd managed it without her noticing.

'Well that's why we shuffled you off to the pool yesterday,' Evie grinned.

'*And* why I suggested we stop at the plant nursery on our way home,' Belle added.

'Oh you sneaky people,' Anna laughed. 'I'll be forever questioning your motives now.'

Sam came up then and gave his mum another hug.

'This is a great party Mum, I'm rapt that I could get here. And that food is making my mouth water. I'm feeling really hungry now.'

'Yes, well I'm rapt that you could get here too,' she smiled up at him. 'And I thought *hungry* was your default position? You've always had hollow legs when it came to food. I'm surprised you're able to stay in such good shape. Have you been going to the gym a lot?'

'Yeah, when I can.'

'Maybe it's his girlfriends who are keeping him in good shape,' Evie teased.

'Ahh … hahaha … I'm not getting into *that* conversation. Oh look, there's someone I haven't seen in ages … I really should go and say hello,' he grinned widely, giving Anna another hug before walking off.

'He's such a lovely person Anna,' Belle said. 'You must be very proud of him.'

'Yes, I really am.'

Evie looked over to where Ross was talking to a couple of her pool friends, just as he looked *her* way. A smile lit her face as she watched him excuse himself then walk in her direction.

'Looks like you're quite popular tonight,' Evie smiled at him.

'Yes, so it seems,' he smiled back. 'I've actually been talking to quite a few interesting people. It's a great party, and that food is making my mouth water. I'm feeling really hungry now.'

Evie and Anna looked at each other and laughed.

'Men,' Anna said. 'They're always thinking about their stomachs.'

Ross gave Evie a quizzical look and she laughed, saying he'd just echoed Sam's comment about food.

'What can I say?' he grinned at the two women. 'We men love our tucker.'

They remained talking with Anna until someone else sidelined her for a chat, allowing the two of them to make a bee line towards an esky to replenish their beers. But, stopping only to drop their empties in a bin, Ross then quickly maneuvered her further under the verandah to a spot that was not so well lit. Removing his arm which had been around her shoulder, he then wrapped it around her waist and gently pulled her towards him. Before Evie could say anything he bent down and kissed her, then stopped and looked into her eyes for a moment, before kissing her again.

'Um … wow … that was nice,' Evie eventually said.

'Hmmm … just nice?' Ross grinned.

'Well no … more than nice … a *lot* more than nice actually,' Evie smiled at him. 'I think we need to do that again though … just so I can find the right word.'

'Hmmm … ok … if you insist.'

'Oh I insist … I *definitely* insist.'

At the same time, Gabi and David had wandered off to the *other* side of the garden. Sitting on a bench seat positioned under a wattle tree, he placed his arm around her shoulders, lent in and kissed her cheek.

'Have I said you look beautiful tonight?'

'No. No I do not think you have,' she smiled.

'Well, you look beautiful,' he grinned.

'Thank you David. And you look very handsome.'

'Your friends have been terrifically welcoming towards me; I really like *all* of them.'

'Yes they are all very wonderful people. And this party is wonderful too. It is so good for the celebration of Anna's birthday … but I am still not sure why you would have a party for the heating of a house.'

David grinned, saying, 'Oh Gabi … I *do* love you. I hope you know that? You make me smile and laugh every day. I don't think I have ever been this happy.'

She smiled too, saying, 'Yes, and I love you too … very much. You make *me* very happy also.'

After having a kiss and a cuddle, David explained the whole housewarming deal.

'Oh … well thank you for explaining that to me, as now it makes more sense,' she smiled. 'I had never been invited to one before.'

'*Okay everyone,*' Sam called out, '*time to sing happy birthday to the birthday girl.*'

After kissing once more, Gabi and David joined the others and were soon singing a rousing rendition of the birthday song to a thoroughly embarrassed Anna.

CHAPTER TWENTY-EIGHT

Gabi turned her head to the left and looked out the plane's window as it rose above the clouds. It had been nearly two weeks since the party and she and David were heading off on another holiday. Anna and Evie had dropped them at the airport; hugging their friend tightly and reminding her to take lots of photos.

The sign flashed on indicating they could unfasten their seatbelts but they both decided to leave theirs on for now. David had surprised Gabi with business class tickets and she was quite delighted with the extra roominess this provided for their seating. He'd said that as it was going to be such a long flight they may as well have a bit more comfort. Reaching over and holding her hand, he smiled at her with a glint in his eye.

'Well we're on our way again … I wonder what adventures we're going to have this time?'

'Yes I wonder,' Gabi smiled back. 'But *I* was just thinking of the new journey that Evie is about to begin.'

'Oh … where's she off too? I didn't hear that she was going somewhere.'

'She is not going *away* somewhere, but she has decided to spend the night with Ross … you know … and have the sex with him for the first time.'

'Oh.'

'Yes. It is a big step for her. It means she has committed to having the relationship with him.'

'Oh, okay.'

'Yes, but that is good I think. I really like Ross, and he really likes Evie.'

'Yes well I hope you don't like him *too* much,' David pretended to look concerned.

'Oh you silly man, of course not,' she playfully hit him on his arm. 'I could not like anyone more than you.'

They leant into each other and then looked out the window for a moment before David spoke.

'Well I've said it before but I'll say it again … I really like your friends. I think they're all terrific.'

'Yes they are.'

'And that party was one of the best I've ever attended. I can't wait 'til the next one.'

'Yes it *was* very good. *And* they did it without much help from me. You know that *I* usually organise these events. I hope they do not decide they do not need me anymore.'

'Now *you're* being the silly one. Liz actually said to me how much they'd missed your expertise.'

'Oh … well that is alright then,' she smiled. 'Sam is lovely too, yes? Anna is very lucky to have such a son. It is such a shame that Claire lives so far away though,' she mused.

'Yes I like Sam too. I really appreciated his help with the barbequing.'

'Yes he is very thoughtful. He helped Anna a lot after Jim's funeral. I just wish he would do the settling down and give Anna some grandbabies.'

'Hmmm … well from the conversations I've had with him I'd say he doesn't seem the settling down type. He loves his job and all the travelling that he's doing. I can't see him settling in one spot for a long time yet … or maybe never. Not all people want kids, as you know.'

'Oh yes, that I do know. I told you I never had the strong urge to have the babies, but I thought I would have them one day anyway … that is what usually happens, *yes?*'

'Yes, that *is* what usually happens,' he smiled.

'Maybe if I had married the better men I would not have used the contraception as I did. But … I am happy with no children. From what I have seen it can be very hard being a parent, and also sometimes a grandparent.'

'Yes, it certainly can be sometimes.'

'So … I like to look to the positive. I have been able to move from the other side of the world to this wonderful country, and have many adventures on the way. That would not have been easy if I had the childrens to look after.'

'Yes that's true. That would not be easy to do with children.'

'And you David … did you always *want* to have the babies?'

'Well, yes, I *think* so. It was just sort of *expected* of you to have kids one day. Louise always wanted children … so we ended up with the three girls. Not that I regret that of course.'

'No of course not. They are *beautiful* girls … and *four* grandsons.'

'Yes, not that *they're* babies any more either. I can't believe that Charlie will be twenty-one in November, and the youngest, Aiden, turned eighteen in January. Dianne and Chrissy always wanted kids, but my youngest, Jane, has gone the other way saying she doesn't want to be tied down with having them. She'd always been happy to travel with her friends at least once a year, and even now she's with Andrew I don't think they'll have any. They both love their free and easy lifestyle … and I have to say it does have some appeal,' he smiled.

'Yes, well that is for us now … the free and easy.'

'Yes, it sure is.'

After their lunch had been eaten and the plates removed, they both leaned their seats back and looked at each other.

'That food was better than we have had *before* on the flight.'

'Yep … see it pays to fly business class,' David smiled happily.

'Hmm … well I feel very lucky that you are so generous. But I appreciate it very much. It would not be easy sitting in the economy seat for nearly a day.'

'No it sure wouldn't. And anyway … what good is money if you don't spend it? I have enough … so why not have some extra comfort?'

Gabi nodded and smiled, knowing just how fortunate she was to have met him.

'Well I still *cannot* believe we are on our way to Morocco. *Morocco*! That is very exciting.'

'Yes it's somewhere I always wanted to go. Louise had never been keen though. By the time we could afford to travel overseas she hated the thought of being away from the girls, and once the *grandchildren* arrived, *that* was the end of her going away *anywhere*.'

'So … *we* can do it together then.'

Holding her hand, David smiled and nodded. 'Yes … the two of us together … *always* together I hope.'

'Yes … I hope always together too.'

CHAPTER TWENTY-NINE

Evie and Ross were lying together on the large bed; both smiling with eyes closed.

'Well … that was fantastic,' Ross finally said, still breathing heavily.

'Yes … definitely fantastic.'

They turned their heads and looked at each other; Ross rolling over to put his arm around her, kissing her neck as he did so. Evie snuggled closer and he pulled the sheet up to cover their naked bodies.

'I could look at your body all day,' he smiled, 'but I don't want you getting cold.'

'Thank you,' Evie replied as she curled one leg over his. 'Hmmm … I certainly feel contented … and hungry,' she grinned. 'What's a girl got to do to get a meal around here?'

'Oh I think you've done enough to get a meal … three courses even,' Ross smiled.

'Ha … okay, but I think I'll have a shower first.'

'Okay. Well we'd better have separate showers. If I come with you we'll never end up leaving here.'

Evie laughed again as she hopped out of bed and sashayed towards the bathroom. Glancing over her shoulder she saw Ross grinning at her retreating figure. He then pretended to come after her, making her squeal as she jumped into the shower cubicle.

Half an hour later they were walking through the lobby of the trendy, art deco style motel on their way to the carpark, one level below. Another half hour and they'd parked the car and were walking towards a popular restaurant in Carlton. They'd eaten there a few times since their first date, and now considered it 'their place.' After having a lovely lunch, and one glass of wine each, they finished with coffee before walking back to the car.

An hour later they were driving past Waurn Ponds; heading towards Anglesea. They'd talked about a myriad of things on the drive, and were now discussing where they'd like to go on holiday sometime soon.

'Well I'm probably going to disappoint you, but I have no desire to go overseas anywhere,' Evie was saying. 'I mean, I can truly understand Gabi wanting to go to Morocco with David - she's travelled to so many exotic places already - but

I just don't have the urge.'

'Really?'

'Um … yes … really.' Evie was sure that Ross was disappointed, but went on anyway. 'I'd actually rather see more of Australia. There are a few places I haven't seen yet, and others I'd love to see again.' Aware that Ross had his eyes on her as often as he could while driving, she kept on talking to stall him from replying. 'I do of course have a passport from when I went on a cruise with some friends years ago. We went to the South Pacific Islands. I actually liked the islands. The people there were all so friendly, and there were heaps of amazing places to scuba dive. I thought the cruise was a little boring after a few days though.' She had to stop then to take a breath, giving Ross time to speak.

'Why do you think I'd be disappointed?'

'Well, you've travelled to so many interesting places overseas but I'm sure there's still lots of places you'd like to visit.'

'No … not really.'

Evie's eyebrows raised as she looked at him in surprise, and he went on.

'The fact that I *have* been overseas so much makes me want to check out more places here. Do you know that I've been to Darwin several times but I've never been to Kakadu? I haven't seen Uluru at sunrise or watched the sun set over the beach at Broome.'

'Oh.'

'Yeah, so the fact that you *don't* want to go overseas is

fantastic. I'd had a feeling that you would, and that would have been okay, but I'm so rapt that you don't.'

He was really grinning now as he asked which place was on top of *her* list.

'Well, I'd love to camp under the stars near Uluru and explore the rock for a couple of days. *And* the Bungle Bungles,' she added. 'And I'd *love* to see them from the air as well … *that* would be awesome.'

Ross looked at her a bit amazed, before turning his attention back to the road.

'Well … I'm actually a bit speechless,' he said.

'Oh … why's that?'

'Because I'd *also* love to do that. In fact when I get back from Germany I think we'll have arrange it … what do you say?'

'Yes, okay. I'm ready when you are,' she grinned.

'Great,' he chuckled. 'I'll be looking forward to it.'

For the next half hour they talked about other dream destinations – Ningaloo Reef and Monkey Mia, Kununurra and Cooktown. Their focus changed though as they drove down a small hill towards the shopping area of Anglesea; Ross saying again how much he loved the seaside town.

'I could just about settle here myself one day,' he mused.

Continuing to drive through a round-about then over a small bridge, he unexpectedly pulled over to the left and parked near the river. Evie smiled and looked over at him, a question evident in her expression.

'I just had to stop and look at those paddle boats. You

don't see them much anymore, and I have many good memories of them from when I was a kid.'

'Oh yes they were in Portarlington too when I was growing up. Except I never had any money to actually *hire* one. So I used to *really* annoy people by hanging on to the end of their pontoon and get towed along,' Evie laughed. 'They used to try everything to get me off, even going out quite deep. But it never worried me as I was a good swimmer. After a while I'd just let go and then latch onto someone else's boat.'

Ross grinned at her, then unclicking his seat belt he leaned over and kissed her. 'Come on, let's hop out and sit at that table over there. It's such a beautiful afternoon, and we have the time.'

'Okay.'

Settled on the bench seat they looked to the right and saw a lone paddle boarder slowly make her way down the river towards the ocean.

'I'd love to have a go at that sometime,' Evie commented. 'It looks quite peaceful doesn't it?'

'Yeah, *and* it looks like fun. We'll have to put it on our list of things to do,' he grinned at her.

The relative tranquility was then interrupted by the squealing of young people as they splashed each other from their paddle boats, and a dog as it raced along the river bank, barking at a scattering flock of seagulls.

'It's bit of a coincidence we both grew up at the beach don't you think?' Without waiting for her reply, Ross went on, 'I hated leaving Mauritius to go to school in London; can you imagine the culture shock I had?' Shaking his head he again went on, 'And it was *freezing*. I lived for the holidays to arrive.'

'Yes that must have been awful,' Evie nodded. 'How old were you when you had to go to school in London?'

'Well dad wanted to send me as soon as I was old enough for school, I would have been six I think, but mum put her foot down and said no, thank goodness. She wouldn't hear of me going before I was ready for secondary school.'

'Your mum sounds lovely.'

'Oh yes she was. We were always very close. I also loved my dad, we were close too, but Mum and I had a strong bond; maybe because I was an only child.'

They sat and talked about childhood experiences for a while before Ross asked her if there were any hobbies or interests she wanted to get into one day.

'Hmm … I wouldn't mind trying pottery one day. Getting my hands onto that wet clay looks like fun. What about you?'

'Yeah, that could be okay. But I've always had bit of a secret passion to start a collection.'

'A collection? What did you want to collect?'

'Well you'll probably laugh at me if I tell you.'

'Well … I will try my best *not* to laugh at you … okay?'

'Okay. Well … one day I'd love to start collecting shrunken heads.'

Evie's eyes widened as she stared at him horrified, unable

to say a word. Ross suddenly burst out laughing before saying, 'either that or I'll start ferret racing.'

Evie then twigged that he was pulling her leg and burst out laughing as well. Ross put his arm around her and they sat and laughed while people near them looked and smiled.

'Bloody Liz … she told you to say that, didn't she?'

Ross grinned and nodded his head. 'Yeah she did. She wouldn't tell me why, she just said to get ready to see the expression on your face. And I have to say it was priceless.'

'I'm going to get that woman,' Evie grinned. She then went on to explain to Ross how she'd mentioned those weird hobbies to Liz after she'd first met him.

'Right … I know what I can do to get her back,' she grinned. 'Listen to my evil plan and tell me what you think.'

After telling him what she intended, they were laughing as they got back in the car and headed for Seaview Avenue.

I was in my work room when I heard the doorbell ringing so I was the first there to see who it was. Opening the door I saw a rather distraught looking Ross.

'Ross … hi … are you okay? Where's Evie? I thought you were bringing her home?'

'Oh God Liz, isn't she *here*? I thought she might have asked one of you to pick her up.'

'*Pick her up*?' I asked, now really concerned. 'Why, what's going on. Why didn't you drive her home?'

'Well I finally got her to ask me about my hobbies, like

you wanted me to, but when I said I'd like to collect shrunken heads one day she just stood up and walked out of the restaurant. I went after her but she'd just disappeared. There were so many people in the street I couldn't see her anywhere. I walked all around the streets and I called her mobile but she wouldn't answer. I'm at my wits end. I was just hoping she was here.'

'Oh no, what have I done,' I exclaimed, putting my hand over my mouth.

Just then Evie popped her head around the door frame and said, 'Gotcha,' then burst out laughing.

I was smiling and shaking my head as I put the kettle on. Both Evie and Ross were still chuckling as they relayed the whole story to Anna and Belle, both of whom thought it was hilarious.

'Well I don't think I'll be playing any more pranks on anybody for a while,' I sighed. 'You got me back really good.'

'Yes, well you got *me* really good too,' Evie grinned. 'So let's say we're even and leave it at that.'

'Deal.'

Evie was still grinning as she placed the tea cups onto the kitchen bench, while I stepped out of the huge walk-in pantry with the chocolate cake I'd made the other day. The doorbell rang again, and this time Anna went to see who was there.

'Hey Liz,' she called out, 'Christine's here … did you forget you're going to the movies?'

'Oh bugger, yes I *did* forget,' I called back, my attention now on the wall clock. 'Ooh I'd better hurry. Tell her I'll be down in a sec.' Hurrying into my bedroom I grabbed my bag, scarf and phone then headed for the stairs. 'Sorry peoples but I've got to dash. Enjoy the cake. See you when you're back from Germany Ross.'

'Yes no worries Liz, see you then.'

As Evie filled the kettle, Ross was intently scrutinizing a painting hanging on the dining room wall, and didn't notice that Belle had walked up behind him.

'Do you like it?' she asked.

'Oh … you startled me,' Ross smiled. 'Um, yes I actually *do* like it. I see by the signature that it's one of yours.'

'Yeah I did that one a couple of years ago.'

'Is it for sale?'

'Well … that one's always been bit of a favourite of mine, but I have a couple of others which are similar if you'd like to see them?'

'Yeah sure.'

'Okay come and have a look while Evie gets the tea ready.'

Down in her studio Belle showed Ross a variety of paintings in different sizes and colors. Establishing that he was interested in buying one for his office in Melbourne, she showed him an abstract with the predominant colours of black, white, and brown ochre. Featuring her usual dot work, he loved the aboriginal feel it had, saying it would be perfect for the wall behind his desk. Taking it upstairs he showed the others, who all loved it as well.

After having enjoyed two cups of tea and a large piece of cake, Ross then stowed the bubble wrapped painting in the boot of his car. Now leaning against the door, holding Evie against him, they stood silently for a moment, simply enjoying having their arms around each other. Saying goodbye was hard for both of them as he wouldn't be back from overseas for about four weeks this time.

'I'm going to miss you,' he said as he traced a finger down her cheek.

'I'm going to miss you too,' she replied, before standing on tip toe and kissing him.

'I'll give you a call when I can … I'll have to work out the time difference first though.'

'Yes okay, that sounds good,' she smiled before adding, 'but I really don't mind what time you call.'

'Hmm … okay. Well … I'm going to be thinking about that outback trip we have planned for when I return.'

'Yes, me too. I can't wait, it'll be *great*. I'll check out accommodation and prices. Maybe we could go glamping,' she grinned.

'Yeah I've heard of that. Well whatever you like, I don't mind.'

They kissed deeply, then Ross said he'd better get going. He'd brought his packed bag with him but he still needed to drop the painting at his office before getting to the airport by seven thirty. Hugging again before another lingering kiss, he then reluctantly got in his car and left. Driving off down the road he was thinking about his retirement in a couple of years; anticipating all the travelling they could then do together.

CHAPTER THIRTY

Belle had been in her studio all afternoon, and was now applying more background colour to her latest abstract. Santana's *Smooth* was playing loudly on her stereo as she sprayed water over the canvas. Then, using a damp sponge, she smeared the acrylic paint into pleasing swirls.

'*... you got the kind of lovin' that can, be so smooth ...*' she sang softly before turning round and tossing the sponge into the sink. Before she could continue painting *or* singing, she noticed her studio door opening.

As soon as I walked in the front door I could hear the music coming from Belle's studio, so decided to say hello and check out what she was doing before going upstairs.

'*Hiii* ... I'm *back*. The movie was fantastic, you've got to watch it sometime,' I called out loud enough to be heard over the song.

'Hi Liz,' Belle grinned, then turned the music down so we could talk without shouting.

'Hey I love those colours, that looks fabulous,' I said as I walked further into the room. 'So, what's been happening here today … anything interesting?'

'Well, I sold a painting.'

'Hey that's fab. Which one, and who bought it?'

'It was the one I called *Rock On.* Remember that one that was mostly different shades of ochre, with black and white highlights?'

'Oh yeah … like rocks in the outback … I liked that one. So who bought it?'

'Ross.'

'Oh wow. So where's he going to hang it? His house in *Terrigal?*'

'No, he bought it for his office in Melbourne.'

'Oh fantastic. *Lots* of people will see it there. You could end up selling more.'

'Yeah hopefully.'

'Okay, well I'm starving. I'm going up to make something for dinner. Do you have any preferences?'

'Um … no … anything would be fine … thanks.'

'Okay well if it doesn't matter to Anna or Evie I might try out a recipe that Christine told me about. Come up and have a drink with me while I cook if you like.'

'Yeah okay, I'll be up shortly. I'm just going to do a bit

more here first. This acrylic paint dries really quickly and I don't want to waste it.'

'Okay.'

Twenty minutes later, with brushes, bowls and sponges now all washed clean, Belle stood for a moment and studied her endeavours so far. She usually painted backgrounds in acrylics then used oil paints on top. The oils gave more depth of colour, and as they took a lot longer to dry, she could manipulate them for a longer period of time.

'Hmm ... looks okay so far,' she thought. 'I like how those colours have blended together.' Studying it for a few more minutes she decided she'd continue with it after dinner. Heading for the door she wondered what dish Liz was whipping up ... not that she minded. Anything she didn't have to cook was okay with her.

From the top of the stairs Belle could see Liz stirring something on the stove, and Evie and Anna sitting on bar stools, both holding glasses of wine. Walking towards the kitchen bench she smelt a tantalising aroma.

'Mmm ... what's cooking good looking?'

'Ah there you are Belle,' I turned and grinned. 'Grab a drink and sit down. I'm making a peri-peri chicken pilaf but it's not quite ready yet.'

'Okay ... anything I can do?'

'Apart from grabbing a drink and sitting down ... no,' I grinned.

'Okay, if you insist.'

'We've already offered our services and been knocked back,' Evie said before sipping her wine. 'Come on, sit here and I'll pour you a drink.'

'Yes, sit, sit … Evie's just about to tell us about her *sleep-over*,' I said as I added the rice to the steamy pan of spicy smelling food.

After the meal was eaten and they were considering having desert, talk once more turned to Evie's date.

'So how would you rate him as a lover?'

'*Liz* … you're a shocker,' Evie exclaimed.

'Yes, *that's* getting a bit personal, don't you think?' Anna exclaimed.

'Well I'm sure Gabi would be asking if she was here,' I replied.

'Yeah she would. Oh come on Evie,' Belle prompted, 'none of us have had sex in so long we're just hoping you've scored yourself a good lover.'

Evie felt all eyes on her, so sighing first, she then said, 'Okay … I'll tell you.' She'd been trying to be serious, but a big smile lit her face.

'Oh … I think *that* answers our question,' I said, nodding.

'Yes it probably does,' Evie said, 'but to put it into words … he's a *great* lover. It was *fantastic*. Twice last night and once this morning.'

We all stared wide-eyed at her for a moment before I said, '*What*? You're kidding?'

'No, not kidding.'

'Wow. And he's sixty three … *that's* pretty good,' Belle added.

'Yes I'll say,' Anna said, a surprised look on her face.

'Yep. So … who's for sweets?' Evie said, smiling as she made her way over to the fridge.

'Well not you,' I grinned. 'You've had *your* quota.'

Belle had returned to her studio straight after dinner, and had been immersed in her painting ever since. After having chosen the colours she was going to use she'd thoroughly mixed the medium into the paint, then added water to obtain the consistency she'd wanted. The oil paints she used these days were mixable with water which removed the need to use turpentine, and so no chemical smell permeated the house.

She was humming along to *Maggie May* as she added a deep yellow to the canvas in broad brush strokes. Then after applying several blobs of purple, she ran a small brush randomly over the canvas, spreading little streaks of purple here and there. Standing back for a moment to assess her work, she decided a spatter of bright orange right through the middle might look good.

'Hmmm … interesting,' she then smiled. 'I'm liking it.'

Checking the time on her mobile she realised tonight's

movie was soon to start so began cleaning her brushes. She'd just finished when Anna opened the door, saying the movie was starting in five minutes and not to be long or the cuppa she'd made her would get cold.

Early the next morning, back in her studio, Belle stood and scrutinised her portrait of Aunty Betty. She'd finished it a week ago and was *reasonably* happy with how it'd turned out. As she'd started the project relatively late in the year, she'd had to keep her use of oils to a bare minimum as she was afraid they wouldn't dry in time. This now changed the way she thought about the finished article.

'Hmmm … I've got another three weeks or so before I have to send it off, so it'll be dry by then. It's not as vibrant as I'd have liked … but oh well, it's done now … next time I'll allow more time.'

The exhibition was to open on July 19th but paintings had to be delivered to the Art Gallery of New South Wales by the 27th of June. So, as she didn't want to make two trips, she'd already booked a courier to deliver it in plenty of time; one who specialised in transporting art.

She was hoping that Gabi would be able to come with them when they had their weekend in Sydney *if* her portrait was accepted as a finalist. There was of course an *extremely* good chance that it wouldn't be, as competition was incredibly fierce.

After examining it closely for another minute, she then

returned to concentrate on her unfinished abstract. With Bob Marley wailing *Is This Love* in the background, it wasn't long before she was once more completely engrossed in her painting.

CHAPTER THIRTY-ONE

JUNE 2014

I was happy. Or so I kept telling myself. But the fact of the matter was I'd been holding back depressing thoughts ever since Hugh died. With a lot of effort I'd managed to adopt a happy exterior, and even *felt* happy at times, but every now and then the gloom overtook me.

'Come on … happy thoughts, happy thoughts,' I chanted to myself as I lay in bed, eyes closed.

Knowing I had much to be grateful *and* happy for, only made me feel worse. Several of my friends had lost their husbands and were now doing it really hard financially, and that was one of the reasons I hadn't fully confided in *anyone*. Being as wealthy as I was, I reasoned I wouldn't receive much sympathy *or* understanding.

'Come on girl … think positive. There is only *now*, and *now* I am happy,' I intoned.

Sighing deeply, I turned my head and looked at the greyish green tops of the eucalyptus trees, visible through my bedroom window. Noticing they were completely motionless, I continued staring for a moment, trying to discern some movement, but being unable to I shook my head and brought my focus back to my bedroom.

'Right … I'm going to get up, have a shower, and see who else is facing the day.' I once more reverted to some positive self-talk as I entered my ensuite. 'Life is good … I'm *so* grateful for my life … I have *fabulous* friends …'

'Good morning Evie.'

'Morning … ready for a cuppa?'

'Yes please.'

Opening the sliding door, I walked out and leant against the railing. Even though the sun was shining, the air was jarringly cold without a breath of a breeze. I could hear no sounds, not even the usual birdsong, which had me marvelling at the utter stillness which enveloped me. Something about the pureness of the morning triggered my sadness and before I knew it I was crying.

Large tears streamed down my cheeks and my nose started to run in rivulets. Fishing a tissue from my pocket I tried but failed to stem the copious flow of fluids. It was if a dam had broken and there was no stopping the surge of emotions. It was when I took in a large shuddering breath that Evie noticed my heaving shoulders.

'Liz ... what's the matter. Are you okay?'

'Yes ... yes ... I'm ... I'm okay,' I stammered while rummaging in my pocket for more tissues.

Evie grabbed a handful out of a box on the bench and handed them to me, then put her arm around my shoulders; holding me tightly in silence until my sobs slowly diminished. Finally, after a couple of shaky breaths, I was able to display a small degree of composure.

'Oh ... my goodness ... what was *that* all about?' I tried to make light of what had just happened, but Evie would have none of it.

'Sit down and I'll get your cuppa ... then you can tell me what's wrong.'

'There's nothing ...'

'Uh ... *no* ... there *is* something wrong and you're going to tell me ... *okay?*'

Knowing that Evie wouldn't let it go, I nodded.

'Yeah ... okay.'

'Good. Now I'll be back in a minute.'

True to her word Evie was soon back with two steaming cups of tea, and a rug she draped over my shoulders. I felt a bit embarrassed about my outburst, but also somewhat better at releasing my bottled-up emotions.

'Okay ... I'm listening.'

'Well ... I think I'm a bit depressed. I think I've been a bit depressed ever since Hugh died. I *still* can't believe he's gone. I loved that man *so much* ... I thought we still had *years* ahead of us. And he was *so fit* ... how could he have had a heart attack just like that? It's just so damn unfair. I don't think I'll ever get over it … and I don't think I'll ever be *truly* happy again.'

Evie nodded, remembering that she'd felt exactly the same after Dash had died unexpectedly.

'Liz … it hasn't even been a year … this isn't something you'll get over *or* accept for a while yet. But *please* believe me, things *will* get better for you in time.'

I looked at her then, but before I could say anything Evie went on.

'And I know that sounds like an empty platitude, but it's true. When people said it to me I just wanted them to shut up and go away. I didn't think anyone could understand how I felt … and then one day I realised I was genuinely laughing about something.' She smiled a bit then, saying, 'I have to say I then felt really bad, like I was betraying my feelings for Dash somehow. But I *knew* he'd want me to be happy … so I just … *let* myself be happy.'

I sighed deeply, then nodded and looked at my friend. 'Thanks Evie … thanks for listening … and thanks for understanding. It was just that I have so much to be grateful for I thought I should just get on with life … you know? The fact that all of you were happy to move in with me has been *wonderful*. I don't like to think what I would have done otherwise.'

'Well I think I'm speaking for all of us when I say it's awesome living here, and *we're* all grateful to *you* for *asking* us.'

'Yeah ... but I've felt I've had to put on a happy front when I'm with my other friends too. You know, there are two women in my book club who are really struggling financially since their husbands died. I'm sure they'd rather be in *my* position, so I don't think they'd be very understanding. And a couple of people I play golf with are *relishing* not having their husbands around anymore. They think it's *terrific* to have all the money now, and no one to complain when they buy *another* thousand dollar handbag.'

'Well I think if a person is a *real* friend, it's irrelevant what their financial position is. It just doesn't matter. And if it *does* matter, then they're not real friends. And ... I have to say those golf ladies sound rather horrendous,' she ended, grinning.

I smiled then, nodding in agreement. 'Yeah, they are a bit hard to take. I purposely don't see them much anymore.' Sighing I went on, 'I think I'm just a bit tired of keeping up a cheery front all the time. I mean, there *have* been times when I've felt happy, like when Lisa and Libby came for a visit and when each of you moved in, but often I've been forcing it.'

'You *are* a dill,' Evie smiled. 'You really should have known that you could tell me ... or any one of us.'

'Tell us what?' Anna asked as she and Belle made their appearances.

Evie raised her eyebrows and looked at me, but before I could speak she suggested moving inside where it was warmer. Soon settled in our usual spots around the dining table, I took a deep breath and proceeded to reveal how I'd been feeling since the death of my husband.

'Liz … I can't believe you didn't tell us sooner,' Belle shook her head unhappily. 'I feel bad knowing you've been feeling like that all this time.'

'Yeah, sorry, I *should* have … but … I don't know … I kept thinking I should just get on with things.'

Anna had been quiet, but now asked who wanted a cuppa. After hearing that everybody was needing tea, she left the others to chat while she switched on the kettle. Then, a couple of minutes later, she placed a teapot and four cups in the middle of the table, along with some milk and sugar.

'Ahh lovely, thanks Anna.'

'Yes thanks Anna.'

'Ta … mmm yes … I was needing this.'

While everyone sipped their hot drinks the only sound to be heard was the melodious warbling of a couple of magpies. Until Anna spoke.

'Um … Liz … I really admire that you've admitted to feeling so down at times … it makes it easier for me to say how *I've* really been feeling.'

Three sets of eyes swiveled in her direction, but before anyone could speak, Anna went on.

'I think I'm also a bit depressed. You all know how miserable I was for a while after Jim died, well … it's been *more* than a while … in fact it's never fully lifted. I've *also* been working hard to hide my feelings, and some mornings I don't even want to get out of bed. Thank goodness for all of that,' she waved her hand towards the large garden, 'it's the only reason I've been able to function as well as I have been.'

'Oh Anna … I'm so sorry I didn't pick up on that.'

'That's okay Belle, like I said, I worked hard to hide it.'

'Well you've done a good job of it, if that's any consolation.'

'Hmm … it does seem silly now I suppose. But when Liz suggested we all move in here I thought I'd get over it in *no* time and I'd soon feel *happy* to have that lying, cheating bastard out of my life …'

'Anna I've never heard you swear before,' Evie cut in, grinning.'

'Ha … yes … the *old* me never did,' she gave a small smile before continuing. 'But really, it's like what Liz said … I had so much to be grateful for I didn't think it was *right* to feel depressed. Being in the garden has helped me a lot … up to a point. Night time's the worst of course … lying in bed with time to think. But it's not only what *Jim* did.' She paused for a moment, before continuing on. 'After what Sam and Claire have told me … I have to accept I won't be having grandchildren … but it *is* hard,' she sighed.

Evie reached over and gave her a hug, quietly saying, 'Yes, but at least you have children. I would have given anything to have had a baby. But that ectopic pregnancy I had when I was married to Phil ruined any chance of that.'

There was a moments silence then before Anna spoke

again. 'Oh Evie ... I'm *so* sorry. I sound like an ungrateful cow, I know I do.'

'No, that's okay Anna ... that's just the way life goes sometimes ... but to top off the fact I could no longer have children, that's when Phil left me for Karen and her little boy. He was so desperate for a son he thought his best chance lay with someone who'd already produced one,' she smiled wryly.

I nodded, remembering the terrible time Evie had endured. Anna and Belle nodded too, then Anna spoke again.

'I really *am* grateful I have two healthy children,' Anna looked at each of us then continued. 'I just think the shock I had at the funeral knocked me completely off balance and into a swamp of self-pity. I thought I'd shaken it off after confronting Pamela ... but it didn't last. So ... as I didn't want to be one of those maudlin people no one wants to be around ... I've tried to hide it as much as I can.'

Before Liz or Evie could speak, Belle sighed, then reached over and hugged her friend.

'Okay ... well ... I guess it's my turn. I also have to admit I've been hiding my real feelings, and *also* because I didn't want to bring people down by talking about it.' Taking a big breath she then went on. 'I think a part of me died when I realised I wouldn't be having grandkids. I've never talked about it with Tatiana as I didn't want her to feel bad ... and apart from mentioning it to you a couple of times Anna, I've kept it squashed down inside pretty good. But ... you know what? I've just *now* come to realise that it's pointless dwelling on what might have been. So … Anna … I think it's time we *both* let it go, because I don't want to feel that way *anymore.*'

Anna nodded, then said, 'Yes … you're right. It *is* pointless … and I don't want to feel like this anymore either.' Taking a big breath … then letting it out … she nodded again. 'Okay … I'm ready to let it go … once and for all.'

We all just sat for a moment, then I told everyone to stand up for a group hug. The sound of chairs being pushed back was followed by the sound of Anna crying as we all hugged in a tight circle.

'Sorry … sorry for crying …,' she started, but before she could say anymore I stopped her, saying she'll feel better after a good cry, adding that *I* felt a lot better after mine.

Ten minutes later, with all tears mopped up, the four of us sat back down; Anna sighing deeply, releasing the last of her tension.

'Right … I think this deserves a celebration, or actually … I think *we* deserve a celebration,' I grinned as I stood up and made my way into the kitchen. 'I think a small glass of champagne is called for.'

'*Champagne … Liz … it's not even twelve o'clock yet,*' Anna exclaimed.

'Well as they say … it's twelve o'clock somewhere in the world,' I called out as I opened the fridge.

A moment later I was back with a chilled bottle and four flutes. After popping the cork and pouring the fizzing liquid, I raised my glass. 'Here's to friendship and honesty, and the end of *all* depressing thoughts.'

The other three women echoed the toast then clinked glasses before sipping their drinks. I then asked Evie about Phil.

'What ever happened to him Evie? Did you ever hear what he's doing these days?'

'Ha … yes I did as a matter of fact. He was *furious* when his dad signed the house in Terrigal over to me in the divorce settlement; he'd *always* wanted it for himself. Then several years ago a mutual friend told me that he and Karen had three kids … all girls. *And,*' she grinned, 'apparently his dad told him that if he left her he'd be completely cut out of his will.'

'Ha,' I laughed. 'Karma or what?' Without waiting for a reply I went on, 'Okay ladies, I think we'd better eat something. Who'd like a jaffle?'

CHAPTER THIRTY-TWO

Anna found it hard to believe that winter had arrived a week ago. Although there'd been some really chilly mornings, the last seven days had been extremely pleasant which had allowed her heaps of time to potter in the garden. Autumn had always been her favourite season, but she loved winter nearly as much, unlike her other housemates who weren't keen on the cold. The four of them were now driving out of the Leisurelink carpark; heading home after spending the morning at the pool.

She and Belle had done a deep water aerobics class while Evie swam and Liz walked laps. Afterwards they'd all had a sauna then enjoyed their usual coffee at the pool café. It was then that a few of the other pool ladies had joined them.

Anna was now able to listen to them talking about their grandchildren without becoming dispirited, but she'd had enough of their chatter today, so had been glad when Evie said they'd better get going.

Now turning towards Belle, Anna said, 'Hey, is it just me … or do you think those two are totally obsessed with their grandkids?'

Belle knew immediately who she was referring to, and nodded her agreement. 'Yeah … they certainly are. It's like they're in a competition as to whose grandchild is cuter or more advanced. I think it's a bit sad really … it's like they have no other interests *at all*.'

'Yeah I totally agree,' I grinned from the driver's seat. 'Boooringgg.'

'Now now … don't be bitchy,' Evie admonished, even though she too was grinning.

'Not being bitchy … I'm just a little tired of hearing about the little darlings too.' Then smiling at Anna and Belle in the rear view mirror, I added, 'I must say you two are handling talk about grandkids much better these days.'

'Yeah … we're over it. It's like water off a duck's back now, isn't it Anna?

'Yes … it *is* actually.'

'Hmm … well that's *great*.'

'Yeah … so how's your knee now Liz? Feeling any better?'

'Well … I think so, or at least it's no worse. I think walking in the water *is* helping.'

'Good. Hopefully it'll improve enough so you won't need that knee replacement after all.'

'Yeah I'm hoping. It's a bit unpredictable as to when it plays up though. But I think this time I can blame it on the shoes I was wearing yesterday. My own fault. I rarely wear heels anymore, and I should have known better.'

'*Heels*, what were you *thinking*?'

'Well I was in a rush and *didn't* think which caused the problem. Not that they were *high* heels, but I just grabbed them and put them on as they matched my outfit. Luckily I was sitting down most of the time.'

'You are definitely a dill,' Evie shook her head.

'Yeah I won't argue with that, but it made me think about the stairs in the house. What if they become a problem for us down the track? None of us are getting any younger, and we *all* have a few creaky joints. So last night …'

'Yes, my back *has* been giving me a bit of trouble lately,' Anna cut in, nodding her head.

'Yeah same here,' Belle agreed. 'And my knee's *still* a bit dodgy since I tripped over, and that's months ago now.'

'Well it looks like I'm the only one who's not decrepit and falling apart at the seams,' Evie grinned cheekily.

'Ha, yeah,' Belle nodded. 'Sooo … it looks like it'll be *you* caring for *us* in our dotage.'

'Arrhh … no, no, anything but that,' Evie replied in mock horror.

After we all had bit of a laugh at the prospect of Evie being our personal caregiver, I continued on with what I thought would be a good idea.

'So, as I was saying … last night I rang Rob, the guy who actually built the house, and he said he knows a good company which could install a small elevator in the house if we need one. He reckons it wouldn't be cheap, but I think if we need one, then we need one,' I smiled.

'Wow.'

'Awesome.'

'Really?'

'Yeah really. So if we're having difficulties with the stairs I'll get him to look into it for us. I'm not sure how it would look - probably wouldn't be a fashion statement - but it would save us from having to move somewhere else … what do you think?'

'Um … yes, I guess you're right.'

'Yeah it does make sense.'

'What a terrific idea Liz.'

'Yeah, well we'll see how we go. You never know, if we all stay fit enough it might not become a problem.'

Back home again, Anna was stripped off and ready to hop in the shower; checking herself out in the full length mirror first. She was sporting a new hairstyle these days - a bit shorter than before - allowing her natural curls to frame her face. Scrutinising her body, front and rear, she thought she was in better shape than she had been in years.

'Hmm … yes … not *too* bad for an old sheila. I think all that working in the garden has slimmed me down a bit. I hope I can keep it up over winter.'

She'd been feeling so much better in herself this last week, so had decided to step out of her comfort zone and try some new things. One of the new things was going to the book club which Liz had been attending for the last six months or so. They went yesterday - the members meeting once a month - and she now had a book to read which she wouldn't normally have chosen.

Her other latest endeavour was joining a drawing class. She didn't really feel very creative, but because the others were … well, except for Gabi … she thought she's give it a go. So she'd joined the University of the Third Age, more commonly known as U3A, and was about to start her new class tomorrow. Not sure what type of medium she'd use, she was going to drive into Geelong later to check out pencils, pastels and charcoal.

After having eaten a light lunch with the others, she was now ready to head off. Belle had told her of the two art supplies shops she preferred, so that would make her shopping quicker and easier.

'Are you all sure you don't need anything while I'm in the city?'

'No I'm fine thanks Anna.'

'Um ... yeah I think I'm okay too.'

'Actually can you grab me a tube of acrylic paint?' Belle asked.

'Sure. What brand ... what colour ... and how big a tube?'

'It's the Atelier brand ... brilliant violet ... and actually get me the 250ml tub. A tube won't be enough because I love that colour and use it a fair bit. Hang on a minute and I'll get you some money.'

A sporadic spattering of raindrops began hitting the windscreen as Anna drove through Angelsea, becoming heavier within minutes. Turning on the wipers she noticed there weren't many people strolling about the shopping area, reasoning it was probably due to the inclement weather.

Soon leaving the town behind, she turned up the car stereo, then sat back and relaxed. As much as she loved company on the drive, she also enjoyed being on her own so she could listen – uninterrupted - to her preferred AM radio station.

Forty minutes later she'd parked in the Market Square carpark and was walking towards Geelong Art Supplies; her first stop. After buying the paint Belle wanted she was crossing Ryrie Street when she saw her friend Hilary, whom she hadn't seen since Jim's funeral. Stopping to say hello they decided they both had time for a cuppa, so popped into a coffee shop around the corner in James Street. Ordering their drinks they then found a table near the front window.

'So how are you?' Hilary asked as she pulled her chair in closer to where she sat. 'Are you over the fiasco that Jim created yet?'

'I'm actually good thanks, and yes, I've totally moved on from that now.'

'Oh, well *that's* good to hear. I couldn't believe what a bastard Jim turned out to be.'

'Yes, that's been the general consensus,' Anna laughed.

'So how's it all going; living with three other women? Is it working out okay? I lived with girl friends when I was younger and I loved it.'

'Yes it *is* working out okay. Sharing with the others is actually going *better* than I'd hoped for,' Anna smiled. 'We haven't had *one* argument, not that I'm surprised. We've known each other too long for *that* to happen.'

'That's great. So how do you divvy up the chores? Do you just take it in turns to cook and clean and whatever?'

'Well, sort of. Liz *loves* cooking so she does most of that. Not every day of course but mostly. Then with the groceries … well … we all just add things to a list as we think of something. Liz enjoys tracking down different ingredients so she normally does the shopping, but one of us usually goes with her to give her a hand. Then, as the cook doesn't have to clean up, one of us will do it. The same with the vacuuming … we just take it in turns.'

'Hmm … okay, that sounds pretty good then. So … I suppose you just divide the bills between you all?'

'Yes we do. Well except for the champagne.'

'Champagne? Yum I *love* champagne.'

'Yes, I'm certainly developing a taste for it too,' she smiled. 'It's Liz's favourite but she's insisted on buying it as it's a *bit* expensive for the rest of us. It's amazing how many things we end up celebrating with a glass of two of bubbly,' she smiled again.

'Hmm … well that sounds pretty good to *me*. So, what else have you been up too? Have you missed your garden? I know how much you loved it.'

The waiter arrived then with their cappuccinos, so after thanking him, they both added sugar and continued their chat.

'No, I actually haven't missed it at all as I've got a huge garden at Anglesea to keep me busy. It'd been a bit neglected before we moved in so I've been pretty busy getting it into shape. You'll have to come down sometime and check it out. I can give you a heap of cuttings if you like.'

'Okay, thanks, sounds good. I wish I'd been able to get to your party but I told Belle I had a wedding to go to when she rang. Don't you hate it when you have two marvelous invitations on the same *day*? I was really disappointed, but … my niece's wedding had to take precedence.'

They both had a few sips of their hot drinks before continuing their chat.

'Mmm … nice coffee,' Hilary smiled, 'I must come here

again. So … what about the others? What are they doing to keep busy?'

'Well Evie's been pretty busy with her writing. She's on her second novel, did you know?'

'Oh great; I loved her first one. When do you think it'll it be finished?'

'She's hoping by the end of the year.'

'Well tell her I'll buy one as soon as it's done. I can't wait to read it.'

'Yes me too.'

'And Liz and Belle? What are they doing? How's Liz coping with Hugh's death?'

'She's going pretty well now. Both she and I have had our low moments of course. We were both pretty depressed there for a while actually.' Anna stopped to sip her cappuccino then went on. 'I don't know if time *heals* … but it does do *something*. She's started making her jewellery again, so keep it in mind if you need a special gift for someone.'

'Okay, I will. I love her jewellery. And Belle? We didn't really have much time for a catch up when she rang me with the invitation. Is she still painting? I loved that exhibition she had last year.'

'Yes she's actually submitting a portrait to the Archibald.'

'Oh wow.'

'Yes. She painted an Aboriginal artist in Alice Springs … did a fabulous job too.'

'That's *fantastic*. I can't *wait* to see it.'

'Yes she finished it a couple of weeks ago. Now she's doing a big abstract for a new coffee shop in Anglesea.'

The two friends continued catching up on other mutual friends before Hilary asked after Gabi.

'Oh she finally met a really lovely man and they're off exploring the world for a month.'

Anna then filled her friend in on David's health issues and their desire to see all the places they can, *while* they can.

'Gabi said she absolutely *loved* Morocco and Spain, and they've been in Portugal this last week. Then they're off to the Philippines before coming back home for a while. Apparently David has some specialist appointments he has to keep.'

'Wow … I am *so* happy for her. But how sad … you know … that he doesn't have a long life expectancy.'

'Yes, we've all thought that. But you know … none of us knows what might happen next, so now we're making a list of things we'd like to do and we're going to do at least one thing each year.'

'Oh … what sort of things?'

'Well, I've always wanted to go camping, so we've put that on the list, as well as a trip on the Ghan. Belle hasn't been to Italy yet either so that's on the list as well.'

'Oh I'd *love* to go on the Ghan. Maybe Pete and I could join you.'

'Yes sure. I'll let you know when we're going.'

'Hmm … you're right though, about putting things off,' Hilary added thoughtfully. 'I think I'll talk to Pete tonight about doing our overseas trip *this* year. To hell with the bills,' she smiled.

'Yes … there will always be bills,' Anna nodded, smiling as well.

After finishing their coffees and making a day for Hilary to visit, the two women hugged then left to complete their shopping.

CHAPTER THIRTY-THREE

'I'll go downstairs and pay the bill while you make sure we're not leaving anything behind.' David reached out towards Gabi as she walked past, then hugged her around her waist.

'Okay … I will just check the bathroom again. But I think I have got everything.' Turning around to face David she hugged him back.

'I have so enjoyed these last three weeks. I will remember this holiday forever.'

'Me too. Maybe we can come back another time?'

'Yes I would love that. But for now … Boracay Island here we come,' she grinned.

'Yes. I can't believe I'm finally going there. I've wanted to check out the Philippine Islands ever since discovering my dad was stationed there during the war.' Pausing to give Gabi a quick kiss he then went on. 'I'll be back quick as a flash to carry the bags downstairs.'

'Okay sweetie.'

Half an hour later they hopped out of their taxi at Lisbon airport. After checking in their luggage they found a lovely restaurant and had a leisurely lunch. Neither had eaten much for breakfast as they'd run out of time after packing their things, so both had been quite hungry. Afterwards they walked around for a while, checking out the variety of souvenir shops. They had no need to rush as they still had thirty minutes before their flight was to board, but not really needing any more souvenirs they decided to sit in a café and have a coffee.

Smiling at each other between sips of their hot beverages, Gabi then sat her cup down and reached for David's hands.

'Do you know this feels a bit of the unreal to me. Here we are, sitting in the airport in *Portugal*, waiting to fly to the *Philippines* … it is *crazy*.'

'Haha … yes, it is a *bit* crazy, but I'm crazy in love with you, so it all feels natural to me,' he grinned.

'And you know that I love you … yes?'

'Yes. I am very happy to know that you love me too.'

'I cannot *wait* to tell my friends about everything we have seen, and show them all of the photos. But it seems the bit strange to know we will be back home in another week.'

'Yes,' he smiled, '*home* seems like a foreign country now. But once I get those tests over with we can take off again.'

'Okay … as long as you are feeling up to the travelling again.'

'Oh I'm sure I'll be alright. So … where would you like to go next?'

'I am not sure, what about you?'

'Well I think I'd like to take my girl to Paris … the city of love … what do you think?'

'Oh … *Paris* … yes *please*,' she smiled delightedly.

'And do you know what?'

'What.'

'I think it would be the perfect place for a honeymoon.'

'A honeymoon?'

'Yes, a honeymoon.'

'David, what are you saying?'

'What I'm saying is I want to marry you and take you to Paris for our honeymoon … what do you say?'

Gabi couldn't speak at first, then tears started to run down her cheeks. David was just starting to get concerned when she finally drew a deep breath and smiled at him.

'Oh David … *yes, yes, yes*. Are you *sure*? You want to *marry me?*'

'Of course I'm sure you silly thing. I *love* you. You make me so *happy*. I want you in my life for as long as that happens to be.'

'And I want to be in your life too … *oh my goodness* I am so *excited.* Jumping up she flung her arms around David's neck, who then also stood up.

'Oh I cannot *wait* to tell my friends.'

'Alright, but I don't think there'll be time now before our flight's called.'

'Okay … I will call them from our room when we get to the island then,' she grinned.

'Good idea,' David said, checking his watch. 'Well, no time to celebrate now. How about we have some champagne on board?'

Sixteen hours later they were lying fully clothed on their bed in the Villa Caemilla Beach Boutique Hotel. Completely exhausted they looked at each other, smiled, cuddled up … and fell asleep. They slept right through the day, waking in time for their evening meal. After that they had a brief wander along the beach before deciding to have an early night; hoping to get their body clocks back on track. It seemed to work, as they both arose around seven the next morning, ready for a day of exploring.

'Oh what a fabulous morning,' Gabi smiled broadly. 'We will do lots of the snorkeling today. But I really must phone my friends before we go. I was just too tired yesterday, but today I feel so wonderful again.'

David nodded but didn't say anything.

'Are you okay sweetie? Is there something wrong? Are you feeling tired? We can stay here today if you like?'

'No I'm alright … it's just that I've been thinking. Would you mind waiting until we get back home to tell your friends we're getting married? Only because I'd like us both to tell my daughters … in person, not over the phone.'

'Oh … of course … I did not think of that. That would be a better idea. And of course I can wait … after all we will be home next week.'

'Thank you my gorgeous girl, now let's eat and then go exploring.'

After a quick hug, they wandered downstairs to the hotel restaurant, were they then enjoyed their breakfast with a honeymooning Japanese couple. During the course of the meal the newlyweds talked of their recent flight to Papua New Guinea. They'd spent a couple of days there and loved it, saying it was different to anywhere else they'd ever been before.

Gabi and David had planned to fly directly to Melbourne at the end of their holiday, but as this new destination was more or less on their way, they decided 'why not', thinking it would top off their holiday perfectly. So that afternoon David found a travel agency where the very helpful young man was able to change their flights. Now they'd go from Manila to Port Moresby, then two days later they'd fly to Melbourne, via Brisbane.

After a blissfully idyllic four days swimming, snorkeling, exploring and relaxing, the loved up couple were now on their five hour flight, presently flying over the Celebes Sea. They were both excited and ready for their next adventure; talking about all the things they'd seen and experienced so far, and how much they had to tell their friends and family. After a light lunch they both dozed for a while, then before they knew it an announcement came on saying they'd be landing in twenty minutes.

The humidity was high when they stepped off the plane at Jacksons International Airport. After negotiating a fee for the taxi ride to the Stanley Hotel, the driver drove the short distance and deposited them and their luggage at the entrance.

'Well we are here ... and I think I love it,' Gabi said, gazing around at the rampant vegetation. 'Oh and I just *love* those tropical flowers over there. Aren't they gorgeous?'

'Yes, and *I* love this tropical heat, but come on, let's get to our room and dump our bags. Then we can have a proper look around.'

Later, after they booked a sightseeing flight for the following day, they both felt a little tired so decided to hang around the hotel pool. After ordering some drinks they lay back on a large day bed under a palm frond canopy and smiled at each other.

'I know we should probably be out exploring - sorry darling - but I just don't feel up to it now.'

'There is no need to be sorry as I am also feeling a bit knickered today.'

'Hahaha … oh Gabi you make me smile. I'm so glad I met you. And just so you know … the expression is feeling *knackered*, not knickered.'

'Oh okay, thank you for telling me. And I am also very glad that I met *you*.'

Grinning at each other they raised their glasses and clinked them together.

'To us,' they said in unison, before laughing and sipping their chilled cocktails.

The next morning they arrived at the airport right on time, then boarded along with six other couples. They were all quite excited and were laughing as they took their seats. David insisted that Gabi have the window seat, and she'd then insisted they would swap over later. Smiling at each other they held hands as the small plane taxied down the runway and lifted off.

An hour later, after they'd all been enthralled by the wonders of the coastline and the dense jungle, the plane did a sweeping turn; back in the direction of the airport. Quite unexpectedly the sky darkened. They'd flown straight into a tropical storm and the small plane was soon bucking and rocking; scaring everyone on board.

Gabi and David squeezed each other's hand as they peered through the small window, but were unable to see anything. The rain which was streaming against their window completely blurred their vision. A woman passenger I front of them was crying hysterically; her partner trying unsuccessfully to calm her down.

David reached his arms around Gabi and drew her to him, holding her tightly. The plane unexpectedly banked to the left, apparently trying to turn back, when suddenly the darkness flared incredibly bright at the exact time they heard an earsplitting bang. It was the last sight and sound they all heard as the plane crashed into the side of a mountain; instantly exploding into a massive fireball.

CHAPTER THIRTY-FOUR

I was in the kitchen poring over a new recipe book when Evie made an appearance. She said she'd been writing all morning and had almost finished the first draft. Happy with her progress she was ready to take a break and eat something.

We were soon both perched on stools at the breakfast bar, each with a toasted sandwich and a cup of tea. A light rain was drizzling from a leaden sky, necessitating the lights being turned on even though it was only midday. Hearing my phone ringing in my bedroom I hurried off to answer it, leaving Evie engrossed in one of Belle's art magazines.

'Hello,' I answered brightly, not recognising the phone number. 'Yes, that's me ... who ... from *DFAT*? *What*? No ... no that can't be right ...*no ... there must be some mistake ...*'

Evie must have been able to tell by the tone of my voice

there was something *really* wrong, as she appeared in my bedroom moments later.

'What? *Liz* ... what *is it*? What's *wrong*?'

I continued listening to the voice on the phone for another a minute, all the time staring wide-eyed at Evie, then walked stiffly back to the kitchen where I wrote a phone number down on a notepad. I then slowly nodded before placing my phone on the bench top. Evie looked nearly too scared to ask what was going on, but before she could speak I stumbled into the lounge room and crumpled onto the couch.

'What's *wrong* Liz ... *tell me* ... what's *happened?*'

Tears were stinging my eyes and my breath had caught in my chest, rendering me unable to breathe for a moment, then, after a concerted effort, I spoke in a shuddering voice.

'It's Gabi and David ... they've both been killed ... in a plane crash.'

'*Oh my God ... no no no ... please no ... oh my God.*'

All four of us had cried more tears than we could have thought possible. We were now sitting together, squashed onto one couch, needing each other's closeness.

'They were supposed to be back home tomorrow night,' I said bleakly. 'This is just *too* dreadful ... my brain still won't accept that it's true.'

'Same,' was all Evie could say.

Belle and Anna both just nodded. They'd said the least since we'd heard the terrible news; the shock seeming to have stripped them of speech.

Since the woman from DFAT had rung, everything had taken on a strange, distorted mien. Time either dragged or disappeared, leaving us struggling to make sense of the smallest thing. Knowing we had to reach out to David's daughters, I eventually rang the DFAT number to speak to the woman again. Thankfully she was able to provide us with a contact number for the eldest of David's three girls.

Dianne had fortunately been able to gather her whole family together. She told me they were all completely inconsolable, but supporting each other the best they could. After talking a little longer; promising to keep in contact, we then hung up our phones.

It was now evening, and we were sitting at the dining table with yet another cup of tea in front of us. We'd been sitting on the couch in semi-darkness when Evie had shivered, realising that it had become quite cold. She'd managed to rouse us from our thoughts; suggesting someone turn on the heating while she made us all a cuppa.

'Do you think they knew they were crashing?' Belle then whispered.

No one said anything; none of us wanting to contemplate our friend dying in terror.

'The woman from DFAT said she'll be in contact when they know more details of what happened,' I spoke quietly. 'Until then …' Shaking my head I couldn't go on.

'At least they were both together,' Evie looked at each of us with a spark of hope in her eyes, 'that has be *one* good thing … don't you think?' Her eyes were pleading for someone to agree.

'Yes … at least they were together,' I nodded 'And they'd probably had a wonderful day.'

'Yes,' Evie went on, 'and they would have been happy. Happy to be travelling together, and happy thinking of all the things they were going to tell us when they got back.'

Anna and Belle nodded but didn't speak.

'I'm going to miss that crazy lady so much,' Evie said, doing her best not to cry again. 'I know she wouldn't want us to be sad … well not for *too* long anyway,' she smiled shakily. 'So I'm going to put a smile on my face and remember the fun times we had together. If I don't … then I think I'll be crying forever.'

Standing up she then walked off towards her bedroom. A minute later we heard a tap being turned on … then off. Evie returned a moment later with a freshly washed face presenting a tentative smile.

'I know you're right Evie,' Belle said, 'but I just can't do it yet.' She then dropped her head down and rested it on top of her folded arms.

'That's okay Belle,' Evie said, giving her a hug before sitting down again.

Anna looked completely drained of colour as she silently reached over and gently rubbed her friend's back.

'You're right though Evie,' I said quietly as I stood up. 'I'm going to wash off what's left of my make-up, then I'm going to get us all something to eat.'

For some reason nearly all the lights in the house were on. It was like we were subconsciously trying to dispel the darkness which had enveloped us all. I'd made soup the previous day so that made for an easy meal, although Anna only had a little of hers. It seemed her recently ejected depression had returned with a vengeance, deadening her whole system. When she said she was going to lay on her bed for a while, Belle went with her, not wanting her friend to be alone when she was obviously feeling so desolate.

'Why do things like this have to happen Liz … and to such *good* people?'

Evie and I were in the lounge room again, sitting in front of the glowing fire.

'I don't know,' I sighed. 'I just don't know.'

We sat like that for some time, oblivious of time … oblivious of everything except for the mesmerizing flames which were dancing in front of us. We were both startled when Belle spoke; Anna standing next to her.

'Um … do you think we can all sleep together in the lounge room tonight? I can inflate the big airbed, and there's heaps of room on the couches.'

'Actually I think that's a good idea,' I smiled wanly. 'I don't feel like being alone tonight either.'

Evie agreed as well, and it didn't take us long to be in our pyjamas, and under our doonas. We were all positioned to have a view of the fire, and after a very short time we all fell into an exhausted, restless slumber.

Morning came, and the sound of the front door bell ringing woke each of us. We were all slightly perplexed at first, as to why we were in the lounge room … and then our faces fell as we remembered.

'What time is it,' I asked grumpily, scanning the room for my phone.

'Nearly nine-thirty.'

'Oh God, who's here at this time of the morning,' I groaned as I stood and looked for my dressing gown.

'It's okay Liz, I'll go,' Evie offered as she headed for the stairs.

The rest of us headed to our bedrooms to make ourselves look better presented, not knowing who might be at the door. It turned out to be Jason and Simon. With everything that had been going on, I had completely forgotten that I'd invited them for Sunday brunch. I heard Evie quickly explain the situation to them, and as the two men walked up the last of the stairs, their faces showed how shocked they were.

'*Oh my lord,*' Jason flung his arms around me. 'How absolutely *terrible* … I can't *believe* it. Not Gabi and Davy … I *loved* those people.'

After sharing what little details we had, I set about preparing a mountain of food … mainly to give me something to do. I glanced outside at the gloomy sky which heralded an imminent downpour, and noticed Anna sitting next to a window, her focus seemingly outdoors as well. The tree tops were thrashing wildly in the gusting wind and I shivered involuntarily before turning my attention back to my cooking.

The others were seated in front of the fire with their coffees, and after some discussion they decided there were other people who would want to know what had happened. Belle volunteered to make a list of people, asking now and then if anyone knew a person's phone number that she didn't know. After a while she moved to a quieter part of the lounge room, then set about phoning the friends who had been close to Gabi. The repetitive telling of the basic details seemed to help her to somewhat come to terms with the tragedy.

Evie said she was determined to cling to the only positive thought she could muster; Gabi and David being together. She said she was concentrating her thoughts on the wonderful day they must have enjoyed - flying over the spectacular jungle and coastline - knowing they must have been extremely excited and happy.

No one seemed to notice when Anna went to her room and put on her coat and scarf. She could no longer listen to Belle going over the same story to the people on the other end of the phone. Sliding open her door she exited to the verandah, then walked down the steps to the garden. Hands in pockets she walked to the furthermost end, then sat at the outdoor setting where they'd all enjoyed many a glass of wine together. The cold wind was making her eyes water, but she didn't care. Being indoors had been making her feel terribly claustrophobic. Staring at the footprints she'd left in the damp lawn, she let the tears roll.

Nature had always been her salvation. Being the youngest of five children to farming parents, she'd often been left to amuse herself. Wandering around the acres of farmland and adjoining bush, she'd always been happy collecting bird feathers, unusual seed pods and any flowers she came across. Then later in life, with her children at school all day and her husband rarely at home, she'd once more gravitated to spending as much time as possible in her garden.

Sighing deeply she now felt completely wrung out and didn't think she could ever be truly happy again. Life just seemed so … *unfair* sometimes. Thinking how suited Gabi and David had been, and what a fun-filled life they had in front of them, had her shaking her head in bewilderment.

'Oh Gabi … I am so going to miss you.'

Letting her mind wander through some of the funny times they'd had, Anna hadn't realised she was becoming wet until Simon appeared in front of her.

'Come on luvie, out of this weather or you'll end up with pneumonia.'

'Oh, okay … thanks Simon. I wasn't aware it had started to rain.'

As they made their way through the garden, Simon spoke again.

'Now I *know* this will sound a bit trite … and heaven forbid that *I* should ever sound trite … *but* … you are *so* fortunate to have such good friends, and together we will *all* get through this ghastly time.'

'Thanks Simon.' Anna put her arm through his and nodded. 'Yes I *am* very fortunate,' she smiled tentatively up at him. 'I'm so glad you and Jason are here. We all love having both of you in our lives.'

'Oh … thanks Anna … you're going to make *me* cry in a minute,' he said in an attempt to lighten the mood.

'No I mean it. You're both always ready with a helping hand whenever it's needed.' She stopped for a moment and looked up at him. 'Thanks for being such a good friend, it really means a lot.'

Simon reached his other arm around her and gave her a hug. 'It's my pleasure lovely lady. Now come on, let's get out of this damn rain.'

Back inside, Anna went to get changed out of her wet clothes while Evie and Belle finished restoring the lounge room to its usual tidy state. Jason was busy emptying the dishwasher so Simon removed his damp jumper, hanging it over the back of a chair near the fire, then went down to the car to get his jacket. That also gave him the chance to have another good cry, before composing himself again. Wanting to be a support for his friends, not a blubbering mess, he took a couple of deep breaths, then headed back upstairs.

CHAPTER THIRTY-SIX

It had taken three weeks to have Gabi's belongings returned to Angelsea, then another week for the memorial service to take place. After some discussion with David's family they'd decided to hold a dual memorial; honouring both David and Gabi. It had taken place five days ago … they were now trying to get used to a *new* normal.

Evie was sitting on the bed in Gabi's bedroom, sighing and thinking of what could have been. Knowing that Gabi no longer had any living relatives, she was at least happy that her friend's possessions could remain with them. Looking at a large photo of the five women, taken at Anna's last birthday party, she shook her head.

'That seems such a long time ago now,' she murmured, studying their laughing faces.

Then, examining an equally large photo of Gabi and David also taken at the party, Evie wanted to cry … but smiled a shaky smile instead.

'What a waste,' she thought, shaking her head again. 'They should have had so many more years together.'

Because David had wanted to ensure that Gabi could definitely move in after he died – even if that wasn't for several years – he'd asked if he and Gabi could move some of her things into her proposed bedroom. The four women had of course said yes. So before they'd left on their overseas trip they'd brought round some of Gabi's much-loved things.

Evie ran her hand over the fluffy, cherry red cushions on the bed beside her. She couldn't help but smile, remembering that all shades of red were Gabi's favoured colours. Apart from the bed, which was a spare one Liz had brought with her, everything else in the room let you know that it was Gabi's domain, from the multi-coloured scarves and hats hanging from a rattan coat stand, to the paintings and photos which decorated the walls. There was a slight fragrance, just discernable, which Evie concluded must be ingrained into Gabi's things. She hoped it would always remain there.

Feeling a bit down now, she let her eyes wander around the room again. It was then that she felt Gabi's irrepressible personality radiating around her, giving Evie an unexpected tingly sensation. She could not help but smile, believing Gabi's spirit had come for a visit.

'I will always remember you my friend,' she said out loud, then immediately felt a sense of peace enveloping her. Still smiling she just sat for a while and enjoyed the warm glow she now felt inside.

A few minutes later after taking a big breath in … then letting it out … she left the room and wandered out to the kitchen. Peering outside she saw last night's storm had not yet abated, the dark sky necessitating lights being turned on in the kitchen and lounge room. She decided to sit out on the deck for a while, all the better to watch the storm, but after a few minutes she found she was too cold without a jacket, so returned inside to get one.

Now suitably rugged up with a scarf as well, she once more sat down and scanned her surroundings. Gigantic gray clouds jostled for prominence while icy darts of water raked across the sky. The bitter wind, blowing straight from the south, was whipping through the tree tops in a wild fury rendering parts of 'Anna's garden' quite bedraggled.

Evie had the house to herself for a couple of hours as Anna and Belle had gone to the pool, and Liz had gone to meet a friend in Torquay. Apparently the friend was hoping Liz had time to make a pendant for her daughter's upcoming birthday. They were meeting at a coffee shop and would probably stay and have lunch.

Sighing loudly Evie thought she really should be writing, but just didn't have the urge today. She'd nearly finished the third draft which would normally have made her happy, but today she'd woken in an 'off' mood, but wasn't sure why.

'Hmm … it could be because I'm missing Ross. It was so thoughtful of him to fly back for the memorial service. I'd forgotten how good it is to have a supportive man in my life.' Evie nodded to herself as she thought about it. 'Yeah … that's probably it. Oh well … can't do much about that,' she sighed again.

Ross wasn't due back in Australia again for another two weeks, and then only for a week before he had to fly to Dubai. Evie knew he loved his job, but had wondered lately if he planned to retire at the end of next year when he turned sixty-five. Thinking how she'd love to see him more often, she was loath to bring up the topic of retirement; not wanting to appear the clingy type.

'Which I'm not and never have been,' she said to herself, knowing that it was usually *she* who was absorbed in her own busy life.

After a bit more thought she wondered if her mood was due to her new awareness of how short life could be sometimes; now more keen than ever to make the most of what she and Ross had.

Her thoughts then went to Simon and Jason, and all the help and support they'd given over the last four weeks. They too had reassessed their lives, and now *really* wanted to get married. As they knew they couldn't legally marry in Australia they were planning to go to New Zealand soon, to do the deed there. The four women were going as well, along with a heap of other friends, all intent on making it a sensational weekend to remember.

Finally unable to disregard the cold creeping through her clothing, Evie went back inside. After divesting herself of jacket, scarf and Ugg boots, she made herself a hot chocolate then moved into the lounge to sit in her armchair; tucking her legs underneath her. The warmth of the glowing fire soon erased the chill from her body and she remained sitting there for quite some time … eyes focused on the flames … and enjoyed *not* thinking.

Realising her cup was now empty brought Evie back to the here and now. Deciding to have another, she slowly stood, stretching her now stiff legs as she did so. Muttering under her breath that she was definitely getting old, she ambled into the kitchen.

As she opened a new carton of milk she remembered they were all going to dinner later with friends at St. Leonards. Val and Claudia had often talked about the exceptional food at their local Greek restaurant, so tonight had suited everyone to get together for a meal. Hoping the rain would ease off by then, Evie nonetheless thought the cold weather would give her a chance to wear the new coat she'd bought recently.

Her thoughts then turned to her childhood home in Portarlington, as they'd drive past it on their way to St. Leonards later. Evie hadn't been there for quite some time and was interested to see if her old home was still standing. She'd loved growing up in the small seaside town and had been sorry to leave when she was eleven. But after her dad had gone missing during a night time fishing trip, her mother had sold the business and house where they'd lived and moved the family of six kids into Geelong. She sighed, remembering the shock she and her siblings had received thirty two years later, after discovering what had actually happened on the fateful night of his disappearance.

'Hey Evie … hope you've got the kettle on.' Belle's voice called from downstairs, interrupting her reminiscing. 'The power went off at the pool café so we couldn't have a coffee.'

'Oh no … how completely unacceptable,' Evie called back. 'Hang on … I'll put it on now. Or would you like a hot chocolate? I'm having one.'

'Ooh yes, that sounds perfect. What about you Anna?'

'Yes, hot chocolate for me too please.'

After leaving their damp coats and footwear downstairs, and depositing their swimming gear in the washing machine, both women made their way up to the living room. Unless they were going out somewhere straight from the pool, none of the four women showered there. Instead they would just strip of their togs and pull on trackie pants and a top to wear home.

'My goodness it's *pouring* outside.'

'Yes. We ran for the car but still got pretty wet. Oh it's so lovely and *warm* in here,' Anna smiled, rubbing her hands together. 'So how's the writing going Evie? Did you get much done with us all gone?'

'Well it's a bit slow at the moment, but I'm definitely getting there,' she replied grinning.

After they'd had their hot drink, and a piece of Liz's famous passionfruit sponge, the two women filled Evie in on a bit of gossip, then went their separate ways to shower off the pool chlorine. Evie tidied the kitchen, wiped the bench tops and then headed to the small lounge room where she'd left her laptop set up.

She loved the spot she'd chosen for her work space as it gave her a wonderful view of the tree tops and sky. The others didn't mind her using it as her 'office' as they were rarely in there, preferring to relax in the larger lounge room. Upon entering the room her eyes were drawn to her collection of books which nearly filled the sizable bookcase. She smiled, thinking how good they looked there, before once more settling down to work.

Having left the computer turned on, she was soon reading over the last sentences she'd written. When she realised she was reading them again for the third time she knew she couldn't concentrate properly.

'Hmm … annoyment,' she grinned. 'Oh well … looks like I might have to leave this 'til later.'

Making sure she'd saved what she'd written so far, she then shut the computer down. Still feeling a bit pensive, she retrieved her outdoor gear, rugged up warmly again and stepped out through the sliding door. She had a comfy chair positioned there for when she felt the need to have bit of a break and some fresh air. Thankfully the rain and wind had eased considerably, although it was still extremely cold.

Her earlier thoughts of having to relocate to Geelong as a child had brought to mind how she'd met her second husband, Dash. She'd been divorced, living in Newtown - a suburb of Geelong - when Dash had moved into the upstairs flat next door to her.

During the next six months or so, she and Dash had become a couple, as well as Liz and Hugh. Then Liz had moved into Hugh's fabulous house at Eastern View, and she and Dash had moved to Terrigal with his daughter Marley and granddaughter Blue, along with Blackie, a young boy they'd fostered.

Blackie now lived in the Northern Territory, working as a helicopter pilot. He and his wife had visited every Christmas until the last one, as they now had a little son, and another baby due in another two months.

'I must go and see them again soon,' Evie decided. 'But … it might be best if I hold off on a visit until after the baby's born. Hmm … I can't wait to see little Jack again, he's such a cutie.' Shaking her head in disbelief she continued her musings. 'I can't believe he'll be one in a couple of months; how quickly time flies. I wonder if he'll be jealous of the baby. Hopefully he'll be too young to worry about a new addition to the family.' Smiling at the thought, she felt a welcome relief - having something joyful to think about –

and made a mental note to ask Ross if he'd like to go with her.

Twenty minutes later after watching the now depleted rainclouds move majestically out to sea, she was pleased to notice a glimpse of blue in the sky after a full day of grey. Finally feeling more settled than she had earlier, she headed indoors to get ready for an enjoyable evening at St. Leonards.

CHAPTER THIRTY-SEVEN

Belle's portrait of Aunty Betty had been couriered to the Archibald Committee about six weeks ago; one week before hearing of Gabi's death. It hadn't made the cut to be a finalist though; that being totally inconsequential, considering how shattered she'd been at the loss of her friend. None of them had felt like attending the show; deciding to go next year if she entered another portrait.

Since then she'd been keeping herself busy with several new commissions. Her latest was from an old friend who'd asked for a portrait of his wife - an intended 40th anniversary gift - and the photo he'd provided was stunning. It was a head and shoulders picture of a very attractive woman, but it was her eyes which really stood out. They were a gorgeous green and contrasted beautifully with her pale skin and dark brown hair. Belle was hoping to get the colour just right, but had an abstract to finish first.

She was now half-heartedly setting up her work area when she stopped and thought for a moment. Shaking her head and sighing, she had to accept she just wasn't in the mood to paint today which was definitely a rare occurrence. Instead she decided to phone Tatiana.

'Hi Mum.'

'Hi darling.'

'This is a lovely surprise. What are you up too?'

'Not much. I have a big abstract to finish but I just can't seem to settle into painting today, so, I thought it was a perfect time for a catch up.'

'Ahh okay … well it's not the best timing for me unfortunately. I can have a quick chat though.'

'Oh … busy at work?'

'No … doctor's appointment in fifteen minutes.'

'Oh. Are you okay?'

'Yes I'm okay, just bit of a tummy thing … nothing major. So what have you been up to lately? Been anywhere interesting?'

'Well, last night we all went to a Greek restaurant at St. Leonards and had a meal with Val and Claudia. It was really yummy actually.'

'Oh yum, I love Greek food. Hmm … I think I'll suggest it to Nomi later. We haven't been out for a meal for a while. So … how was Val and Claudia, still into their poetry and music I suppose?'

'Yes, both good, and both still performing gigs here and there. But listen, I'll get going so you can get to your appointment. Give me a call one night when you have time.'

'Okay Mum, will do. Thanks for ringing. Bye.'

'Bye love.'

After a quick look around her studio; seeing it was all reasonably tidy, Belle sighed then wondered what she'd do next. Drumming her fingers on the table top for a moment while she thought about it, she decided to get lunch ready for everyone, so headed upstairs. Anna and Liz were going to their book club later, the first time in a while, as none of them had felt like socialising much following Gabi's death. Neither of them were in sight when she got to the kitchen, and neither was Evie.

Flicking the switch on the kettle, Belle then opened the fridge and stood there, trying to decide what everyone might like for lunch. Deciding on the quiche she could see sitting on the top shelf, she popped it in the oven and turned it on, once more appreciative of Liz's culinary skills. Ten minutes later the other three women had made an appearance and were sitting at the breakfast bar in anticipation of being served lunch.

'Mm, mm ... yummy quiche Liz,' Evie smiled. 'Quite delish.'

'Yeah they're not too shabby,' I agreed. 'What are you doing today Belle? More painting?'

'Hmm ... I'm not sure yet. Why?'

'No real reason. Just thought if you're footloose and fancy free you might like to come to the book club with us.'

'Hmm … no … thanks anyway. When I get time to read a book I want it to be one *I* choose.'

'No worries. What about you Evie? What are you up to today?'

'Well I'm on bit of a roll with my writing so don't want to stop, but Helen's asked me a few times to meet her for coffee so I said I would this arvo. I'm meeting her at the Art Gallery first so we can check out the latest exhibition, then we're going for coffee at the waterfront somewhere. You come too if you feel like it Belle.'

'Okay, thanks, I'll see how I feel later.'

With lunch over and dirty dishes in the dishwasher, Evie and Anna went to get ready for their respective outings, while Belle remained where she was; perusing one of Anna's gardening magazines. I was just about to go and get ready myself when I remembered I had something to tell her.

'Hey Belle, remember you said the other day that you'd like to research your family tree, but you're not sure how to go about it?'

'Yeah.'

'Well I was checking out a few things online last night and came across an old friend. Do you remember Delma Tunbridge? I worked with her at the real estate agents for a couple of years, before she moved to the country some-where. Must be close to thirty years ago now.'

'Yeah I remember Delma. What's she up to these days?'

'Well … she just happens to be a *genealogist* now. I messaged her and said hi, and mentioned you were inter-ested in *your* genealogy, and she said you can contact her *any*time.'

'Oh, *great.*'

'Yeah. So she's on facebook under 'Delma Tunbridge Genealogist' so she's easy to find.'

'Okay.' Smiling, Belle went on. 'It's funny but I'd never been into finding any 'long lost' relatives before, but now I'm getting older I have an interest to know more about them. Too late to ask Mum and Dad of course, and I doubt my brothers would have any info, so, yeah … I'll definitely contact Delma later tonight. Thanks Liz.'

'No problemo.'

Belle had decided not to go with Evie, and was now sitting outside her bedroom, under cover of the overhead decking. She'd left the sliding door slightly open so she could *just* hear the music coming from her stereo. A *Doors* song was playing, *Riders on the Storm*, and she smiled as she hummed along, thinking how it really suited the weather. The others had left a while ago and she was enjoying being home on her own, something which didn't happen very often.

They'd each furnished their private outdoor space with a

comfy chair and side table for when they wanted time alone. Liz had one day called hers 'her bunker' so that's what they all called them now. One rule they'd agreed on was that you didn't disturb someone when they'd 'bunkered down' unless it was for something really important. This ensured they could always enjoy some 'alone time' if it was needed.

Except for hers, which was downstairs, the others had their private areas on the verandah upstairs. Liz and Evie's bedrooms were next to each other on the northern side, so leaving that area for Liz, Evie had set up her personal retreat outside the small lounge room where she did her writing; also on the northern side but the other end of the deck. Liz had also screened both sides of her area with a few large pot plants, but left enough room to walk past if needed. Anna loved *her* sanctuary which was directly outside her bedroom. Even though it faced south, it also caught the morning sun, and being an early riser she often enjoyed her first cuppa of the day there.

Belle's secluded area was situated below Evie's. She wasn't at all visible from above though, as there were no gaps in the deck's flooring. Leaning back, her feet on a low foot-stool, she gazed at several fat droplets of water as they clung to the leaves of a nearby Monstera … before they slowly slid down … then plopped onto the ground.

The rain had stopped not long before she'd come outside, but by the looks of the iron grey clouds which were lurking above, there was a strong chance of more on the way. She didn't like the cold weather, but as long as she was well rugged up, as she now was, she quite liked studying the winter sky; marvelling at the many shades of grey a storm could produce.

She was surrounded by a profusion of plants, most of which would flower in the spring, but due to the previous owner's expert planning there were several which were now in bloom. The purple flowers of a Happy Wanderer spiraled down from where it was climbing, contrasting nicely with a delicate white clematis, and two terracotta pots full of pink and magenta cyclamen also added colour to the otherwise green space.

Feeling cocooned by nature, and quite sheltered from the elements, Belle sighed with contentment as she snuggled into her sheepskin coat. Smiling, she was thinking how good it was to be alive ... when thoughts of Gabi suddenly surfaced.

'Hmm ... so unfair,' she couldn't help thinking. 'So *bloody* unfair.'

Whenever the tragedy popped into her head, her mood was quashed by the accompanying gloom it generated. Knowing it was early days yet, she still wondered if she'd ever be able to accept the loss of her good friend.

Remembering what Evie had said a while ago ... that Gabi wouldn't want them to be sad for *too* long, Belle had been making a concerted effort to concentrate on all the fun times they'd shared instead. That worked ... up to a point ... but it gave her hope that it *would* become easier over time.

Thinking of how they'd stopped in front of Evie's old

home last night - Evie surprised to see it still standing - brought up memories of her own childhood. Both were from large families … but there the similarities ended.

Being the eldest of five kids, she'd had to do a lot of housework and child minding. Her four brothers ended up resenting her for what they'd called, 'her bossy ways', never understanding she'd just been doing as she was told. Their mum had been quite unwell after each birth, and their dad had spent way too much time at the pub. He'd also insisted she was old enough to 'look after the little ones' whatever her age. Happy to get away from her noisy brothers whenever she could, she'd then spent a lot of her formative years on her own.

She'd been quite content to live alone since Tatiana had moved out – nearly twenty years ago now – and was quite unconcerned that she'd been classified as bit of a loner. It didn't worry her as she'd always been happy in her own company, and even more so since cultivating her childhood love of art into her passion. Even though most of her friends who'd been widowed or divorced had remarried, she'd had no urge to share her life with another man - Grant being her one and only love.

Her lack of interest in watching 'reality' television, or following any of the usual sporting teams had often made her feel on the outer when socialising though, as most conversations seemed to revolve around those topics. She'd very quickly become bored, reinforcing her preference to stay home and read a good book. Going out with her best friends was the only way she could guarantee having a great time. It had been that fact which had swayed her to consider Liz's proposal.

She'd known the only way she could possibly share a house would be to have plenty of her own space, and had been delighted to discover how well they all respected each other's privacy. Having *thought* it would be good to have company in the evening, she now knew that she'd been right.

Suddenly sneezing, she decided to head back indoors, so giving her nose a quick blow, she stood up then re-entered her bedroom. Leaving her coat and scarf on a chair, she pulled off her boots and slid her feet into her sheepskin slippers.

'I hope Tatiana's feeling better now,' she thought as she walked upstairs. 'Tummy bugs can be *really* unpleasant.' Deciding to phone her later that evening, she'd just switched on the kettle when she heard Anna and Liz arrive home from their book club.

CHAPTER THIRTY-EIGHT

I was now sitting in my work room after spending the last hour or so at the book club with Anna; catching up and laughing with some friends. But now alone at my work bench a wave of sadness had washed over me. I knew why … it was twelve months today since I'd lost my darling Hugh. I wasn't sure if I should mention it to the others though, as I didn't want to put a downer on things when we were still coming to terms with Gabi's death.

'Hmm … yes, I *will* tell them … later. I'm not going to hide my feelings again … best to get it out there I think.'

I knew if I kept it to myself I'd dwell on it – and probably become a bit depressed - and didn't want to go to that dark place again. Sighing, I contemplated the resilience of the human spirit; praying that in time my happy memories of Hugh would displace the sadness. Then, hearing Mum's voice in my head saying, 'This too shall pass,' I immediately smiled as images of her rushed into my mind.

Being an only child we'd always been incredibly close, even more so after dad had died when I was a teenager. I knew I'd been lucky to have a young, very social mother; one who'd been genuinely interested in whatever I was doing. We'd had heaps of fun; shopping, golfing and traveling together, before she'd been killed in a car accident thirty-one years ago. Thankfully though, she'd still been alive when I'd become a single mum.

I'd been devastated when my boyfriend, along with his mate, had shot through to Queensland the day after I told him I was pregnant. I eventually found out through the grapevine that he'd been killed in a motorbike accident a year later. My dream of him returning one day so we could be a family were then well and truly dashed.

But I'd had Mum, and Lisa had enjoyed having a grandma for eleven fun filled years. Mum had been the *best* role model for me, and then I'd done my best to support Lisa when *she'd* become a single mum. It had been a really difficult time for me though, as Lisa was living in England, and I'd not been able to see her *or* my granddaughter as much as I'd have liked … until Hugh came into my life.

Cherishing the lovely feeling this memory then produced, I took a deep breath in … then let it out slowly. Gazing for a moment at the nearly finished pendant in front of me, I then concentrated on completing it in time for my friend's daughter's birthday.

An hour later I hung the finished article on a hook near the window. The overhead light shone on the central gem, high-lighting the pink of the rose quartz. Pleased with my work, I then tidied up and headed upstairs.

'Coffee or tea Liz? Or a wine?' Belle was standing at the open door of the fridge with a questioning expression on her face.

'Oh I think I'll have a cup of tea thanks, and maybe a small piece of that raspberry slice.'

'Okay, sounds good. I'll just see if the others want a cuppa as well.'

The four of us were now sitting in the cozy lounge room. We all *loved* the gas log fire. It looked so much like a real one but spared us from cleaning up ash residue and bits of wood. As we enjoyed a late afternoon tea we reminisced about different times we'd lived in houses with open fires, or gone camping and sat round a fire late into the night.

'Maybe *we* could all go camping together some time,' Anna then said, looking around at the others. 'I've never *been* camping.'

'Well … I'm not too sure about *that* idea,' I spoke up

straight away. 'I *have* been camping … *once* … and I swore I'd *never* go again.'

'Why?' Evie chuckled. 'What happened?'

'Well it was a long time ago … I was probably in my twenties. The idiot man I went with said he'd had *everything* organised … *huh*. He didn't bring all the tent pegs. He didn't bring any cooking utensils. Worst of all he didn't bring any *wood*. It'd been raining and any wood we found was wet so we couldn't get a *fire* started. I was *not* impressed. I made him take me home and I *never* went out with him again.'

The other three laughed, shaking their heads; imagining the fiasco. Anna then became serious, claiming that *we* could organise a camping trip properly, and that it *could* be fun.

'Well, if we had everything imaginable that we might possibly need, it *could* be okay,' Belle ventured. 'I've been camping too, a *long* time ago, and it was very relaxing. We camped next to Lake Hindmarsh - a very scenic spot -although the Galahs and Cockatoos made a hell of a racket every morning and evening. But … I have to say that I *love* the smell of the bush on a hot day … and swimming in a lake is always lovely … no sharks,' she grinned, adding, 'I'd be happy to go there again.'

Evie said she'd be happy to go as well, not mentioning it was where she'd been with her first husband when she'd had her ectopic pregnancy; ultimately ending her plans of having children.

'Hmm … well … *maybe* I could give it another go, when the weather's better though,' I smiled. 'And if we do, I think we should ask Simon and Jason. I'm sure they'd bring *all* the modern comforts.'

Laughing, we all joked about what the two men would bring; from coffee machines to a wine cooler, and agreed we'd definitely be glamping, not camping, if they came along.

'Yes, well it's definitely too cold to consider it *now*, but we're *nearly* at the end of winter,' Anna continued, not wanting to let go of her idea. 'Springtime might be a nice time to go, but we get a lot of rain in spring, so maybe we wait until summer?'

'Probably not the best idea,' Belle shook her head. 'Lots of snakes in summer, depending where we go of course. I reckon autumn would be better.'

Evie agreed, and I reluctantly nodded my head, hoping that everyone would forget about it by then.

'Hey one thing I *do* want to do next summer is get to the beach more often,' Evie stated seriously. 'I've only gone swimming a couple of times since I *moved* here.'

'Yeah I know, same here,' Belle agreed. 'But by the time we all got settled in the weather had cooled off a lot, and when we did get a hot day I always seemed to be doing something else.'

'Yes that's true,' Evie nodded. 'Well next summer I'm going to prioritise and get in lots of swimming. It's just as well we've been getting to Leisurelink as often as we have though. It really helps with staying a bit flexible doesn't it?'

'Yeah for sure.'

'Absolutely.'

'Yes it does.'

After chatting about other holiday destinations for a while, Anna asked Evie if she was going to continue doing her Feng Shui charts.

'No I've scaled that right down now, although I might do the odd one now and then if a friend asks. But I really don't have the time anymore. Once I finish this novel I want to get started on the next one … I already have the basic plot line in my head,' she smiled.

'Well aren't you a smarty pants,' I grinned, causing everyone to chuckle.

'Well I suppose *someone's* got to earn some money around here,' she responded cheekily.

That evening after dinner we were all once more ensconced in front of the glowing fire; the large, wall-mounted T.V. turned on but muted. The last episode of a favourite series was coming on in another half an hour, and we were filling in time by once again discussing the state of our different physical disorders, having agreed we were now *officially* old since we had this as a topic of conversation.

'I tell you I am so sick of this arthritis,' Anna sighed. 'The anti-inflammatory's don't seem to be doing much good these days.'

'Yeah I'm sick of mine too,' I agreed. 'But that's just reminded me about something I read on Facebook the other day.'

'Ahh … Facebook,' Anna smiled.

'Yes Anna, Facebook,' I smiled as well. 'I know it's not your thing, but there's often some really good information on there.'

Belle cut in then saying, 'Hey Anna, I thought you were going to get on board when Sam was in Canada. Didn't you say he was pestering you about it?'

'Yes he was, and I *did* think about it. But I decided I'd rather phone him and have a *proper* chat every now and then.'

'Yeah, same here, although Tatiana *did* talk me into setting up my profile so I could promote my paintings *and* so we could 'chat'. But because I hardly ever look at it, she got the hint and now usually phones me.'

'Yes, I'm not into all this social media stuff either,' Evie added, 'but it *is* a great way to let people know about my book. I think if you have any sort of enterprise you have to be on it these days.'

'Well I love it. Lisa and I have been using it for years now. It would have cost me a *fortune* to be phoning her in England all this time.'

'Yes that's true. I suppose it does have its place,' Anna conceded. 'So, what was it that you read anyway?'

'Well, they reckon that Cannabis oil is excellent for reducing inflammation pain, so I'm going to see if I can get some. Not sure where from though. I think I'll google it later … or ask Simon … he might know.'

'*Really?* So … do you get *high* on it?'

Belle asked the question but all three women were staring at me expectantly. I had to laugh a bit before I answered.

'No, you don't get high. Apparently the THC is removed so you just get the medicinal benefits.'

'Bugger,' Evie grinned, causing us all to smile.

'Well I'm going to ask my doctor about it next time I see her,' Anna stated. 'I'd be happy to give it a try.'

We all nodded, thinking the same thing.

'Hey what's with chin hair?' I then asked. 'I keep plucking them but they keep sprouting.'

The others smiled, Anna saying, 'Yes, what *is* that all about?'

Different hair removal options were discussed for a while, before talk moved on to muffin tops.

'I swear *mine* just arrived out of the blue one day,' Evie said, shaking her head. 'I was trying on some jeans I hadn't worn for ages when this *roll of fat* appeared that I'm sure wasn't there before … and do you think I can get rid of it … *no.*'

'Same here,' Belle nodded. 'I eat well … *and* exercise … but it seems like it's here to stay.'

Anna was nodding in agreement but before she could comment I cut in.

'Well I'm going to embrace my curves from now on,' I stated smiling. 'Hugh loved me just the way I am, and that's good enough for me.'

We all agreed there *were* worse things in life to worry about … although facial hair *was* a bugger. After asking everyone if they'd like a glass of wine, I then went to the fridge to get a bottle plus four glasses. I'd just sat down again when I remembered I wanted to run something else by them.

'Hey I've been meaning to check something with all of you. Lisa and Libby would like to stay here when they move back to Australia in November, just 'til they find a place in Geelong. Is that okay with everyone?'

'Of *course* it is Liz … this is *your* house after all.'

'Thanks Belle, but no … this is *our* house and we all need to agree about things like this.'

'Well it's okay by me,' Anna said straight away.

'Me too,' agreed Evie. 'They could stay in Gabi's room.'

'Yeah … that's what I'd thought,' I nodded.

'You know what?' Belle then said.

'What?' we all said together, then smiled.

'I think we should always refer to it as "Gabi's Room". What do you reckon?'

'Yes.'

'Yeah.'

'That's a great idea.'

'Okay, that's agreed then. Gabi would love that.'

After a bit more talk about Lisa and Libby relocating back home, I said I had a toast to make. All eyes turned to me at the same time, but before anyone could speak I continued.

'It's been twelve months today since my Hugh died. I wasn't going to say anything about it, but decided not to bottle it up inside.' I could tell that the others were going to speak so I put my hand up to stop them. 'I don't feel the need to talk about it … I just wanted to acknowledge it. That's why I've left it to tell you just before the show starts,' I smiled. 'So … I would like to propose a toast to Hugh … the most incredible man I've ever known.'

'To Hugh,' everyone echoed as we clinked glasses.

I then unmuted the TV just as the music heralding the start of the show began.

Belle went downstairs to phone Tatiana during the first commercial break and was now waiting for her daughter to pick up.

'Hi Mum.'

'Hi love, I won't keep you. I just wondered if your tummy is any better.'

'Oh, yes, all good, nothing to worry about. What are you up too?'

'We're just watching the last episode of 'A Place to Call Home'. We all *love* that series. What about you?'

'We've just finished dinner. Your phone call has got me out of clearing up,' she said, a smile in her voice.

Belle heard Naomi in the background saying, 'Hey I heard that.'

Belle laughed, then said she'd get going as she didn't want to miss the show. 'I'll call you again tomorrow as I've been thinking of coming for a visit in the not too distant future.'

'Oh, well that's a bit freaky. I was just going to ask when

you'd be able to get over this way again. Seems like ages since we saw you.'

'Oh … okay. I didn't think it was *that* long ago, but yeah I can come again soon. That'll be lovely. I've just begun a portrait though, and have to have it finished by the end of the month, so … how about we synchronize a date in a couple of weeks?'

'Perfect, we'll look forward to seeing you then. Okay, bye Mum.'

'Bye love.'

CHAPTER THIRTY-NINE

SEPTEMBER 2014

'Hi Mum.' Tatiana had a huge smile on her face as she greeted Belle at the airport.

'Hi love, how are you?'

'I'm feeling terrific. It's great to see you again. I've been hanging out for your visit. These last couple of weeks have really dragged, don't you think?'

'Um … well … I'm not sure about *dragged* … but yes it's great to see you again too. You're … looking very well,' Belle said hesitatingly. 'Whew it's pretty hot here for the first day of spring. Come on, I've just got my carry-on bag so let's get out of here.'

Tatiana chatted about this and that as they drove; Belle listening while admiring the view. She never tired of feasting her eyes on the colours which were an iconic part of the Alice Springs surrounds. Loving the way that the glaring blueness of the vast skyline clashed beautifully with the rusty red of the earth, Belle sighed with contentment and relaxed back in her seat.

'Hey your portrait of Aunty Betty looks good in the gallery next to her work,' Tatiana said, glancing across at Belle. 'That was a great idea to send it over to her. She seems pretty happy with it too.'

'Yes, well, I could have kept it but thought she might like to have it. I'm really hoping to see her again while I'm here so I might pop into the gallery tomorrow and have a catch up.'

After a few minutes discussing who's portrait Belle would like to paint next, they drove into the girls' driveway; Naomi opening the front door as soon as they arrived. She gave Belle a hug as she stepped inside, then took her bag to deposit in the spare bedroom. She was back quick as a flash, then stood looking from Tatiana to her mother, a big smile on her face. Belle knew there was something strange afoot, as Tatiana had seemed unusually happy to see her and had talked non-stop since picking her up.

'Okay … what's going on?'

Naomi walked over and stood next to Tatiana who turned side on, then smoothed her loose top down over her tummy.

'Oh my God,' Belle whispered when she saw the unmistakable bump. Lifting her eyes to look at her daughter's happy face, she suddenly became speechless.

Tatiana and Naomi were both grinning and nodding, and now had tears running down their faces.

'Yes Mum … we're pregnant.'

'Oh my God, oh my God, oh my God. How did this *happen … no don't tell me … yes … no … yes* tell me. *How did this happen?'*

The two girls were really laughing now, telling Belle to come and sit down and they'd have a cuppa and tell her all about it. She walked over towards the dining table in a slight daze while Naomi dashed into the kitchen to pour boiling water into the teapot she'd had all prepared. Back in no time with cups, teapot and a plate of celebratory cream puffs, she sat down with the other two, a huge smile on her face.

'Okay,' Belle said, then took a deep breath, 'tell me … how did this happen … *the usual way?'* she asked with raised eyebrows. 'And who's the father? Or did you go to a sperm bank? And how far along are you? When's your due date?'

'*Mum …'*

'I know, I know … one thing at a time,' she managed a smile.

'Yes,' Tatiana laughed. 'Okay … so … we are half way along, four and a half months. Our due date is January 16th.'

'Okay.'

'And we didn't do it *the usual way,* as you put it, but we did use an actual guy. Not a sperm bank.'

'Oh … okay … so who's the guy?'

'Well his name's Snowy. I've known him for a long time, and he's really lovely. He said he didn't want children of his own, but he was happy to give a hand, *literally*,' she smiled, 'so that we could have a baby.'

'Oh.'

'Yes, so he won't be responsible financially. We don't want that do we Nomi?'

'No way. We're totally ready and prepared for the added costs involved. We've been wanting this for a while now.'

'Oh, *really?*'

'Yes, so he'll probably visit occasionally and buy a birthday and Christmas present, that type of thing, but the actual bringing up of the child will be *our* responsibility.'

'Okay.' Belle sat and let all this totally unexpected news sink in for a moment, while Tatiana and Naomi sat and smiled at her. Then, as if a light had been switched on inside her, she suddenly stood up and hugged them both.

'*Congratulations* … I can't believe I haven't *said* that already. I am *so* happy for both of you … *and* for me … I'm just having a hard time believing that … *I'm going to be a grandmother.*'

Belle was in a quandary on her flight returning home. She'd been gazing out the window at the layers of clouds - a smile lighting up her face - when the thought of telling Anna her extraordinary news popped into her head. She was amazed then, at how quickly her feelings changed from happiness to hesitancy; uncertain as to how she would ever tell her friend.

Finally deciding to sort out that dilemma later, she chose instead to think about her last week's stay in Alice Springs … then shook her head in wonder. When she'd first set eyes on her daughter in the airport she'd noticed she'd put on a bit of weight, but hadn't liked to say anything. Then later, after hearing the fabulous news, she'd realised the whole 'giving up alcohol for a while' was because Tatiana had been in the early stage of pregnancy. She'd understood their reasoning behind not telling her their plans, as they'd not wanted her to get her hopes up, just in case the whole thing was unsuccessful. She *had* been surprised to hear though, that they'd been wanting to have a baby for the last year or so.

Smiling again, she shook her head once more, still having trouble accepting she was finally going to have a grandbaby. Naomi's parents had died some time ago, so Belle knew she'd be the only grandparent; not that she was worried about that of course. Her thoughts travelled forward to imagine all the experiences that would now open up for her, but all too soon an image of Anna appeared again; overshadowing her joy once more.

'How on earth am I going to tell her?' Sighing deeply, she then decided to simply enjoy her news before she arrived back home, so took a deep breath and allowed the smile she'd been suppressing full access. When the air hostess asked if she'd like anything, she nodded, asking for a glass of champagne.

Later, after leaning her seat back as far as it would go, she sighed and closed her eyes. Her thoughts were now on booties and bunny rugs, toys and teething. She couldn't *wait* to start buying baby clothes, her mind trying to decide on which colours to choose.

'Hmm … soft green … or mauve? Or maybe pastel *rainbow?*'

Evie picked Belle up from the Gull depot and could immediately see she was super excited, but after asking what was going on, Belle insisted she couldn't talk about it 'til they were all together. Evie had been intrigued, but happy to wait 'til they were back in Anglesea again, so talked instead about some mutual friends who had just left for an around Australia holiday.

Belle gathered us all together then hit us with the startling news that Tatiana was pregnant. We were all momentarily speechless before we *all* said how thrilled we were. There followed lots of hugging and a few happy tears; Anna shocking us all with her enthusiastic acceptance of the surprising news. I then opened the bubbly and we all sat around the dining table, eager to hear *everything* as to how this had come about.

'So … how did the actual … *conception part* take place?'

'Well … apparently the guy came round for the evening,

then he went into the bathroom and … took things in hand, so to speak … um … then he gave them the end product in a cup, and then they used a syringey thing to do the rest.'

'And it *worked*?'

'Yep … it worked.'

'Wow.'

'Definite wow.'

'Unbelievable.'

'And so who is this guy anyway? Have they known him long?'

'Yeah, from their university days, and then they ran into him again in the pub, earlier this year. They said he's a really lovely guy, and that I'd get to meet him sometime soon.'

'How extraordinary … you must have been gob smacked when you first found out,' Evie asked, shaking her head.

'Oh yeah absolutely. I think I still am actually.'

'Well this is the best news ever,' Anna smiled. 'I hope you're going to share him or her with us. Oh, do they know the sex yet?'

'No they've chosen not to know until he or she arrives. And of *course* I'm happy to share. I can't *wait* 'til they're able to bring the baby here. Of course you may not be thrilled to share if said baby cries all night.'

Everyone laughed at that, picturing us all taking it in turns to walk the floor with a screaming baby in our arms. Still feeling quite amazed, I then rustled up a meal, with all talk centered on the incredible news for the rest of the evening.

CHAPTER FORTY

Anna was so proud of herself. Six months ago she would have been in the depths of depression after hearing Belle's news, but now she could happily share in her friend's good fortune. She was presently taking advantage of some spring sunshine by attacking a heap of weeds which had sprung up in the vegie garden. As she gently hoed between rows of carrots and capsicums - stopping occasionally to throw the weeds into the wheelbarrow - she contemplated how much her life had changed.

She now accepted that life didn't always go the way she'd prefer, which had freed her to take life as it came along. Gabi's death had nonetheless affected her profoundly. Consequently she was now much more appreciative of so many aspects of her own life. She had good health and healthy offspring, great friends, a wonderful home and a fulfilling lifestyle. The book club meetings were always a lot of fun, and her U3A art class was a day she looked forward to each week. Even though it often had more to do with socialising than drawing, she loved exploring her newly discovered creative side, as well as getting to know the others in the class.

Her present contentment was also due to Sam having rung last night, saying he was back in the Alice, so she was *finally* able to go for a visit. She'd planned to catch up with him ages ago but he'd been needed back in Vancouver for a while, then after a quick stint in Australia he'd then had to go to Hong Kong. Even though Belle had only returned from the red centre two weeks ago she had of course offered to keep her friend company on her trip. Anna smiled thinking of how excited Belle had been at having a valid reason to visit Tatiana again so soon.

'After all,' Belle had said happily, 'I know the place so well now, I could show you around when Sam's working.' So they were travelling together this time; catching the midday flight tomorrow.

As she straightened up she stretched from side to side – attempting to unkink a few tight muscles – then heard Evie call to her, saying she was making a cuppa if she'd like one. Anna decided her body was in need of a rest so signaled she'd be there in a minute. Washing up in the laundry first, she then quickly went to her bedroom and sent an email to her daughter.

From annanowiki@gmail.com
To clairebaumann@yahoo.com.au

Hello Claire,
Just letting you know that Sam's finally back in Australia so I'm
off to see him in Alice Springs tomorrow. He had to go to Hong
Kong for a while, so organised a stopover in Singapore for his
return flight so he could catch up with Grace and Pamela.
Anyway, I'll be home again in a week. Hope all is good with you
and Gunther.
Love to both of you
Mum xx

Evie was on her mobile in the kitchen as Anna joined Liz and Belle at the outdoor setting. They were chatting about going to see a French movie coming to the Village Cinema, and as Evie took her place at the table, she and Anna both said they'd like to see it as well.

'Hey, changing the subject … that was Ross on the phone. He said he's going to be in Melbourne for a few days and asked if I was free to catch up and stay overnight. I said I was, so, I can take Belle and Anna to the airport tomorrow if you like Liz?'

'Oh that would have been handy but I've already arranged to meet Simon and Jase for lunch tomorrow so I'm going there anyway. But that's okay, we can all go together. We can drop these two off at the airport, then I'll drop *you* off. I'm intending to stay over at their new apartment anyway, not that they know that yet,' she smiled, 'so that works out great. You call me tomorrow when you've finished with lover boy and I'll pick you up and we can drive back together.'

'Okay … sounds like we have a plan then.'

'You're kidding,' Jason said the next day. 'They used a syringey thing?'

'Yep, so Anna said.'

'Wow … that's *amazing … and* fantastic.'

'Yeah it's all pretty incredible isn't it?'

'Yes … but good on them. So when's the little bundle of joy expected?'

'January 16th.'

'Oh … a little Capricorn.'

'Or an Aquarian if it's four days late,' Simon added smiling.

'Oh, right. I hadn't thought of any of that.'

Simon then happily informed us of the positive and negative traits of the two signs, until we were interrupted by the waiter taking our orders.

Later, after eating an enjoyable lunch - lingering over our coffees for as long as we could - I bid the men adieu as they returned to their separate jobs. I had let them 'talk me into' staying the night (ha-ha) and agreed to meet them at their apartment after they'd finished work. Before venturing out into the throng of the city, I phoned Evie for a quick chat; letting her know our proposed plan was a goer. After agreeing on a time and place to pick her up tomorrow, I smiled, anticipating my full day of shopping ahead.

Popping my phone into my bag I headed off to my first destination; The Block Arcade. I was needing a new casual jacket and some dressy pants - thanks to bit of a weight gain - but I was also going to look in Dafel Dolls and Bears for a teddy bear for Belle's expected grandbaby. I couldn't help but smile when I realised it was *that* quest which excited me the most.

CHAPTER FORTY-ONE

The Alice Springs sun was dazzling as usual, and Belle and Anna were taking full advantage of it while they could. They'd arrived at the girl's house an hour ago and had been swimming or relaxing around the pool ever since. Anna smoothed a bit more suntan cream over her legs before stretching out again.

'Have I said *this is the life?*'

'Yes,' Belle laughed, 'a couple of times now.'

'It's glorious though isn't it? It's quite hot for early spring. I think it must be getting close to thirty degrees.'

Just then Anna's phone rang so after bit of a struggle to get up from the banana lounge – not quite as elegantly as she'd have liked – she went inside to answer it. Bringing the phone back with her a few minutes later, she sat back down.

'I love these chairs but they're a bugger to get out of

aren't they?' As Belle chuckled, Anna continued on. 'Okay, I've arranged to meet Sam for a meal at Monte's tonight at seven. He *had* planned to pick me up but said he has something to do straight after work and he could possibly get held up. So … he suggested you might like to go with me and we can have a drink while we wait for him. He said he'll buy us both a slap up meal when he gets there.'

Bell laughed saying it sounded like a great idea.

'Okay, that works out good then. I'll be here with you to meet Snowy, and then you can come with me and meet Sam.'

'Yeah that works perfectly.'

'I can't believe you haven't met him before, after all we've known each other for so long now.'

'Yeah I know.'

'I must remember to give him this address tonight so he can drop in whenever he has some free time while we're here.'

'Good idea. Hey what did he say about his visit to Singapore? Did it all go well?'

'Yes it did. Apparently Grace *loves* the idea of having a big brother. He said at first she just stared and smiled at him, not saying more than hello. But after about ten minutes she wouldn't *stop* talking; asking him all about Australia. She even asked if she could *visit* him here one day.'

'Oh. What did he say?'

'He said that one day she might be able to when she was older, and if her mum said it was okay.'

'Wow. Is it still completely unbelievable that Sam and Claire have a half-sister?'

'Well … no. I'm actually used to the idea now. I think the fact that I ended up liking Pamela helps … and Grace *is* a delightful little girl. I'm not sure if Claire will ever accept the situation though.'

Naomi and Tatiana arrived home then as they only worked half a day on Saturdays, which put an end to that conversation. Belle had insisted she and Anna would get a taxi from the airport earlier that day, so this was the first time they'd seen one another since they'd arrived. After lots of hello's and hugs they were soon all back outside with cold drinks in hand. Talk immediately turned to morning sickness, weight gain, and all things pertaining to pregnancy and childbirth.

The sun was completing its slide westward so Naomi suggested they go inside and have some nibbles while they waited for Snowy to arrive. After settling down in the lounge room, talk then alternated between preferred gender, baby names and colours for the nursery. Their laughter and chatter was soon interrupted by the front door bell ringing.

Belle and Anna watched as Tatiana walked over to the door and opened it. A tall, well-built man with dark, curly hair stepped inside. He bent down and gave Tatiana a kiss on her cheek then stood and noticed the people in the lounge room who were all staring at him. His eyes alighted on Anna and he frowned, then smiled.

Anna had sat frozen to her seat for a moment before standing up saying, '*Sam?*'

'Hi mum … what are you doing here?'

'What am *I* doing here? I'm here to meet the father of Tatiana's baby.'

'Oh … well that's *me*. I was going to tell you tonight over dinner.'

Silence hung in the air for several, very long seconds, then it seemed that everyone spoke at once.

'*What?*'

'*You're Snowy?*'

'You're Anna's *Son?*'

'*Oh my God.*'

Anna had hugged Sam and introduced him to Belle, before they'd all sat down at the dining table; all still quite stunned. Everyone just looked at each other before Tatiana finally spoke.

'This is so bizarre I don't know where to start.'

'Well, I think *I* know where to start,' Anna said. 'How do you know Tatiana, and how come she calls you *Snowy* and not *Sam?*'

'Oh … yeah … well … we actually met at Uni … years ago now. We did a couple of different classes together and became friends. We never actually kept in contact, but we ran into each other at Monte's, not long after I moved here, and just picked up our friendship again.'

'Okay … but what about your name?'

'Well one day a mate of mine at Uni saw my name written down as S. Nowiki. He started calling me Snowiki, then that got shortened to Snowi. People thought it was funny because I've got black hair, and it just stuck. It's like calling a redheaded person Bluey.'

Everyone just looked at him for a moment, then Anna started laughing. That set Belle off, and soon they were all laughing.

'This is going to go down as the craziest day of my life,' Anna said, still smiling. 'So what you're saying is that *you're* the father of Tatiana and Naomi's baby … which makes *me* the *grandmother* of Tatiana and Naomi's baby.'

Sam nodded, then Anna screamed.

'*Arhhh … Belle …* I don't *believe* it. We're *both* going to be grandmothers.'

CHAPTER FORTY-TWO

'Okay … fill me in. How was your sleepover,' I grinned at Evie before turning my attention back to the road.

'Terrific as usual, and guess what?'

'What?'

'Well … Ross said he's going to retire after the present job he's working on is finished.'

'Oh wow … how come?'

'Well he would have retired anyway at the end of *next* year when he turned sixty-five, but he said that Gabi and David's death really affected him. He said he has enough money, and doesn't want to wait another year before we can spend more time together.'

'Wow that's *fabulous*.'

'Yeah,' Evie smiled. 'We *both* want to see a lot more of Australia … and each other.'

'Soooo … does this mean you'll be moving *in* together?'

'No. We both want to keep things the way they are. I mean we'll definitely be spending *heaps* more time together, travelling and that, but we still want to have our own space. It's great. And you know what? I'm not sure I'd *want* to live full time with a guy again. So we've decided to just see how things go, which suits me perfectly.'

I breathed a sigh of relief. I'd hated the thought that Evie might want to move out.

'Well I am *so* happy to hear that. It's fabulous that he's retiring, and even *more* fabulous that you're not leaving our little hacienda.'

'I wouldn't call it *little*.'

'Well no … but you know what I mean.'

Turning towards her friend, Evie smiled. 'Yes … I know what you mean.'

We drove without talking for a while, listening to some oldies but goodies on the stereo, when Evie suddenly spoke.

'Oh I just remembered that I was going to tell you something; I'd forgotten all about it until now. Blackie rang me last night … he and Robyn have had their baby … a little girl they've called Bronte.'

'Oh I love that name.'

'Yes same here.'

'And guess what … Bronte and Jack are born on the same day, just one year apart.'

'Oh wow. So they have a new born and a one year old? Busy times up there then.'

'Yes. I want to visit them soon. Ross said he'd also love to come so I'll wait 'til he's back and we'll head up to Katherine then. I have to say it was one of the best thing Dash and I did when we fostered Blackie all those years ago.'

'Yeah, it worked out fab for everyone didn't it.'

They continued reminiscing about old times until they rolled into their driveway at Anglesea.

That evening as we were watching the Project, Evie's phone rang just as a commercial started. After I listened to her saying, 'Hi … uh huh … yes, I can … what time … okay … bye,' she hung up and turned to me. 'Hmmm … that was interesting.'

'What?'

'Well that was Anna saying they're coming home tomorrow, and could you or I pick them up from the Gull depot … but she sounded *extremely* happy about something.'

'Hmm … maybe Sam's moving back to Geelong?'

'Yes … maybe. Wouldn't she just *say* that though?'

'Hmm … maybe they've had a great time and she's just feeling *really* happy?'

'Well … then you'd think she'd be feeling a bit *disappointed* at leaving … don't you think? And I thought they were staying a couple more days … *weren't they?*'

'Um … I think they'd left their return date open; dependent on Sam's work schedule.'

'Oh okay. Well he must be off again, and that's why they're coming back.'

The commercial finished so our attention went back to the T.V. show once more.

The next morning I received a txt from Belle asking if I could *also* come with Evie for the arranged pickup at the Gull depot. All she added was that they had a little surprise for us both.

'Hmm … curioser and curioser,' Evie smiled after I told her. 'I said there was something going on. I wonder what it is.'

'No idea.'

'Hmm … well they won't be in Geelong until five thirty so we've got a while to wait before we find out.'

'Yeah … bugger. I really want to know *now*.'

'Well I'm going do some more writing. I've just about finished the final draft so I want to keep on with it while I'm on a roll.'

'Okay. I think I'll make a cake, and if we're celebrating something later we might also need a Pavlova.'

'Ooh yes, we'll *definitely* need a Pavlova.'

That afternoon Anna looked fit to burst with excitement as she alighted the small bus. Belle wasn't too far behind in the excitement stakes either. Evie and I looked at each other with puzzled expressions, wondering what on earth was going on. We were waiting next to the Range Rover, the rear door already opened, ready for the bags.

As the two women pulled their carry-on bags behind them, their smiles radiated towards us. So infectious was their happy mood we were all soon laughing and hugging. Then, holding them at arm's length we looked at them expectantly, curious to hear their obviously exciting news.

'I'm going to be a grandmother,' Anna shouted, uncaring of who heard her.

'What?' Evie and I said as one.

'It's true,' Belle nodded, smiling widely.

Seeing the puzzled expressions on our faces Anna went on.

'It's *Sam. Sam's* the father of Tatiana's baby.'

'What? Really?'

'Yes really.'

'Oh my God that's … *fantastic.'*

'That's, that's … *unbelievable.'*

After more hugs and some tears, I took control, telling everyone to get in the car so we could go somewhere and talk properly.

Ten minutes later we were sitting in the bar of the Lord of the Isles Hotel. As we each picked up our glass of bubbly, I proposed a toast.

'To Anna and Belle and their soon to arrive grandbaby.'

'To Anna and Belle,' Evie echoed.

'To us,' the other two grinned, raising their glasses.

After sipping some of her drink Evie then wanted to know how Sam had become 'Snowy'.

We'd just had the one glass each at the hotel as I had to drive, but now we were home I opened another bottle. It had become quite chilly so the fire had been turned on, warming us as we sat at the breakfast bar. The mouthwatering aroma of garlic bread wafted from the oven as I gave the spaghetti bolognaise a stir and Evie poured the drinks.

'Okay the food won't be long, in fact we can have the garlic bread now if you like.'

'Oh we like,' Anna said first, followed by the other two.

I smiled as I took the foil rolls out of the oven and sat them on a board in front of us. Once unwrapped we were soon tearing pieces off, savouring each hot, garlicky morsel.

'Mmm … I'm starving now,' Belle said, licking butter off her fingers. 'We didn't eat much on the plane did we Anna?'

'No, not really,' she agreed, licking her fingers as well. 'We were too busy talking,' she grinned.

'Yes, well no wonder,' Evie nodded, 'this whole situation is crazy. *Fantastically* crazy.'

'Yeah … but how perfect,' I added. 'You're both going to be the grandmother to the same child … amazing. Have you decided what name you'll be called? Nana? Grandma?'

'Well … I like Gran,' Anna said, looking at Belle. 'Just Gran, not Grandma.'

'And I like Nan,' Belle said. 'I had a lovely nan, so I'd like to be Nan as well.'

'Okay, so one last toast before dinner,' I raised my glass. 'Here's to Gran and Nan … may you never have *too* many poopy nappies to change.'

CHAPTER FORTY-THREE

MARCH 2015

It was the first week of autumn and one year since we'd commenced living together. We all agreed we should mark it in some way, so after some discussion we decided to order in Thai food later and have a few drinks. But first we were off to the pool. Belle, Anna and I were going to do a deep water aerobics class while Evie would swim laps.

We ended up staying longer than we'd planned. While having coffee with some friends at the pool café, one friend, Ingrid, had become quite upset. She told us her husband of thirty-eight years had recently left her for a woman he'd apparently met online. Now she was living alone in a large four bedroom house; feeling devastated and at a complete loss.

Belle had suggested she share with a friend, and straight away Rose said she'd *love* to share with someone.

After we had another coffee and discussed the situation at length, Ingrid was able to see the positives in sharing, so asked Rose to think about moving in with her. Rose was quite excited about the idea as she'd been living on her own for years, and doing it a bit tough financially. It wasn't long before they left together; Rose to follow Ingrid to check out what could be her new home.

We were then about to leave the pool and head home when Maureen told us she had a friend overseas who'd bought some cannabis oil, and how it had reduced her inflammation pain dramatically.

'Oh, we were talking about that ages ago,' I said surprised, 'but I hadn't been able to find out where to buy any.'

'Yes well it worked for her, so I can recommend trying it if you can get your hands on some. I read that Tasmania's been suggested as a growing site, so hopefully it'll become more available soon.'

Everyone at the table was interested; making a note of the web address pertaining to the Tasmanian proposal before we said our goodbyes. In the car on the way home Anna said she was definitely going to try and buy some and would get on her laptop as soon as she was home.

Anna had actually showered, dressed and dropped her wet swimming gear into the washing machine before she turned on her computer. Now sitting at the small desk in her bedroom, she suddenly decided to write an email to Claire first.

From *annanowiki@gmail.com*
To *clairebaumann@yahoo.com.au*

Hello Claire,

Thanks again for phoning to let me know you and Gunther arrived home safely. It was terrific you were both able to fit the quick trip into your schedules. Hopefully you can stay here longer next time.

Sorry you had to stay at the Motel but Tatiana, Naomi and Annabelle booked the spare room first this time. (You can be happy you didn't get woken at 2am and 6am by a certain little hungry girl though!) But you now know there's a spare room here for you anytime.

I have to say again that Sam was thrilled to see you both. I think he's loving being a dad ... even if it is in a limited capacity. I'm glad you like my new home. Maybe you can come for a week or so in the summer next time, and we can spend the whole day at the beach like we used to years ago. Okay I'd better go. Hi to Gunther. Love to you both.

Mum xx

P.S. I'm so happy we had a talk and sorted out so much 'stuff'.

Smiling happily she hit 'send'. Then after retrieving her note book out of her bag, she began her online search for cannabis oil. It didn't take her long to find the relevant site, and after reading all the info she was even keener to buy some. Quite pleased with herself for being willing to try something so controversial, she hoped that it would soon be readily available. Smiling in anticipation of being pain free sometime in the future, she shut everything down then went outside to join the others.

We began our celebrating outdoors as it was a gloriously balmy afternoon with the gentlest of breezes stirring the air. The hum of bees could just be heard as we passed by a lavender bush; it's strong fragrance attracting the ever busy workers.

'Anna this looks absolutely stunning,' I said with my arms outstretched, genuinely admiring the manicured garden.

'Yeah Anna, it really is.'

'Yes you've truly outdone yourself.'

'Thanks everybody,' she smiled and gave a small bow.

We all wandered around the lawn area for a while, breathing in the unmistakable smell of freshly mown grass; one of my favourite scents. We'd agreed to hire a lawn mowing person to keep the grass in check, and now had a lovely young woman coming every two weeks. After appraising the fragrant shrubs and flowers, and the variety of herbs and vegetables growing in their raised beds, I had to compliment Anna again.

'Everything's looking so healthy Anna. It's no wonder *we're* all so healthy … eating these beautiful vegies.'

'Thanks. Yes it all helps I think.'

We then retired to the outdoor setting where some nibbles were waiting, along with an ice bucket holding a bottle of champagne.

'What a year hey,' I said as I began to open the bottle.

'Yes absolutely.'

'Yeah you can say that again.'

'Yes … definitely an epic year. And before we go any further, I feel the need to thank Gabi for bringing so much joy into my life,' Evie said, 'or should I say, *our* lives.'

We all nodded, and let Evie continue.

'Gabi was one of a kind. Funny, caring, and the life of any party. I hope *I'm* remembered with as much love when *I* sign off. Actually … I think I still feel her presence every now and then … anyone else?'

'Yes me too.'

'Same here.'

'I thought it was just me.'

'That's great,' she grinned. 'I thought she was floating around here somewhere. So … I'd like to propose a toast to our very good friend who will always be deeply missed … to *Gabi*.'

We all raised our glasses and repeated the toast, then sipped our chilled bubbly.

'Okay, now to stop us from feeling a bit maudlin I'm going to put some music on. Does anyone have any requests?' Evie looked at each one of us again.

'Rod Stewart.'

'Belle, you *always* play Rod Stewart. How about K.D. Lang?

'Ha … Anna … *you* always play K.D. Lang.'

'How about …'

'It's okay … *I'll* choose something when I get inside,' Evie grinned as she walked off.

Five minutes later, Cream's *Layla* could be heard across the expanse of lawn, as Evie smilingly made her way back towards them.

'Ooh I love this song.'

'Me too.'

'Me three.'

We all had bit of a laugh, then settled down to talk some more.

'I think Anna's had the most changes to contend with this past year,' Belle said thoughtfully.

'Yeah, absolutely,' I nodded in agreement.

'Yes … it's certainly been eventful,' she smiled. 'I've gone from being a boring, depressed, frumpy wife … to an outgoing, happy, trendy grandmother.'

'Well I don't think any of us can top that,' Belle laughed. 'Although I *can* relate to the grandmother bit.'

'Annabelle is *so* adorable … any idea when Tat and Naomi are bringing her for another visit?' I asked.

'Probably not until Christmas, but we're planning to visit them again in a month or so, aren't we Belle.'

'Yep … and I can't wait,' she grinned.

We all had bit of a chuckle, before Evie asked how Sam was adjusting to having a daughter.

'Well he's been a bit surprised at how much he *loves* her. He said he wasn't expecting that. I think he really loves that her middle name is Samantha as well,' Anna grinned.

'Yes, it's gorgeous how they combined all your names. I *love* it,' I enthused.

Anna and Belle looked at each other and smiled. They'd both been over the moon when they were told the baby's name straight after she'd been born. And then Naomi had assured them it was not going to be shortened either … she'd always be called Annabelle.

'Yes, it was so thoughtful of them,' Belle agreed. 'And I love that Tatiana was aware of incorporating Annaliese's name as well. It means a lot to me to have my other little girl remembered.'

'Yes that was a beautiful thought,' Anna nodded, to which the others agreed as well.

'So is Sam very involved in Annabelle's life?' Evie then asked.

'To a degree, but Tatiana and Naomi are her parents. He had agreed to be a silent partner, so to speak, and he's been honouring that. But I know the girls will be more than happy to have him in her life. And I have to say again how happy I was that Claire and Gunther made the trip here to meet

Annabelle. I think she's actually going be a doting aunty,' Anna smiled.

'Yeah, Claire seemed really taken with her didn't she?' I grinned. 'Especially when Annabelle smiled directly at her.'

'Yeah … how can you resist *that* smile?'

'It was terrific to see you two getting along better too, Anna.'

'Yes. Thanks Evie. We've managed to sort out a *few* issues lately. A lot of stuff regarding her dad have been laid to rest now, thank goodness. She *actually* even *phoned* me yesterday,' she grinned. 'But you know … I hadn't been aware she'd felt pressured to give me a grandchild. Apparently she'd felt that she'd really let me down, and *that* was one of the reasons she'd chosen to settle overseas.' Anna smiled and went on. 'I'm so glad that she told me. It's freed us up to talk properly again … we're actually getting on better *now* than we ever have.'

An hour later the sun had begun to slip behind the tree tops, producing elongated shadows which were swiftly stretching across the lawn. Hearing the whine of a mosquito as it zoomed around my ear, I quickly ducked then frantically waved my hand around my head.

'Bloody mozzies … I hate them,' I said, quickly scanning the air around me. 'Well I don't know about you ladies but I'm feeling a bit chilly *and* hungry, and now the damn mozzies are out I reckon we head indoors and order the food.'

Relaxing on the couches in the darkened lounge room, we were all feeling quite content. We'd demolished our Thai food, and a wicked cheesecake I'd whipped up earlier, and were now enjoying a cup of tea. I was drawn to stare at the fire as it threw dancing shadows across the wall, then became aware of the soft fragrance emanating from several scented candles which Evie had placed around the room.

'Well, what a delightful day. I think we'll have to do this every year.'

'Yeah I agree Anna,' I nodded. 'It's been a fabulous day.'

'Yep.'

'Definitely.'

'It's great we could celebrate the sale of your house too Belle,' Evie said, '*and* for such a good price.'

'Yeah it *was* a good price. But Kaye was happy. She'd said all along she wanted first option to buy if I decided to sell. And after renting it all year she knew there were no undisclosed problems.'

'Hmm … it makes me question whether I *should* sell mine,' Evie mused. 'I think Blue will settle in Perth with Marley and Zac when she returns from her year of travelling. But … I'll see how it works out with the family I have renting it now. They've said they're rapt to be living there, and according to my old neighbour they're really taking care of the place.'

'Oh, well that's good to know. Maybe just keep it then if you've got good tenants. Hey what time did you say Ross was picking you up tomorrow?'

'Well it may not be 'til the afternoon because he stayed over in Williamstown last night. Jimmy wanted him to stay and Ross said he couldn't say no.'

'Ha … yeah it *is* hard to say no to grandchildren. Does he stay there very often?'

'Yeah sometimes. Now he's retired he's able to stay over if Becky and Greg want to see a show or something. But Jimmy prefers staying with Ross now that he's bought his house in Lara. Did I tell you he recently bought Jimmy a small dirt bike to ride? He figured with having three acres there was plenty of room for him to ride it.'

'Oh that kid will *love* that.'

'Yeah he does. I think he'll be visiting *quite* a lot after we're back from our holiday,' she smiled.

'Okay so if you're not being picked up 'til the afternoon, do you want to come with me to see Lisa's new house? We can have lunch there, then Ross can pick you up when it suits him. It'll save him from driving down here as well.'

'Um … yeah, that should work out okay. Where *is* the house anyway? I'll have to let Ross know.'

'Manifold Heights.'

'Oh, anywhere near where Gabi had her unit?'

'No. Lisa's place is over the other side … not far from Clonard.'

'Ahh okay.'

'What about you two,' Evie looked at Anna and Belle, 'are you coming as well?'

'No we'll go next time. We've already arranged to meet Rose and Ingrid at the art gallery to see the Early Images of Geelong exhibition.'

'Oh yes, I forgot about that.'

'Yeah, then we're going to have dinner before we go and watch a movie … not sure which one yet, we'll all decide when we get there. So by the time we have coffee afterwards we probably won't be home 'til eleven-ish.'

'Hmm … looks like I'll have the house to myself for a while after I get back from Lisa's then,' I smiled.

'Yep … I hope you'll be able to cope without us for a while,' Belle grinned.

'Yeah … I think I'll be able to manage.'

The next morning after loading her bags into my Range Rover, then hugging Belle and Anna goodbye, Evie and I set off. After laughing about the huge farewell she'd just received, Evie said it felt like she was going away for longer than a month. I smilingly agreed, then asked what time they'd decided to head off.

'Well Ross wants to go as soon as he picks me up. I mean, we *could* wait 'til the morning and get a fresh start, but he's wanting to hit the road straight away. So, depending on what time he gets away from Williamstown, we'll probably stay overnight in Port Fairy.'

'Sounds like a plan,' I grinned.

'Yes. I have to say I *am* a bit excited. And I'm *so* looking forward to driving across the Nullabor. It's something I've *always* wanted to do. Ross said the same.'

'Yeah, and you'll have a fab time catching up with Marley and Zac. I *love* Perth, it's really laid back. So you'll see Ross's son as well while you're there?'

'No, I forgot to tell you. Adrian's met a girl and they've moved to Margaret River so we'll go there first. It makes more sense to do that, then we'll drive up to Perth. We'll stay about four days in each place then mosey on up the coast a bit.'

'Sounds fab.'

'Yes, it does. And of course with using a hire car we can leave it there and fly back.'

'Yeah great idea. I loved travelling with Hugh. We used to have so much fun.'

'Hmm … maybe you could start thinking about meeting someone else now? Even just someone to go to dinner with occasionally?'

'No … not yet. Maybe sometime down the track. Hugh is still so much part of my life … if that makes any sense … that I just don't have the need to meet someone new yet.'

'Fair enough. And it *does* make sense.'

We then talked for a while about Ingrid's and Rose's decision to share Ingrid's big house, thinking it could work out perfectly for both of them. Belle had given them a tip on ensuring they had their own space; everyone laughing when they heard about the bunkers.

Half an hour later, after a bit more natter about Jason and Simon's recent holiday in Cairns, and how they'd *insisted* we all go with them next time, we pulled up in front of Lisa's new house. It was two story, had a glimpse of the bay, and was within easy walking distance to Clonard, the school which Libby would attend for the next two years.

'Oh this looks lovely.'

'Yeah, it's lovely inside too. Come on … let's go in.'

That afternoon, after Ross had found the address without too much trouble, he and Evie departed on their holiday. Later, after helping to clear up the remains of our dinner, and promising to visit again soon, I headed back to Angelsea.

Smiling as I pulled into the driveway at Seaview Avenue, I was startled to see an Asian couple walking towards me. They seemed a bit startled as well; moving to the side to allow me room to drive right in. I assumed they were lost tourists, so hopping out of my car I turned to see what I could do for them.

'Hello … is there something I can help you with?'

'Yes, hello. Are you living here? Are you Liz?'

'Ahh … yes I am.' I was slightly quizzical.

'Hello Liz, I am Hiroki and this is my wife Kimiko. Gabi

told us all about you and her other friends who are living here. We are the people who told them about our trip to Papua New Guinea. We are so very, very sorry … but it is because of us that they died.'

I was feeling a bit stunned at what my unexpected visitors had told me. They'd left a few minutes ago and I was still standing by the front door. I then felt a small smile begin to form, so shaking my head a little, I closed the door and headed upstairs.

'Well … wait 'til the others hear about *this*,' I spoke out loud. Perched on a stool at the breakfast bar, I slowly swiveled to and fro as I thought about what I'd just heard. The lovely Japanese couple had felt compelled to visit, so they could relay the wonderful news which Gabi had been so excited about on that fateful day.

Apparently Kimiko had told Gabi she was on her honeymoon. Gabi had then excitedly said she and David were going to Paris for *their* upcoming honeymoon. She'd said she couldn't *wait* to tell her good friends whom she lived with, and wanted to have the wedding ceremony at the house they now all shared. They'd chatted for a while before Hiroki mentioned the trip they'd done the day before, and that was when Gabi and David had decided to have a stopover in Papua New Guinea on their way home.

I'd told them not to blame themselves, and that it was just one of those things no one could explain as to why it had happened. I'd then thanked them for traveling so far to tell us, saying how pleased I now felt, knowing how happy my friends had been. They'd then left to catch up with David's family.

I suddenly felt a lovely lightness envelop me, knowing without doubt that Gabi had been the happiest she'd ever been in her life. I could clearly picture her squealing in delight at the thought of marrying David ... *and* telling us all about it.

Being in an empty house was a bit unusual for me these days, so I decided to make the most of it. Choosing a CD off the top of the stack, I popped it into the lounge room stereo; turning it up loud enough to be heard in the bathroom. I was soon singing along to ZZ Top's *Gimme All Your Lovin'* as I turned the taps on over the bathtub. Then, after adding bubble bath and several drops of 'relaxation blend' essential oils, I lit a couple of scented candles.

Back in the kitchen I removed a bottle of my preferred beverage from the fridge; automatically checking the contents of the shelves as I did so.

'Hmm ... there's diddlysquat in there ... lucky everyone was eating out tonight.' I then smiled, thinking I'd have to tell Evie that 'diddlysquat' was my new favourite word ... it was definitely more impressive than 'shopping'.

Deciding to make a grocery list tomorrow, I poured a glass of champagne, then thinking for a moment, I took the bottle with me … just in case I felt like having a second drink later. Smiling at my indulgence, I deposited my wineglass and bottle in the bathroom then hunted in my bedroom for the novel I was reading.

I was finally relaxing in the steamy, fragrant water; book in one hand, drink in the other. Soon realising I needed both hands for the book though, I had a mouthful of champagne before placing it on a small table, next to the bottle.

'Ahhh … this is the life,' I smiled. I hadn't read much of my latest book club novel so thought now was the perfect time to get into it, but after a couple of pages I changed my mind and put it aside. Instead, I enjoyed my champers; humming along to *Sharp Dressed Man* for a few minutes before leaving the empty glass on the table beside me.

The blend of bergamot, mandarin and geranium oils had been thoroughly diffused in the hot water, leaving me feeling totally relaxed. Sighing, my mind wandered to the changes that I and my housemates had experienced during the past year. As I thought more about it I slipped down 'til the hot water and bubbles reached my chin … sighing again as I closed my eyes.

I must have zoned out for a while because I was completely startled when an unexpected downpour began to pelt loudly on the corrugated iron roof. The unmistakable smell of rain then wafted through the open window and I breathed it in deeply; savouring the fresh scent. It prompted me to reflect on how quickly things could change; sometimes for the better … sometimes not.

'You just never know what's around the corner do you,' I quietly reflected. 'Still … I'm really excited thinking about the future. If it's anything like the last few years it'll be eventful at the very least. Hmmm … I'm just *so* thankful I had the inspiration to ask those women to share this house with me. I'm not sure what my life would be like if I hadn't.'

I then sat up, blew some bubbles off my hand, and poured myself some more champagne. Lifting the wineglass I smiled … then proposed a toast.

'Here's to *me*, and to my fabulous female friends. If they hadn't been willing to give my idea a go, none of us would now be living a new and *different* life … cheers.'

THE END

FROM THE AUTHOR

Hi, thanks for checking out 'A New and Different Life' … I hope you find it an enjoyable read. This is my second novel, the first being 'Six Skene Street'. I'm currently writing my third, which will be quite different from the other two, but I'm hoping it will be just as well received.

Now a little about myself. I'm still living in Geelong (I love it here) and love having my grandchildren come for sleep-overs. I'm now 64 … getting a bit creaky … but still loving life. In my spare time I'll either be catching up with friends for coffee, (love my coffee … oh … *and* my friends) painting another abstract, or going for a long walk … no doubt stopping somewhere for coffee!

I'd love to hear your feedback regarding 'A New and Different Life' so if you feel inclined you can contact me at: alisonmorantauthor@gmail.com

Cheers, Alison.